COLLECTION 18

Kristy and her friends love babysitting and when her mum can't find a babysitter for Kristy's little brother one day, Kristy has a great idea. Why doesn't she set up a babysitting club? That way parents can make a single phone call and reach a team of babysitting experts. And if one baby-sitter is already busy another one can take the job. So together with her friends, Claudia, Mary Anne and Stacey, Kristy starts THE BABYSITTERS CLUB. And although things don't *always* go according to plan, they have a lot of fun on the way!

Catch up with the very latest adventures of the Babysitters Club in these great new stories:

And coming soon. . .

COLLECTION 18

Book 52
MARY ANNE
AND TOO MANY BABIES

Book 53
KRISTY FOR PRESIDENT

Book 54
MALLORY AND THE DREAM HORSE

Ann M. Martin

■SCHOLASTIC

Scholastic Children's Books,
Commonwealth House, 1–19 New Oxford Street,
London, WC1A 1NU, UK
A division of Scholastic Ltd
London ~ New York ~ Toronto ~ Sydney ~ Auckland ~
Mexico City ~ New Delhi ~ Hong Kong

Mary Anne and Too Many Babies
Kristy for President
Mallory and the Dream Horse
First published in the US by Scholastic Inc., 1992
First published in the UK by Scholastic Ltd, 1994

First published in this edition by Scholastic Ltd, 2000

ISBN 0 439 99504 3

Typeset by Rowland Phototypesetting Ltd,
Bury St Edmunds, Suffolk
Printed by Cox & Wyman Ltd, Reading, Berks.

1 2 3 4 5 6 7 8 9 10

CONTENTS

MARY ANNE AND
TOO MANY BABIES

This book is for Alice,
my friend from around the world

1st
CHAPTER

I was thirteen years old before I became a sister, and guess what? My new sister was my age, thirteen. Were we long-lost twins, separated at birth and reunited thirteen years later? No. Although that's much more interesting than the truth. The truth is that my sister is actually my stepsister. Earlier this year, my father got married again, and he happened to marry the mother of Dawn Schafer, who was already one of my best friends. So Dawn and I went from being best friends to being best friends *and* sisters. Not many kids are that lucky.

My name is Mary Anne Spier. I'm an eighth-grader at Stoneybrook Middle School (commonly known as SMS) in Stoneybrook, Connecticut. I was born here and have lived here all my life. Before Dawn came along, I had a very small family. Two people. My dad and me. Of

3

course, I had a mum in the beginning, but she died when I was really small. I don't even remember her. After she died, Dad brought me up.

He did a good job, even if he was strict, but I always wished for a bigger family; at the very least for a baby brother or sister.

When I was twelve and in the seventh grade, a new family moved to Stoneybrook – Dawn and Jeff Schafer and their mother. The Schafers had just been divorced, and Mrs Schafer wanted to bring up her kids in the town in which she'd grown up. That town was Stoneybrook. Unfortunately for Dawn and Jeff, *they* had grown up in California, so the move to cold, snowy Connecticut was something of a shock to them. Dawn was determined to make the best of things, though, and she adjusted to her new life fairly quickly. For one thing, she made new friends straight away. I was her first friend, and I introduced her to my friends in the Babysitters Club, which is a business we run. (I'll explain that later.) Straight away, Dawn and I started spending a lot of time at one another's houses, and guess what we discovered one day when we were looking through our parents' high school yearbooks. We found out that a long time ago my dad had dated her mum. They'd been sweethearts. But then they graduated from high school, and Dawn's mother went off to college in California and met Mr Schafer and married him and then had Dawn and Jeff. Meanwhile, my dad had also got married, although he'd remained in Stoneybrook.

Well, Dawn and I knew just what to do with our secret. We arranged for our parents to meet again, and after a while they began going out together, then *finally* they got married. (In case you're wondering, Jeff moved back to California to live with his father. That happened before his mum married my dad. He was simply never happy in Connecticut. He missed his old life too much. I love Jeff, but I hardly ever see him.)

"Dawn? How come the hedge clippers are in the bread bin?" I asked one day. It was a Monday afternoon. School was over, and Dawn and I were prowling around the kitchen, making a snack.

Dawn shrugged. "Mum's responsible, I'm sure. I'll put them back."

Dawn took the clippers from me and headed for the door to the garage. She was smiling.

Dawn's mother, whom she calls Mum and I call Sharon, is just a teensy bit, oh, scatterbrained. Sharon is really nice, and I'm lucky she's my stepmother, but I'm just not *used* to finding hedge clippers in the bread bin, or my sweater in the freezer, or the TV remote control on a shelf in the bathroom. I grew up with a father who could have run for the presidency of the Neat People's Society. Dawn grew up with a mother who wouldn't have been allowed within miles of a meeting of the NPS. Actually, she isn't so much messy as she is completely disorganized – as opposed to my father, who colour-codes his socks. How they became friends is beyond me. How they became husband and wife is, I think, beyond even *them*, but they do love each other. And the four of us are learning how to live together without going batty. A few months ago, I might have freaked out if I'd found a pair of hedge clippers in the bread bin. Now I can handle the situation calmly.

Dawn came back from the garage, and we sat at the kitchen table with snacks in front of us. Mine was a nice, normal after-school snack – an apple and a handful of chocolate chip cookies. Dawn's was a salad bar – a carrot, some celery sticks, a radish, a little square of tofu and a small container of uncooked peas. This is an example of the difference between Dawn and me, and between her mum and my dad. Dad and I eat the kind of food we were brought up on, a little of everything – fruits, vegetables, dairy stuff, meat, sweets. Dawn and her mum think it's practically a crime to eat meat. Or sugar. A really great dessert for Dawn is something like, some berries. Now, I am not, I repeat *not*, addicted to junk food the way our friend Claudia Kishi is, but excuse me, berries are not dessert as far as I'm concerned. Cake is dessert. Chocolate mousse is dessert. A large brownie is dessert. *Maybe* berries are dessert, but only if a piece of cheesecake is underneath them.

Dawn poked around at her peas, and I bit into my apple.

"I saw the twins' baby brother this morning," said Dawn. (We have friends – not close friends, just school friends – who are twins. Their names are Mariah and Miranda Shillaber, and they have a brother who is just a year and a half old.)

"You did?" I said. "Where? Is he adorable?"

"Yeah, he's pretty cute. He was with Mrs Shillaber. They'd dropped off Mariah and Miranda at school."

"The twins are so lucky," I said. "I wish our parents would have a baby. They still could, you know. It isn't too late."

"And if my mum doesn't want to give *birth* to another baby," added Dawn, "then she and Richard could adopt one." (Richard is my father.)

"I know. It worked for Kristy's family."

The parents of one of our close friends, Kristy Thomas (who's also a member of the Babysitters Club), adopted a two-and-a-half-year-old Vietnamese girl. And they already had six kids between them.

"My mother wouldn't even have to give up work," said Dawn. "Kristy's mother still works. Of course, her grandmother lives there now."

"Yeah. I'm not sure we could convince a grandparent to pack up and move in with us. A baby *is* sort of a big job."

"I suppose so. But who could take better care of a baby than us? We're expert sitters, after all. I mean, we do belong to the Babysitters Club."

"By the way, what time is it?" I asked.

"Four-thirty. Our meeting won't start for an hour."

"Okay. I just don't want to be late. You know Kristy."

Dawn rolled her eyes. She knew all right.

We went back to our snacks. After a few moments, Dawn said, "Do you *believe* that new course we have to take? Instead of career class?"

"What? Modern Living?" I replied.

"Yes! I've never heard of such a thing. We're going to learn about marriage and job hunting and family finances? And *divorce*! I think I already know enough about divorce, thank you."

"I suppose it is pretty weird. At least Logan will be in my class." Not to brag or anything, but Logan Bruno is my boyfriend. We've been going out together for a pretty long time – even though we have definitely had our ups and downs.

I'm the only member of the Babysitters Club to have a *steady* boyfriend. If you knew Logan you'd understand why I like him. He's kind and caring and funny. He's really gentle, but he also plays great baseball and football. He's good-looking, too.

"My class tutor," Dawn spoke up, "said we have to take Modern Living because – and this is a direct quote – "it's important that we explore and experience the realities of being an adult in today's changing society."

"That sounds like an introduction to a really bad social studies video," I said.

Dawn giggled. "I don't think it's fair that only the eighth-graders are subjected to this torture. Don't the sixth- and seventh-graders need to know how to be adults, too?"

"Yes," I answered, "but they'll get their turns when they reach the eighth grade."

I finished the last of my cookies, swept the crumbs off the table, and stood up. Dawn cleared away our serviettes. (Her mother may be messy, but Dawn is neat and organized.)

"We'd better go," said Dawn.

"Okay. Oh, I have to feed Tigger first!" Tigger is my grey, tiger-striped kitten. When Dad and I moved out of our house and into the old farmhouse Dawn's mum had bought, Tigger came with us. He's our only pet. I love him to bits. (I think

Sharon is still getting used to him. I don't know what's taking her so long. He's absolutely adorable.)

I scooped up some cat biscuits into Tigger's dish. Dawn looked at her watch again. "Now we'd *really* better go," she said.

"Okay. I'm ready." My sister and I left for Claudia Kishi's house.

2nd CHAPTER

I still feel a little funny riding my bike to Claud's. That's because I used to live just across the road from her. Riding my bike from one side of the street to the other would have been sort of silly. But my new house isn't nearby. I can still run inside the Kishis' house without bothering to ring the bell, though. Kristy and I did that when we were little. (Kristy also used to live opposite Claud, next door to me, but she's moved, too.) And we continue to do it. So do the rest of the members of the Babysitters Club (or BSC).

Dawn and I dashed upstairs and raced past the door of Claud's older sister, Janine the Genius. She wasn't there, though. Then we ran into Claudia's room, picked our way over the junk on her floor, and flopped on to her bed. I was pleased to see that we were not the last club members to arrive.

"Hi, everyone," Dawn greeted Claudia, Kristy, and Jessi Ramsey.

"Hi," they replied. (If we didn't sound overly enthusiastic, remember that we'd seen each other at school just a couple of hours earlier.)

Kristy Thomas was sitting in Claudia's director's chair, her visor perched on her head, a pencil stuck behind one ear.

Kristy is the chairman. (Of the BSC, I mean.)

Jessi, one of our junior officers, was leafing through the club notebook.

As I found a comfortable position on the bed, I glanced at Kristy. She was staring at Claud's digital dock. That clock is the official club timekeeper, and when the numbers flip from 5:29 to 5:30, Kristy begins a meeting, whether all the club members are present or not.

I suppose Kristy has a right to do that. After all, she's not just the club chairman, she's the person who started the BSC. The club was her idea. What is the BSC? It's really a business, and a successful one. This is how it works. Three times a week – on Mondays, Wednesdays and Fridays, from five-thirty until six – my friends and I gather in Claud's room and wait for parents needing babysitters to call us. When a call comes in, one of us agrees to take on the job. This is great for parents. They make one phone call and reach seven people, seven expert babysitters. So they're bound to line up a sitter quickly. They don't have to phone one person after another, trying to find someone available.

How do parents know when to phone us? How do they know when we hold our meetings? Because we advertise – you know, leaflets and posters. Also because we've been in business for a while now. We have a good reputation.

Anyway, Kristy is the chairman, since she started the BSC. She is overflowing with fantastic ideas. Kristy is the one who thought of keeping a club notebook, which is like a diary. Each time one of us finishes a sitting job, we're supposed to write about it in the book. Then, once a week, we read through the recent entries to find out what happened on our friends' jobs. This has turned out to be really helpful.

Kristy also came up with the idea for Kid-Kits. Every member of the club has made a Kid-Kit. A Kid-Kit is a large box that has been painted, decorated, and filled with child-centred things – our old games, books, and toys, art materials, activity books, and so forth. Our sitting charges just love to see us show up with our Kid-Kits. They may have the most spectacular toys ever created, but show them something new (even if it's old, it's new to the kids), and suddenly it's more interesting than anything they've got themselves. Somehow Kristy knew that.

Kristy seems to be a natural with kids. She certainly spends enough time with them at her own house, although for a long time only one of her brothers and sisters was younger than she was. Hmm – that's pretty confusing. What I mean is, Kristy's mum got remarried just like my dad, and when that happened, her family changed. A lot. When Kristy and I used to live next door to each other, her family consisted of her two older brothers, Sam and Charlie; her little brother, David Michael; and her mum. Her dad had walked out when David Michael was just a baby. Several years later, her mum began seeing this guy Watson Brewer, who happens to be a millionaire. He also happens to be divorced, the father of two little kids. After Mrs Thomas and Watson Brewer got married, the Thomases moved to the other side of town into Watson's mansion. That was when Kristy's family began to grow. The Brewers adopted Emily Michelle, a little girl from Vietnam. Nannie, Kristy's grandmother, moved in to help look after her. And, Watson's children, Karen and Andrew, live at their father's every other weekend. Also, they acquired a dog and two goldfish, and Watson already owned a cat.

Did I tell you that Kristy is my other best friend? Actually, she's my first best friend, since we grew up together, and I didn't meet Dawn until the middle of the seventh grade. A lot of people think Kristy and I make a pretty weird duo. That's because we're so different. Kristy is extremely outgoing and is known for her big mouth. (Well, she is.) Also, she loves sports and even coaches a softball team for little kids. (Her team is called Kristy's Krushers!) I, on the other hand, am shy. I'm whatever you call the opposite of out-going. (Ingoing? Ingrown?) I think before I speak. I'm romantic (maybe that's why I ended up with a steady boyfriend before any of the other BSC members did), I cry easily (nobody likes to go to the cinema with me), and I do *not* enjoy sports. However, Kristy and I look sort of alike. Everyone says so. Our faces are the same shape, we both have brown hair and brown eyes, and we're short for thirteen. We dress differently, though. Kristy's happiest when she can just drag on a pair of jeans, a polo-neck, a sweatshirt, her trainers and maybe a baseball cap. (Her uniform.) She never bothers with jewellery or make-up. (Well, hardly ever.) I wear clothes that are a little more trendy – as trendy as my dad will allow me to look. Mostly, I suppose I dress on the casual side. I don't have pierced ears (neither does Kristy), but I do wear jewellery, including clip-on earrings. And I experiment with my hair sometimes.

Nothing way out, though. So, Kristy and I are quite different. Maybe that's why we've been such good friends. We complement each other, personality wise.

You know who's the opposite of us in almost every way? Claudia. Yet she's a good friend, too. We voted Claud as the vice-chairman of the BSC. We thought that was fair, considering we meet in her room three times a week, mess it up (usually), take over her phone and eat her junk food. The phone – that's another reason we hold our meetings in her room. Claud has not only her own extension, but her very own phone number. That means that when job calls come in, we don't tie up someone else's line, just Claud's. You may think Claudia's job isn't difficult. I know it sounds like that, until you realize that not everyone remembers to call the BSC during our meetings. When parents call during off-hours, Claud has to deal with those jobs.

In what ways is Claud different from Kristy and me? All right, let me see. First, she comes from a smaller, less complicated family. It consists of her parents and Janine. No pets. And Claud's interests are art, junk food, mysteries, babysitting and fashion, although probably not in that order. Claudia is a fantastic artist, and she's addicted to junk food and Nancy Drew mysteries. Chocolate, crisps and books are hidden all over her room. (They're hidden because her parents disapprove of both addictions. They wish she would eat healthy food and read the classics.)

Claud is also very fashion conscious, unlike Kristy and me. To begin with, she's exotic-looking. No brown hair and brown eyes for her. Claud is Japanese-American. Her hair is jet black, long, and silky. Her dark eyes are almond-shaped. Her skin is creamy and clear (despite the junk food she consumes). She loves experimenting with her hair, plaiting it, twisting it up, wearing ribbons and hair slides and ornaments in it. And her clothes are outrageous. Her parents let her dress in whatever style she likes. A typical Claudia outfit might include a sequinned shirt, ski pants (maybe black), low black boots, dangly turquoise earrings, and ribbons woven through tiny braids in her hair. And she wouldn't forget sparkly nail varnish.

Another thing about Claud. She's a *terrible* pupil. She could be a good one if she tried, but school doesn't interest her. Sometimes her awful spelling drives me crazy – but I love her anyway.

"Hi, everyone!"

"Hey, Stace!" we replied.

Stacey McGill had dashed into club headquarters, followed closely by Mallory Pike. They had arrived just in time. As soon as they had sat down (Mal on the floor with Jessi; Stacey backwards in the desk chair), Kristy announced, "This meeting of the Babysitters Club will now come to order. Any important business?"

"Subs day!" cried Stacey. She's the treasurer, and one of her jobs is to collect subs from the seven main club members every Monday. (Two more people belong to the club, but they do not attend meetings and don't have to pay subs. They're associate members, kids we can call on to babysit if a BSC call comes in and none of us can take the job. Guess what. One of the associate members is . . . Logan!) Anyway, Stace is great at maths, so she's the perfect choice for keeping track of the money in our treasury, which is a brown envelope. We use the money to cover our expenses: to help Claudia pay her phone bill, to buy new items to replace used-up ones in the Kid Kits, and so forth.

Like Claud, Stacey is a real fashion freak. She dresses wildly, wears lots of jewellery (her ears are pierced; so are Claudia's), and her mum lets her get her blonde hair permed. Stacey grew up in New York City. In fact, like Dawn, she didn't move to Stoneybrook until the seventh grade.

Recently, her parents got divorced, which has been hard on Stace. Now she lives with her mum, while her dad is back in NYC. Stacey has no brothers or sisters.

Also no pets. She's funny, outgoing, caring, wonderful with children and a teensy bit boy crazy. I really admire Stacey. She's been through a lot, and her troubles seem to make her a stronger person. Apart from the divorce, Stacey has to cope with a medical problem. She has a disease called diabetes. Her body can't break down sugar the way most people's bodies can, so she has to monitor her diet extra carefully (no sweets or desserts), test her blood several times each day, and (this is the gross part) give *herself* injections of insulin. Even so, Stacey ends up in hospital from time-to-time, but she always bounces back and is usually pretty cheerful.

What happens if Stacey or one of the other club officers has to miss a meeting? No problem. Dawn takes over for that person. As alternate officer, that's her job. She has to know everything about running the club, but that's easy for Dawn Schafer, since she's almost as organized and neat as my father is.

Dawn is also very much an individual, which is one of the reasons she became the second of my two best friends. I like her independence, even though I eventually learned that individuality plus independence does not necessarily equal self confidence. Dawn has some chinks in her armour just like everyone else. In general, though, she's easy going and not likely to be swayed by what other people are doing or thinking.

Dawn has the most amazing hair I have ever seen. It's at least as long as Claud's, just as silky, but as light as Claud's is dark. It's nearly white, sort of the colour of sweetcorn. Dawn's eyes are blue and sparkly, she's tall and thin, and her clothes are as individual as her personality is. She wears what she feels like wearing and manages to look both trendy and casual at the same time. Her mum is not at all strict about what Dawn wears – which may explain why Dawn's ears are double-pierced, so she can wear two pairs of earrings at the same time, although she often wears four non-matching earrings!

Dawn, Kristy, Claudia, Stacey and I are eighth-graders at SMS. The other two main members are eleven-year-old sixth-graders at SMS. They are Jessi Ramsey and Mallory Pike, our junior officers. "Junior" just means that their parents will allow them to babysit only after school or at weekends; not at night unless they're sitting for their own brothers and sisters. Mal and Jessi are another pair of best friends, and I can see why they're drawn together. Each is the oldest kid in her family: Jessi has a younger sister and a baby brother, and Mal has *seven* younger sisters and brothers. Each loves kids and is a terrific babysitter. And each feels that her parents treat her like an infant. They *were* finally allowed to have their ears pierced (only one hole per ear, of course), but Mal, who wears glasses, is not permitted to get contact lenses, and both have to dress kind of like . . . oh, like me, for instance. On the tame side.

Mal and Jessi adore reading, especially horse stories, but other than that, their interests are pretty different.

Jessi is a ballet dancer, a good one. She takes lessons at a special dance school in Stamford (the city nearest to Stoneybrook). In the mornings, she wakes up early to practise at the *barre* in her basement, and she has performed in lots of big productions. I think she will be a star one day.

Mal, on the other hand, likes to write and draw. She makes up stories and illustrates them. Also, she keeps journals. I bet she will become a children's book author one day.

In terms of looks, Jessi and Mal are pretty different, too. Jessi's skin is a deep brown, her hair is black, and she has the long legs a dancer needs. Mal is white, her curly hair is red, and she'd give just about anything to get rid of her glasses. Also her brace, even though it's the clear kind and doesn't show up too much.

Ring, ring!

"I'll get it!" cried Claudia.

Stacey had finished collecting the subs,

21

and now the phone was ringing with what was probably our first job call of the day.

Claud grabbed the receiver. "Hello, Babysitters Club." She listened for a moment. "Yes?. . . Oh, hi, Mrs Salem," she said. (We met Mrs Salem when we were taking an infant-care class. She and her husband have twin babies, a boy and a girl.) "Of course," Claud was saying. "Okay, I'll call you back in a few minutes. "Bye." Claudia hung up the phone and turned to me. "That was Mrs Salem. She needs a sitter for Ricky and Rose next Tuesday afternoon. Who's free?"

I think I forgot to mention that I am the secretary of the BSC. I'm in charge of the club record book. (Guess who thought of keeping a record book.) I write down any important BSC information and I schedule all of our jobs.

I looked at the page for the following Tuesday. "Hey, guess what. I'm the only one free," I said. "And I'd *love* to sit for the twins. Babies. I can't wait!"

Claud phoned Mrs Salem to give her the good news.

3rd CHAPTER

"Do you, Mary Anne Spier, take this man to be your husband?"

"I do."

"And do you, Logan Bruno, take this woman to be your wife?"

"I do."

"I now pronounce you man and wife, for as long as you are members of my Modern Living class."

I had never been so embarrassed. It was the second session of Modern Living, and everyone in our class had to pair up and get married. At least Mrs Boyden hadn't asked Logan to kiss me.

Why were we getting married? Good question. I'll give you Mrs Boyden's answer. "Class," she had said during our first session, "you are in the eighth grade. Most of you are thirteen years old now. Some of you are fourteen, a few of you are twelve. Despite how old or young you may feel, the truth is that you are now biologically capable of becoming parents, or you will be soon. How many of you think you are capable of parenting, of being part of a couple, or of living on your own?"

I didn't know about living on my own or getting married, but I certainly knew a lot about looking after kids.

So I put up my hand.

I didn't realize Mrs Boyden would call on me. I'd thought she was just asking for a show of hands. But she said, "Mary Anne?"

"Yes?" I replied. "Oh. Um, well, I babysit all the time," I said, my face flushing. "I can change nappies and everything."

Mrs Boyden hadn't seemed too impressed. She just nodded. and then she started talking about getting married. "The best way to experience adult life is to live it," she said. "That's why you are going to pair up, get married, and stay married until this class is over. You may choose your partners if you wish. I will assign partners to those pupils who do not choose their own."

Nearby, someone whispered, "As if getting married to someone you see three times a week is realistic."

I glanced at Logan then, who was sitting on my other side. He smiled at me. We were going to "get married". It was an exciting prospect. *I* knew we were ready to take the big step. Well, I thought we were. Okay, I wasn't sure at all, but I definitely wanted to find out. Especially if it meant we could spend more time together.

Our class spent the rest of that first session talking about things like how old our parents were when they got married, and what being married *really* means. I had dared to put up my hand to contribute to the conversation, but only after Shawna Riverson had said, "I think getting married *really* means that you have a plastic bride and groom on your wedding cake, right, not those little bride and groom mice or something. Or maybe you could have a giant plastic wedding bell, right, and some bluebirds or something."

The class sniggered, and even Mrs Boyden looked surprised.

Well, after a comment like that, nothing I said could sound any more stupid. So I raised my hand. "I think marriage really means commitment. It means you love your husband or wife so much that when you have a problem, you try to work it out so you can stay together."

"You are definitely on the right track," Mrs Boyden said to me. "Thank you, Mary Anne. Class, there's a little more to marriage than the wedding. That's just the first day."

Even so, we had our shot at weddings in the very next session of Modern Living.

"Are all of you engaged to be married?" asked Mrs Boyden at the beginning of class. Four boys put up their hands. "*We* aren't," they said, looking disgusted. And Gordon Brown added, "There are nine girls and thirteen boys in this class, Mrs Boyden. All the girls have been taken."

"We have not been 'taken'!" cried Erica Blumberg. "We are not pieces of property. You can't claim us."

"Okay, okay," said Gordon. "All right, the girls have all been used up."

Erica's face practically turned purple. "We are not hot water, either. We aren't some commodity. You can't use us up."

"Commodity?" I heard Shawna whisper. "Doesn't she mean condiment?" Shawna looked really pleased with herself.

"Okay, okay, kids. Please calm down," said Mrs Boyden, holding her hands in the air. "We'll discuss this some other time. Gordon, you're right. Two of our couples will consist of boys only. Can you deal with that?"

"I am *not* going to be a girl," said Howie Johnson.

"Well, neither am I," said Gordon and the other boys.

"Do they have to decide ahead of time who's the wife and who's the husband?" asked Logan. "Maybe they could decide later. Maybe they wouldn't even have to tell us their decisions."

26

Mrs Boyden opened her mouth to say something, but before she could start speaking, Howie said, "Yeah, yeah. We'll decide later."

"Okay," replied our teacher, in that tone of voice grown-ups use when they *mean*, "If that's the way you want it, but I think it's a pretty poor idea. I suppose you'll just have to find out for yourselves."

The girls and the remaining boys had paired up by themselves. Mrs Boyden created two couples out of the other four boys because they refused to do it for themselves. Then the marriage ceremonies began, and soon I was Logan Bruno's wife and he was my husband and I was being silently thankful that we didn't have to kiss in front of our entire Modern Living class, not to mention in front of Mrs Boyden.

"From now on," said our teacher, when the weddings were over, "when you are in class, you will sit together as couples. In fact, when you are in class you will *be* couples, and I'll expect you to think and behave as such. You may be asked to be couples outside class," she added, and her words sounded somehow ominous. (I glanced at my "husband", and he shrugged his shoulders as if to say, "that doesn't make any difference to us. You and I are already a couple.")

Guess what Mrs Boyden assigned us for homework. She asked each couple to get together, discuss money and finances, and decide whether they could be a financially independent couple.

"Huh?" said Shawna. "You mean like really rich?"

"No, not independently wealthy," said Mrs Boyden patiently. "Financially independent. Could you support yourselves? Could you live in your own place and buy groceries and clothes and pay your electricity bill and phone bill and taxes and so forth?"

"Don't all married couples support themselves and pay their bills?" asked Gordon. "Don't all families?"

"No," our teacher replied. "Most do, I suppose, but it doesn't happen by magic. You don't get married and suddenly come into money. So your homework is to work out how you would fare if tomorrow, say, you were married and on your own." She paused, then she smiled and added, "Actually you *are* married and on your own. How are you going to cope?"

Logan and I found out that afternoon. I went to my husband's house as soon as school finished. The house didn't feel like my husband's, though, since my husband's younger brother and sister and mother were also there. Kerry, who's nine, and Hunter, who's five and has terrible allergies, were in the kitchen with us, waiting for Mrs Bruno to take a bag of popcorn out of the microwave.

"Put it into two bowls, Bubby," said Hunter stuffily to his mother. "If you don't, then Kerry hogs it. She eats faster than be."

"I do not!" exclaimed Kerry.

At that moment, the doorbell rang and so did the phone. Mrs Bruno reached for the phone, and Kerry ran for the door.

"Dear," Logan said to me, "I apologize for the noise here today. Let's go and work in the dining room. We can close the doors."

"All right, sweetheart," I answered, grinning.

"Ugh!" cried Hunter. "Dear! Sweetheart! You two sound like you're barried or subthig." He sniffed loudly.

"We are," replied Logan. "Hunter, this is your sister-in-law."

I was eager to get to work. "Come along, darling," I said to Logan.

We closeted ourselves in the dining room. We were equipped for an afternoon of work – newspaper, writing pad, pens, calculator, a packet of biscuits and a flask of iced tea.

"Let's see," I said, when we'd seated ourselves at the table and spread out our things. "First we'll need a place to live."

"Right." Logan opened the paper to the ads for flats for rent. "We'll have to start small," he said. "We probably won't be able to afford a house straight away. How many bedrooms do you want?"

"I think two will be enough at first. One for us, one for guests."

"Okay . . . two bedrooms. Here's one. The rent is . . . oh, my lord, it's two thousand dollars a month!"

"Two *thousand?*" I repeated. "What does the flat come with? Fourteen bathrooms and a private plane?"

"I don't know. Maybe it's in a really posh block. There must be cheaper flats. Or maybe two *thousand* was a misprint. Maybe a zero was added by accident."

But it wasn't a misprint. The rent for the cheapest two-bedroom flat we saw advertised was eight hundred dollars a month.

"We'd have to earn nine thousand, six hundred dollars a year just to pay our *rent,*" I said. "How much money do you earn each year, Logan?"

Logan estimated how much money he earned babysitting and doing odd jobs. I estimated how much money I earned babysitting. We added the figures together. Then we stared at each other with our mouths open.

"We couldn't even pay a month's rent," said Logan.

"Let's look at smaller flats," I suggested. "We could live in a studio flat for a few years. That would be okay."

"Only if we found one that cost about thirty cents a month. Remember, we have to buy food and clothes."

"And pay all those bills and taxes and stuff," I added.

Then Logan said, "Just for laughs, let's turn to the ads and see if there are any really big discounts on at the supermarkets."

There were. But we also saw that steak cost a fortune, even at sale prices. "So we won't eat meat," said Logan. "It's not good for you anyway."

"I don't think we'll eat much of anything," I replied. "Everything is expensive. Even junk food."

"There's just one solution," said Logan.

"What?"

"We'll have to live at home. We are not financially independent."

"Whose home?" I asked.

"Mine. I'm the husband."

"So what? I'm the wife and there's more room at my house."

"But I don't want to live with your dad. He would watch me all the time."

"Well, I don't want to live with my nine year-old sister-in-law and my five-year-old brother-in-law. Anyway, I want us to have our own place. I want to hang curtains and paint cupboards."

"I don't think they let you do that if you aren't paying rent," said Logan. "We haven't found one of those thirty-cents-a-month places yet."

I sighed. "I know. But there *is* more room at my house."

"Yeah. You're right. Okay. We'll live in your bedroom."

Logan and I wrote up our findings. I knew Logan would be embarrassed to admit in front of the other boys in our class that he'd be living in a girl's bedroom, but that was our only solution. And no matter how silly we found Modern Living, we wanted to do well in the course.

4th CHAPTER

The Salems' house was quiet.

"Ricky and Rose are asleep," said their mother. She sounded quite relieved. Also, she looked sort of tired.

"Is anything wrong?" I asked.

"Oh, not really. It's just, you know, *twins*."

That didn't worry me much. Especially considering that the BSC once sat for fourteen children for a week. And that I've babysat for Mal's brothers and sisters tons of times and even gone on family holidays with the Pikes, as a mother's helper.

I had arrived at the Salems' house for my afternoon babysitting job. School had just finished. I'd gone to my job straight from school. Now I was standing with Mrs Salem in the kitchen.

"All right," she said. "Let's see. The twins will probably wake up in about half

33

an hour. They'll be hungry then. Their bottles are all ready. After they've eaten, you can take them for a walk. The buggy's in the garage. They should probably wear sweaters. The emergency phone numbers are here on the fridge door. . ."

Mrs Salem is so organized. That's one reason my friends and I like to take care of Ricky and Rose. We haven't had too many opportunities, though. The Salems wouldn't let us babysit until the twins reached six months. But now they phone us *fairly* regularly.

Mrs Salem left for her meeting, and I sat at the kitchen table and started on my homework. First I looked over my notes from Modern Living class. We were talking about parenting. I didn't see that it was such a big deal; not for a babysitter anyway. If everyone would just take a child care course, they'd be prepared.

I was opening my maths book when I heard a noise from the first floor. I paused and listened. Definite cooing. I tiptoed upstairs and stopped at the doorway to the bedroom the babies share. Even from out on the landing, I could smell that baby smell – powder and wipes and lotion and clean clothes and wet flannels.

I waited for the sound of tears, but instead I heard only cooing. The babies were talking to each other; at least, that's how it seemed.

"Hi, Rose. Hi, Ricky," I called softly from the landing. I walked into their room quietly. The twins have reached that touchy "fear-of-strangers" phase, and I didn't want to make them cry.

They didn't. The cooing stopped, though. They sat in their cots, watching me solemnly and silently.

"Hey, Ricky. It's me, Mary Anne. I've taken care of you a few times now." I crossed the yellow carpet to Ricky's white cot. I just adore the way the Salems have decorated the twins' nursery. It's bright and airy. Yellow striped curtains hang at the windows. A small shelf is already jammed with picture books. A blue wooden chest of drawers, decorated with a painting of Winnie-the-Pooh, holds most of their toys. Under the window stands the changing table. Around the middle of the wall runs a colourful frieze of teddy bears and balloons.

I didn't approach Ricky too closely yet. Instead, I stepped over to Rose's cot and whispered to her.

"Want to be . . . *tickled*?" I finally said.

Rose's face cracked into a smile. A few teeth showed. I tickled her toes gently. When she began to giggle, I lifted her from her cot and laid her on the changing table.

A lot of babies don't like to be changed, for some reason. I can't understand that.

Personally, if I were wearing a wet, smelly nappy, I wouldn't even wait for someone else to change it. I'd learn to do it myself.

Rose lay on her back and kicked her feet in the air. She let me remove her nappy, which I dropped into the nappy bucket. I know, it sounds old-fashioned. But so what? Mrs Salem does not put disposable nappies on the babies. She found out how bad they are for the environment, and she switched to cloth nappies, even though she and her husband have to wash *loads* of nappies almost every day. They never complain about this.

I pinned Rose into a fresh nappy. Then I looked around the room. "I suppose I'd better dress you in a fresh outfit," I said. From the twins' wardrobe I took a pale blue dress, smocked across the front. I slipped it on to Rose, then completed her outfit – frilly socks and dainty blue cloth shoes. She looked like a princess.

Ricky's turn. He also let me change him without fussing. Then I dressed him in a red-and-white sailor suit. "You look very handsome," I told him.

I carried the twins (one at a time) to the kitchen. I found that I had to plan ahead with the babies. Managing them took some work. For instance, to move them to the kitchen, I had to put Rose back in her cot, carry Ricky downstairs, fasten him in his high chair, return to the bedroom for Rose, then carry *her* down-stairs and fasten *her* into *her* high chair. But so what? The babies were as good as gold.

They even gave themselves their bottles. Mr and Mrs Salem must have been pretty happy when the babies learned how to hold on to things.

"Ready for a walk, you two?" I asked.

Ricky smiled at me, and a drop of milk trickled down his chin.

Rose burped, then grinned.

"Charming," I told her, giggling.

I fastened the twins in their double buggy and pushed them down the Salems' drive. If I do say so myself, they looked really cute, sitting side by side, all dressed up, smiling and cooing. I almost wished they were wearing matching outfits so people would know for certain that they were twins, and not just two unrelated babies.

We set off down the pavement. We passed an older woman who paused to smile at Ricky and Rose. Then we met up with a man who stopped to say, "Goodness. Ricky and Rose. You two are certainly getting big. Don't you make a fine-looking pair."

In response, Rose kicked her feet, and Ricky waved his arms around. They gurgled and grinned.

A few minutes later, a couple of little

girls flew through the front door of a house and dashed across their lawn. "Hi, Rosie! Hi, Ricky!" they cried. Then they looked at me. "Miss, can we play with the twins, please?" asked the younger girl.

Miss? Honestly, was I getting *that* old? I thought. But what I said was, "Okay, for a few minutes. I'm Mary Anne. I'm babysitting for the twins. What are your names?"

"Sara," said one.

"Bea," said the other.

The girls bent over the babies. They tickled them. They played peek-a-boo and pat-a-cake with them. They exclaimed over their outfits.

"I can't wait until I can babysit," said Bea.

"It's the best job in the world," I replied.

"Is it ever hard?" Sara asked.

"Hard? Nah," I said, completely forgetting about the time Jamie Newton refused to go to sleep, and the day Jenny Prezzioso ran a temperature of 104° and I had to call an ambulance, and the many things that had been broken by Jackie Rodowsky, the Walking Disaster. "It's always fun," I added. "I can't wait until I have children of my own." Or better yet, a baby sister, I thought.

"The twins were *angels*," *I* told Dawn later that afternoon.

It was almost dinnertime. Dad and Sharon had not yet returned from work.

Dawn and I had finished tossing a salad and had just stuck a casserole in the oven. It was some vegetarian thing Sharon had concocted. I didn't ask what was in it. I have found that it's better not to know.

"Rose and Ricky are pretty sweet," agreed Dawn.

"They didn't even cry today. Not even when I changed them."

"Babies are wonderful."

"I know. I don't understand why Dad and Sharon won't have one. I thought that was supposed to be part of a marriage. Look how badly Watson and Kristy's mum wanted a baby after they got married."

"Would you want a little brother or a little sister?" asked Dawn.

I hesitated. "I know I'm supposed to say I don't care as long as the baby is healthy, but well, I would sort of like another sister," I said. "She would be so much fun to dress up. We could buy her jewellery and hair ribbons and some of those headbands – you know, the stretchy ones."

Dawn sat in a kitchen chair and said dreamily, "What would you want to call our sister . . . or brother?"

"I don't know about a brother, but I think a beautiful name for a girl is Tara. Or Charity. Or Bea. Isn't Bea cute? I met a little girl today called Bea. Maybe Will would be nice for a boy."

"I think Dawn and Mary Anne are lovely names."

I jumped a mile, then whirled around to see who had spoken. It was Sharon. Dawn and I had been lost in another world, and we hadn't heard our parents come home.

"Are you two talking about babies again?" asked Dad.

"Yes," I replied.

I couldn't bring myself to say anything else, but luckily Dawn jumped into the conversation. "We've noticed a pattern," she said. "People get married, then they have babies. Or they adopt babies or children."

"Not everyone," said Sharon. "Besides, between Richard and me we already have three children. And a cat."

"But don't the two of you want to have a baby together?" I asked.

"No," Sharon answered gently. "Not at this point in our lives."

"We're happy just the way we are," added Dad.

His voice carried that final note, the one that means, "End of discussion". The one that means, "I don't want to hear another word about it."

Dawn got the message, too. "Dinner's almost ready," she said.

So we ate dinner. No one said anything further about babies. But I couldn't stop *thinking* about them. Especially what to name a baby. I doodled in the margin of my maths homework that evening: Tara, Lizzie, Margaret, Tara, Adele, Tara, Frannie, Tara, Charity, Bea. . .

5th
CHAPTER

When Logan and I had worked out our finances for Modem Living class, we'd drawn some pretty negative conclusions: flat rents were much higher than we'd expected; food was expensive; everything was expensive. And we could not yet be financially independent.

"What are we supposed to say in the lesson tomorrow?" Logan asked. "Somehow, I have the feeling that "we can't afford anything" isn't what Mrs Boyden wants to hear. We could have told her that without doing *any* homework."

So Logan and I had written a two-page paper outlining how much money we earn, comparing the rents of different-sized flats, and trying to work out what percentage of someone's salary should be spent on rent alone, and therefore how much we would need to earn to afford even the tiniest little flat. We made four professional-looking graphs, too. (We used Magic Markers, coloured dots, rulers, even a protractor.)

Guess what. The day those homework assignments were due, we never even discussed them. We walked into our Modern Living classroom to find Mrs Boyden sitting at her desk, her hands clasped in front of her. On the desk was a carton of eggs, the lid open. Mrs Boyden said nothing as we filed into the room.

Something was going to happen.

"Logan," I dared to whisper, "do you think Mrs Boyden is angry with our class? Have we done something wrong?"

Logan shrugged. "Beats me."

To be on the safe side, I handed in our homework assignment. I laid it silently on the edge of our teacher's desk. The other kids watched, then did the same thing.

When we were all sitting quietly, Mrs Boyden got to her feet. She smiled. "Congratulations," she said. "You have all become parents."

"Huh?" said Shawna.

"You've been married for a while," Mrs Boyden continued, "and now you have had babies. Congratulations."

I noticed a lot of confused faces in the room.

Mrs Boyden indicated the carton of eggs.

"Your children," she said. "When I call

your names, please come to the front of the room and receive your egg. Logan Bruno and Mary Anne Spier."

Feeling both confused and self conscious, Logan and I made our way to Mrs Boyden's desk. She held out an egg, which Logan accepted (because my hand was sort of shaking). When she didn't say anything else, we returned to our seats.

Pair by pair, the other kids were given eggs also. While Logan waited for everyone to sit down, he played with our egg. He placed it in the middle of his desk, tapped it, sent it rolling, then caught it just before it sailed over the edge.

"Each of you now has a child," Mrs Boyden announced, closing the lid on the carton. "The eggs are your children. For the next few weeks you are to treat the eggs as you would infants."

At that moment, Logan had just rolled our egg to the edge of his desk again. He caught it in a hurry. He handed it to me.

"Your babies," Mrs Boyden was saying, "must be fed regularly, clothed, taken to the doctor, and especially, watched over. Just as you would never leave a human baby alone, you must never leave your egg alone. Someone must be available to care of it at all times. You will be in charge of your egg-babies for a month. At the end of four weeks, a paper will be due. I will expect you to write about your experiences, any problems you encountered, the solutions to those problems, and so forth. We'll talk more about the papers later this week. By the way, as parents you are responsible for your children, starting immediately. Of course, I won't be able to see that your babies are cared for when you're out of school, so everyone is on his or her honour this month. Every eighth-grader will become a parent to an egg, and I trust you to keep an eye on each other. Only you can make the honour system work.

Now, any questions?" our teacher asked.

As you can imagine, nearly everybody raised a hand.

"Shawna?" said Mrs Boyden.

"Do we really have to take our eggs to the doctor?" she asked. "I might feel sort of silly. I mean, what will the doctor think?"

Mrs Boyden closed her eyes momentarily. "No, you don't actually have to take your egg to a doctor. But you are going to be a mother for a month, so I expect you to know when and why your child might need to see a doctor. Remember to plan for check-ups."

Logan nudged me. "How are we supposed to feed these eggs?" he asked.

I shrugged.

Shawna put up her hand again and spoke without waiting to be called on. "About food—" she began to say.

"No, you do not need to prepare food and pretend to feed your egg," Mrs Boyden broke in. "Let me explain the project in more detail. When you leave this room at the end of the period, either you or your partner – your spouse – must watch over your child every moment. You wouldn't leave an infant unattended, so do not leave your egg in your locker during school hours. The egg will accompany you to classes. You must also tend to your egg after school and at night."

"Hey, what about after-school sports?" exclaimed a boy in the front row. "I can't watch an egg while I'm at baseball practice."

"Ask your wife to watch your child, then," said Mrs Boyden.

"But I take piano lessons," spoke up the wife. She hesitated, then added, "I suppose I could take the egg along with me."

Mrs Boyden nodded. "That would be an acceptable solution, as long as you keep your eye on the baby throughout the lesson."

Mrs Boyden mentioned some facts about babies. Not everyone was aware, for example, that small babies cannot hold their own bottles. "What does that tell you about feeding your baby?" asked Mrs Boyden.

"I suppose we have to be *with* our egg at mealtimes," spoke up Trevor Sandbourne. "The baby can't eat by itself."

"Right. In fact, you need to *hold* the egg," pointed out Mrs Boyden. "Small babies can't sit up, either. Understand?" We nodded. "One last thing," our teacher went on, glancing at the clock. "From now on, I would like you to refer to your children *as* children, rather than as eggs." Mrs Boyden didn't explain this – the bell rang just as she finished her sentence – so I didn't have a chance to ask her *why* we weren't supposed to call our eggs eggs.

Around me, my classmates were getting to their feet. But not Logan. He turned to me with this incredible, horrified expression on his face. Then he looked at our egg. I mean, our child. It was resting on my desk inside a little barricade I had created with my notebook, purse, and two textbooks. For the time being it was safe, but—

"We can't carry that, um . . . we can't carry *that* around all day," said Logan, pointing at our child.

"Just what I was thinking," I answered. "But we have to."

"Yeah. Okay. Where will it be safe? In my school bag?"

"Not the way you sling that thing around. I'll put our child in my bag. She'll be safe there."

"Are you sure she won't suffocate? And how do you know it's a girl?"

"I don't. I just want a girl. And she won't

suffocate. My bag doesn't close, see?" (My bag was a big woven bag. It was great for school because I could throw lots of stuff into it, and I didn't have to worry about zipping or unzipping it all day.)

"Okay," said Logan uncertainly.

"Hey, come on, this is going to be fun," I told him. I was standing up, settling our daughter in my bag.

"But what about gym? You and I have gym at the same time now. What are we going to do with her then? I'll be playing baseball. I can't bring her out on the field with me. It's too hot. Anyhow, I'd probably sit on her."

"Don't panic," I said, although I felt a teensy bit panicky myself. "I'll be doing aerobics in my gym class. I'll bring my bag with me and leave it where I can see it. She'll be fine.'"

"All right. I suppose I'm just a nervous father."

"Well, relax. You're with kids all the time. You're great with them. Pretend you're babysitting or something."

Logan relaxed. He looked fondly at our child, now nestled in a wad of tissues in my bag. "Maybe we should name her," he suggested.

"Yes, but not now, dear. We're going to be late for our next class." I picked up my books and slipped my bag over my shoulder.

Logan peered worriedly inside the bag. "Take care of our child," he said. "Be particularly careful during gym. Why don't you give her to me at lunch and I'll watch her for the rest of the day?"

"Oh, no," I said. "You are not putting our daughter in your schoolbag. This afternoon we'll get together and work out a way to carry her around. I don't mind watching her today."

I had thought I might feel silly worrying about our child all day. I mean, how was I supposed to explain to my gym teacher that I needed to keep my bag nearby during aerobics so that I could babysit for an egg? But of course I wasn't the only pupil with that problem. A lot of other girls who had also attended their Modern Living classes earlier that day were in the same situation. And I saw a couple of them just put their eggs on the floor and leave them. How would they be able to tell them apart at the end of the lesson?

"Logan!" I exclaimed, when I met him in the cafeteria at lunchtime. "We have to label our baby or something. What if she got lost? We wouldn't be able to tell her from any other egg. I mean, baby."

"This afternoon we'll paint her with food colouring," said Logan. "It's painless *and* non-toxic. You have to think of those things."

I nodded. "Listen, I'm sure she's hungry by now. Why don't you eat while I feed her? Then I'll eat while you finish feeding her. We should probably feed her again at. . ."

6th CHAPTER

Tuesday

When I accepted the job with the Papadakis kids, I expected to babysit for just three children — Linny, Hannie, and Sari. I mean, the Papadakises only have three children. But I ended up bringing a fourth with me. My new son, Izzy the egg. My husband, Alan Gray, wanted to watch Izzy after school, but he wouldn't have been able to watch him in the evening, so I just brought Izzy home with me that afternoon, and at 3:45, carried him across the street to the Papadakises'. I think Izzy kind of confused the kids, but what would you expect?

Well, of all things. Alan Gray has been Kristy's enemy (okay, her pest) for as long as I can remember. And who does she end up marrying in her Modern Living class? Alan. How unfair.

How unfortunate. Kristy had a cow.

But that was on the day they got married. On the day they became parents, Kristy changed her mind about Alan. He turned out to be a pretty good father. First of all, he named Izzy.

"A son called Izzy," he had said dreamily to Kristy as he'd held his child for the first time.

"Izzy?" repeated Kristy. "What kind of name is that? Especially for a boy. I've never heard of a boy called Izzy."

"It's short for, um. . ."

"It's short for Isabelle or Isadora or Elizabeth," said Kristy.

"Oh, it must be short for some boy's name," said Alan offhandedly. "Anyway, don't you think it's a nice name?"

"It *is* sort of cute," Kristy had agreed, pleased that Alan was at least taking an interest in the project.

By Tuesday, the day of Kristy's job at the Papadakises', both she and Alan were taking more than a little interest in Izzy. They had made this elaborate "environment" for him in a shoe box. The box was lined with pieces of flannel so Izzy would always be comfortable. The sides of the box were covered with felt so Izzy wouldn't hurt himself if he bumped into a wall. Alan had placed a tiny music box in the environment so Izzy would feel comforted and develop an appreciation for music. And Kristy had stuck tiny charts and pictures on the felt so Izzy's learning cells would be stimulated. She claimed she read aloud to him at night, but I don't know.

Also, unlike a lot of the couples in Modern Living, Kristy and Alan fought over who got to take their child home after school (as opposed to who got *stuck* with him after school). They were conscientious parents. Which is why Kristy never even considered leaving Izzy at her house while she went to the Papadakises'. Of *course* he went along with her.

The Papadakis kids are good friends of Kristy's younger brothers and sisters. Linny, who's nine, plays with David Michael. Hannie, who's seven, is one of Karen's two best friends. And Sari, the little one, sometimes plays with Emily. Kristy and the kids are pals. So Kristy decided that her first order of babysitting business should be to explain Izzy to them.

As Mrs Papadakis backed down the drive, Kristy sat at the kitchen table with Linny and Hannie. Sari, who had just woken up from a nap, was sitting sleepily in her high chair.

Kristy placed Izzy's environment on the table. She pointed to her son. "This," she said, "is Izzy Thomas-Gray."

"That egg?" replied Linny, after a moment's hesitation.

"Well, yes," answered Kristy. "Only he isn't—"

"*He*?" interrupted Linny.

"—he isn't just an egg," Kristy continued. "He's my son."

"You mean your pret*end* son . . . don't you?" asked Hannie. She peered into the shoe box and stared at Izzy.

"Well, yes. My pretend son," Kristy agreed. Then she tried to explain Mrs Boyden's Modem Living project to the kids.

"Okay, so you're pretend-married," said Linny, "and this egg is your pretend son. And you're babysitting for him, as well. Right?"

"Right."

"Where is Izzy's food?" asked Hannie.

"The food is pretend, too," Kristy answered. "I just have to spend time with Izzy as *if* I were feeding him. A bit like when you play with your dolls. You don't give them real food. Only with Izzy I have to remember to feed him every day, as often as—"

Ring, ring!

Linny bounded to his feet and made a grab for the phone. "I'll get it!" he cried.

He picked up the receiver and said politely, "Hello, Papadakises' residence. Who's calling, please?. . . For Kristy?. . . Okay." Linny held the phone towards Kristy. "For you. I think it's your pretend husband."

"Hello?" said Kristy. "Alan? What's up?"

"I'm just checking on Izzy," he replied. "I was sitting here thinking about him, and. . . Is everything okay?"

"Oh, yes. Fine. Izzy's napping."

"Napping? Shouldn't he be eating? I don't think he eats enough. We don't want him to get scrawny."

"Alan, trust me. He's fine," said Kristy. "Um, except for—"

"WHAT?" exclaimed Alan. "Except for what?"

"He seems kind of nervous here."

"I thought he was asleep."

"He is now. But when we first got to the Papadakises', he was really shy."

"Well, you know, new faces."

"Yeah, but I'm concerned that he's not socializing properly."

Kristy and Alan discussed Izzy's social development. They talked for quite a while. They talked for so long that the kids became bored, and Linny lifted Sari out of her high chair, nudged Kristy, and whispered loudly, "We're going to the playroom."

"Okay," Kristy answered distractedly. Ten minutes later, she finished her conversation with Alan, hung up the phone, and headed for the kids' playroom. Halfway there she realized she was without Izzy, and she dashed back to the kitchen. The table was empty. Had Izzy been in the kitchen when Kristy finished her phone conversation? She couldn't remember. She glanced round the room, decided he wasn't in it, and headed for the playroom again, calling, "Linny? Hannie?"

"Yeah?" Linny called back.

"Have you got Izzy?"

"Huh?"

"I said, "Have you got Izzy?" " By then, Kristy had reached the playroom. The first thing she saw was Izzy's environment. The box was on Hannie's small colouring table. "Never mind," said Kristy. She ran for the box.

It was empty.

I mean, it was empty of Izzy. Everything else was there – the flannel, the cell-stimulating pictures, the music box. Only Izzy was missing.

"Where *is* he? Where's *Izzy*?" cried Kristy with a gasp.

"Hey, funny!" exclaimed Linny. "Good joke. Get it? Where is *he*? Where's Izzy?" He laughed loudly.

Hannie began to laugh, too. "Where Izzy? Where Izzy?" she sang.

Even Sari laughed and joined in.

"This isn't funny, you lot," said Kristy,

her heart pounding. "Izzy is my baby. Remember? I'm responsible for him. Who brought this box in here? Linny?"

Linny's smile had faded. "Yeah, I did," he answered. "You were busy talking on the phone, and I thought Izzy might want to see the playroom."

"Okay." Kristy tried to calm down. "You brought this box in here? Then what? Did you take Izzy out of it?"

"Very, very gently," Hannie answered for her brother. Then she added, "*Very* gently. Honestly. Cross my heart."

"I believe you," said Kristy. "Just tell me where you put Izzy."

Hannie frowned. She looked at Linny, who was frowning, too. "Linny was holding on to Izzy tightly and he walked—"

"How tightly?" Kristy interrupted.

"Not *that* tightly," said Linny.

"Linny showed Izzy around the playroom," Hannie continued. "He showed him the bookshelf and Sari's rocking horse and the art cupboard and the trucks and cars, and then. . ."

"Yeah?" prompted Kristy.

"I think he stopped to look at his collection of bottle caps."

"Oh, that's right," agreed Linny. "So I put Izzy on the floor and, um, that's all I remember. Until you came in."

"Everybody, spread out and search!" yelped Kristy.

"Hmm. If I were an egg, where would I go?" muttered Linny.

"How about the fridge?" suggested Hannie.

She and Linny got the giggles. While Kristy tossed aside books and toys and sweaters, looking for her missing son, Hannie and Linny cracked jokes and laughed helplessly.

"Maybe Izzy is off looking for Humpty Dumpty," said Hannie.

"Egg-sactly!" cried Linny. "Or maybe he had a great fall."

"Egg-cellent," said Hannie.

"I hope nobody found Izzy and then . . . cooked him and ate him," added Linny. "That would set a bad egg-zample."

By that time, Kristy was no longer listening to Hannie and Linny. "Come on, Sari. You'll help me, won't – Hey, Sari, what are you doing?" Kristy knelt beside Sari, who was squatting on the floor. At her feet was a doll's blanket. Sari was patting it and saying, "Baby, baby."

Kristy poked the blanket. Then she pulled at it. Inside was Izzy. "Oh, thank heaven! You're safe!" cried Kristy. "It's okay, Linny, Hannie. I found him. Guess what. Sari was taking care of Izzy for us."

"Drat. No more egg-citement," said Linny.

Even Kristy couldn't help laughing. "Linny!" she exclaimed.

"Sorry," he said. "It's just . . . I don't know. Your *son*? An egg named Izzy? I never heard of anything like that."

"Egg-straordinary, isn't it?" said Kristy. And then she replaced Izzy in his safe environment.

She decided not to tell Alan what had happened.

7th CHAPTER

Our daughter had a name. She went without one for four days without one and I argued over what to call her. I was holding out for Tara, but Logan didn't like the name. He wanted to call her Sally, which I thought was much too plain. Finally we compromised.

We named our child Samantha.

I thought Samantha was almost as beautiful as Tara, and that Sammie was an adorable nickname. Logan liked Sammie, too, because it sounded like Sally.

We lined a wicker basket for Sammie with scraps of pink fabric. The day we had been given Sammie, we had painted pink flowers on her with food colouring. The day we named her, we added this:

S

"Now we'll always be able to recognize her," said Logan.

"*And* she's beautiful," I added. "Our beautiful daughter."

As soon as Sammie's basket was ready, Logan took on more than his share of the work in caring for our daughter. He took her home with him almost every afternoon. He carried her around school as often as possible.

He was a natural father.

Of course, he couldn't care for Sammie *all* the time, though. And one morning he met me at school, basket in hand, and said, "Just as I was leaving the house, Hunter reminded me that I promised to take him and Kerry to the playground this afternoon. I'm worried about taking Sammie with me. I don't want her to get too much sun."

"I'll take her," I said. "I'm babysitting for Rose and Ricky after school, but that shouldn't be a problem. It'll probably be easier for me to look after three babies than for you to take care of one baby and two active kids. I mean, the twins can't walk yet.

How much harder could three babies be than two?"

I found out at the Salems' house. Three could be plenty harder than two, and even two could be . . . a nightmare.

The bad dream began shortly after Mrs Salem left the house, when Ricky woke up from his nap.

He woke up crying.

I had been sitting in the kitchen with Sammie's basket in my lap while supposedly I gave Sammie a bottle, when I heard snuffles and tears from the twins' bedroom.

"I'm coming!" I called gently, so as not to wake the other twin.

I stood up. "Sorry, Sammie," I said. "You'll have to finish your bottle later." I knew that wasn't quite fair. If Sammie had been a real baby, I would have had to work out how to feed her *and* rush upstairs. As it was, I had to bring her with me.

I entered the babies' room and found a very unhappy Ricky. He was sitting at one end of the cot, wailing, tears streaming down his face.

"Shh, Ricky, shh," I whispered. "What's the matter?"

I put Sammie on the changing table and picked up Ricky. I rocked him and walked him around the room until I realized that Rose was stirring. Then I took him into the hallway – and realized I'd left Sammie behind. A small baby should never be left on a changing table unattended. So I went back to retrieve her, and Ricky's cries woke Rose, who also began to cry.

"Hey, come on, you two. I can't hold both of you," I said, remembering at the same time that I hadn't finished feeding Sammie. Then the thought occurred to me that the twins were probably hungry. Also, that they could hold their own bottles. So I settled the babies in their high chairs and handed each one a bottle. Perfect. They could feed themselves while I fed Sammie.

Well, that worked in theory. In reality, Rose continued to fuss, so I held Sammie in my lap and fed Rose myself. This arrangement lasted until Ricky threw his bottle on the floor.

I stopped what I was doing, picked it up, handed it to him, and went back to Rose. Ricky threw down the bottle again. I decided Sammie had eaten enough and stood between the twins, holding Rose's bottle with my right hand and Ricky's with my left.

When the bottles were empty, I stepped back and examined the babies.

"You two look simply delightful," I told them. (I didn't mean it.)

They were far from the beautiful babies I'd dressed on my last sitting job. They were wearing crumpled T-shirts and damp nappies. Their cheeks were tearstained and their chins were milk-covered.

"Time to clean you up," I said decisively.

With difficulty, I returned Sammie, Rose and Ricky to the twins' room. I put Rose in her cot, Sammie on the windowsill, and Ricky on the changing table. I removed Ricky's wet nappy.

"Wah!" he wailed.

He cried the *entire* time I changed him.

"You aren't getting ill, are you?" I asked. I felt his forehead. No temperature. And his appetite had seemed fine. When he was dry and powdered, I returned him to his cot and placed Rose on the table. She cried noisily while I changed her.

"Having a bad day?" I said to the twins. They stared at me from tear-filled eyes. At least their bottoms were dry.

"How about a walk?" I suggested. Walks are good for stopping tears.

I removed two lovely outfits from the wardrobe. For Rose, a white ruffled dress with matching knickerbockers and a hat, and her pink shoes. For Ricky, a frog jumpsuit with a matching shirt and hat, and his tiny high-topped trainers.

The babies eyed all those clothes warily. They turned on the tears before I'd even so much as lifted Ricky's arms. In the end, they left the house wearing fresh clothes, and socks. No earrings or frills for Rose.

No hat for either of them. Not even shoes. At least they'd whittled down their crying to sniffles and hiccups. They weren't happy, but they were quiet.

I hung Sammie's basket over a handle of the double buggy. Then I set out with the three babies. For a while, they were quiet. They seemed content. I managed to convince myself that Sammie had had enough to eat and I hadn't neglected her *too* badly. I relaxed.

And Rose began bumping back and forth in her seat and making these awful whiny noises. She wasn't exactly crying, but—

Time for distraction technique. "What a beautiful day!" I exclaimed. I pointed to the sky. "Look, I see a bird. Bird."

"Ba!" said Rose.

"That's right. Bird. And there's a cloud."

We stopped next to a garden. "Ooh, pretty flowers," I said.

Ricky reached for a tulip, got a grip on the stem, and pulled.

The plant uprooted, sending dirt flying.

"Ricky!" I cried. I whirled round and looked at the house beyond the garden. What if someone had seen us? "Ricky!" I said again. "No, no, no!" I took the flower from him and dropped it in the garden. I tried to bury it under some leaves. Then for good measure, I said "No!" to Ricky once more.

Both babies, looking bewildered, burst into tears.

Uh-oh. "Sorry, Ricky. I'm sorry," I said. "Rose, I'm sorry. I didn't mean to shout. But Ricky, you can't go around pulling up plants. That flower isn't yours. It belongs to someone else." (As if he could really understand me.)

I wheeled the buggy away quickly and hurried down the pavement with my cargo of crying babies. If Logan had been at home, I *might* have phoned him and asked him to come and get Sammie. But I coped as well as I could.

"That was a nightmare, all right," Dawn said that evening, when I described my job at the Salems' to her.

"Yeah. I suppose it could have been worse though."

"How? If the house had burned down?"

"No, if, um, well, I'm not sure. I mean, this just wasn't realistic, that's all. I don't usually babysit for three babies at once. I have to admit, I thought the job wouldn't be too bad since the babies can't walk. I should have realized how silly that is. I still have only one pair of hands, and most people take care of just one baby at a time. Anyway, nothing bad actually happened this afternoon. The babies were fussy, but you have to expect that. I still want a little sister, don't you? A real one, I mean. Not an egg one. Even a little brother would be okay."

"Yeah, I still want a sister or brother," Dawn replied. "And you know what came in the post today?"

"What?"

"The Kumbel catalogue."

"The *Kum*bel catalogue?" I shrieked. The Kumbel catalogue sells everything. Dawn knows what my favourite section is. Baby supplies and furnishings. "Where is it?"

"In my room. I'll go and get it." Dawn dashed across the landing, then returned to my bedroom, clutching the fat catalogue.

I found the baby section in about three seconds. "Ah, look!" I exclaimed. "Look at that cot. It would be perfect for a girl *or* a boy. White with yellow stars and a moon."

"It is adorable," agreed Dawn. "And we could get that matching chest of drawers and rocking chair. A yellow-and-white baby's room would be so cute."

"If Dad and Sharon had a baby," I said thoughtfully, "I suppose you and I would end up sharing a room again." (We had tried that once. It hadn't worked.) "My room would become the baby's room."

"No, the baby could have Jeff's room, I think."

"Oh, whatever. Hey, look at *that*! A baby's lamp with a stars-and-moon shade. Tara would *have* to have that."

"Tara?" said three voices.

Drat. Dad and Sharon had overheard us talking again.

"Yeah. Our . . . baby sister?" I ventured.

"No," said Dad.

"No way," said Sharon.

"Double drat," I replied.

8th
CHAPTER

Ten people attended the next meeting of the Babysitters Club. Seven humans and three small babies. (Okay, three eggs.) Sammie, Izzy and Bobby.

Bobby was Stacey's little boy. (Claudia's child was over at his father's house.) He lived in a plastic mixing bowl. His father was Austin Bentley, a friend of Stacey's and Claudia's. Austin sometimes invites one or the other of them to school dances or to parties, but he isn't their boyfriend. (A good thing, too, because I think he'd have trouble choosing between them.) The three of them are just good friends.

Claud had fixed a sort of nursery in her room. The nursery was an area on her dressing table on which sat Sammie in her basket, Izzy in his shoe box environment, and Bobby in his mixing bowl. She had placed pillows on the floor around the dresser in case one of the babies fell off.

"Why don't you just put the babies on the floor?" asked Mal practically. "Then they wouldn't be able to fall."

"Too draughty," Kristy answered.

"So how are your kids getting on?" Jessi inquired politely.

"Sammie's fine," I said, "but Logan—"

"Order! Come to order, please!" said Kristy.

(I checked the official club time keeper. Sure enough. Five-thirty.)

My friends and I straightened up. We adjusted ourselves.

"Any club business?" our chairman wanted to know.

No one answered her. So I said simply, "Logan is hogging Sammie. Lately, he is almost always looking after her." Tears welled up in my eyes. "This is the first time I've brought her home after school since the day I babysat for the Tragedy Twins."

Stacey giggled. "You mean Ricky and Rose?"

"Yeah." I couldn't even laugh at my own joke.

The phone rang and Claud picked it up. "Hello, Babysitters Club. . . Mm-hmm, mm-hmm. . . In Karen Brewer's class. . .? Oh. . . Thursday afternoon? I'll check and call you straight back." Claud hung up and said, "That was someone called Mr Gianelli. He said his son is in Karen's class at Stoneybrook Academy."

"Gianelli," repeated Kristy. "He must be Bobby's father."

"Right," said Claud. "The Gianellis have two kids, Bobby and his little sister, Alicia. They need a sitter on Thursday afternoon."

I looked at the appointment pages in the record book. "You can do it, Stace," I said. "Want the job?"

"Okay."

Claud phoned Mr Gianelli back while I scribbled in the BSC record book. I love filling in those blank pages.

"I don't know why you want to spend so much time with an egg," Stacey said to me. She brushed her hair out of her eyes.

I gasped. "Sammie is my *daugh*ter!" I exclaimed.

Stacey made a face. "Honestly, Mary Anne."

"You heard what Mrs Boyden said."

"Yeah, yeah. And I'm doing the project. So's Austin. We're very fair and careful. We each take care of Bobby exactly half the time. One day I bring him home, one day Austin brings him home. But what a pain. I don't think I have time for Modern Living class. Always having to stop and think about feeding Bobby or giving him a bath or something. On Monday I took him shopping with Mum

71

and me. I thought a baby would need new vests and nappies and things pretty often. So I lugged the mixing bowl round four baby departments while Mum shopped for fun things, like books and presents. All I saw were baby thermometers and baby minders and baby trainers and baby toys and baby bottles and baby blankets. Babies certainly need a lot of equipment. I never even had a chance to look at clothes for *me*."

"Oh, but buying baby things is fun," I spoke up. I was thinking about the Kumbel catalogue.

"For five minutes," said Stacey.

"Well, anyway, I – I—" (I was trying to think of a nice way to say I didn't agree with Stacey.) "I suppose I don't mind shopping for baby things. And I *still* wish Logan wouldn't hog Sammie."

From her place on the floor, Mal tried to hide a giggle.

"What's so funny?" asked Dawn.

"Mary Anne keeps saying Logan is *hogging* Sammie. And "hogging" makes me think of bacon. And Sammie is an egg. Get it? Bacon and eggs?" Mallory snorted with laughter.

Jessi began to laugh, too.

But us five older club members remained serious. After a few moments, Claud said, "You two don't understand. You aren't parents yet."

Mal and Jessi calmed down.

We took a few phone calls. Then Kristy got up from the director's chair, crossed the room to the dresser, and peeped into Izzy's box. "I think Izzy is getting spoiled," she said.

"Too much attention?" I asked.

"No, I mean I think he's spoiling. Smell him."

Kristy is forever asking me to smell disgusting things. I don't know why she thinks I'll do it.

"No, thanks," I replied.

But brave Dawn stood up and sniffed around in the box. "I can't smell anything," she said. "You're making up worries."

"I am not," Kristy replied. However, she sat down again.

"You lot, what's being married like?" asked Jessi.

"Yeah, what's it like?" echoed Mal.

"Well," Stacey began after a moment, "I don't know what to compare it to. But a lot of it is communicating. With your husband or wife. You have to be able to talk about who's going to watch the baby when, and who has to remember to do which things with the baby."

"And you have to agree on things," added Kristy. "And trust your husband. That's really important. You have to trust him."

"Being married is expensive," I added.

"Nobody has said anything about love," pointed out Jessi.

The room grew silent.

"Yeah, aren't you supposed to be in love?" asked Mal.

"I suppose that *would* make things easier," said Stacey slowly. "If I were actually in love with Austin, I'd want to spend more time with him. And I'd want our child to spend more time with us. Maybe being married wouldn't seem like *quite so* much work."

"I know what you mean," I said. "Marriage would still be difficult and expensive. But, boy, if I didn't love Logan – Um, if I didn't *like* him a lot—" (I was blushing.)

Dawn smiled. "You can say 'love', Mary Anne."

"Okay. If I didn't love him, I could never be married to him and take care of Sammie with him. It's hard enough when we do love each other. . . Oh, I almost forgot. I have to feed—"

The phone rang. Jessi picked it up. "Logan? Okay, hang on a sec." Jessi handed the phone to me. "It's your husband."

"Hi, dear," I said.

"Hi. Did you feed Sammie?"

"I was just about to."

"Okay. By the way, is Claudia's room warm enough?"

"Yes." Logan reminded me of Kristy and Alan.

74

"Maybe you should add a little blanket to the basket."

"But it's almost seventy degrees outside . . . *dear*," *I* said. "Sammie is fine. Or she will be after I feed her."

Logan let me hang up and feed Sammie. Kristy fed Izzy, and Stacey fed Bobby. "You know," said Kristy, "if we really had to feed babies, we'd have to stop and prepare their feeds. That would take even more time. I think we're getting off easy."

"*I still* wish Logan would let me look after Sammie more often," I said. "Sometimes I think he doesn't trust me."

"Oh, he's just being overprotective," said Claud.

There seemed to be a lot of that going around.

"Well, I think you should all just feel lucky that you *don't* actually have babies," said Jessi. "That this is just a school project."

"And that it will be over in less than a month," added Mal. "I remember when my mum was pregnant with Claire. If she had been at school then, she would have had to drop out."

"Mallory. She had six other kids to look after," said Kristy.

"That's not what I mean. You don't know how tired you feel when you're pregnant. And you're even tireder after the baby comes. Busier, too."

Hmm. I wondered if Sharon could handle her job, as well as being "tireder" and busier than usual. Well, of course she could. Dawn and I would help her whenever she wanted. She would only have to do one third of the usual mothering. Now, if she and Dad would just come to their senses.

9th CHAPTER

Thursday

Who knew an egg could be so scary? Well, maybe I should have known. When I was five I went through this phase during which I was terrified of pigeons for no good reason. Anyway, I sat for Bobby and Alicia Gianelli this afternoon, and Alicia... well, when she first saw my son she screamed. Mrs Gianelli hadn't said anything about Alicia having an egg phobia, so I suppose it was the surprise of finding an egg underneath the flannels in the mixing bowl. Maybe she expected a kitten or something. Also, the egg's name was the same as her brother's. I suppose that was confusing.

The Gianellis were new clients of the BSC. None of us had babysat for them before the afternoon of Stacey's job. Kristy knew Bobby slightly because he's in Karen's class at school. That was how the Gianellis had heard about the BSC. But basically they were uncharted territory. You know, a new experience.

Uncharted territories and new experiences make me nervous, but Stacey enjoys a good challenge. She was looking forward to her job at the Gianellis'. She adores meeting people, especially kids.

Stacey walked straight to the Gianellis' house after school. She ran up their front steps, stuck her finger out to ring the bell, and realized there was a piece of tape over it. (Over the bell that is. Not over her finger.) To the left of the bell was a small sign that read, CHILD SLEEPING, PLEASE KNOCK.

Stacey knocked lightly on the door, and it was opened by this tall man with a moustache. "Hi, I'm Mr Gianelli," he whispered.

"I'm Stacey McGill," Stacey replied.

Mr Gianelli ushered Stace inside, quietly explaining that Mrs Gianelli was at work, Alicia was napping, and Bobby had not yet come home from school. "He takes the bus," said Mr Gianelli in explanation. Then he noticed Stacey's mixing bowl. "What's that?" he asked.

Stacey began to tell him about Mrs Boyden and Modern Living, but Mr Gianelli interrupted her. "Ah, the egg project," he said. "I know it well. I used to be a teacher. Good luck."

He gave Stacey some instructions, showed her where important things (like the first-aid kit) were kept, handed her a list of emergency phone numbers, then left to go to a meeting in Stamford.

Stacey sat at the kitchen table and waited for Bobby to come home or for Alicia to wake up. While she waited, she talked to her own Bobby, the one in the plastic mixing bowl.

"Pretend I'm feeding you," she said wearily to the egg. "By the way, you're going over to your father's house tonight instead of tomorrow. I can't take care of you tonight. I'm way behind in everything, thanks to—"

"Are you the babysitter?" asked a sleepy voice.

Stacey whirled her head round. She hadn't heard anyone come into the kitchen. Standing a few metres away, apparently keeping her distance, was a dark-haired, dark-eyed little girl with olive skin. She looked curiously from Stacey to the mixing bowl and back to Stacey.

"Hi!" Stacey said brightly. "Yes, I'm your sitter. My name is Stacey. Stacey McGill. You must be Alicia."

The girl nodded. Then she held up four fingers. "I'm this many," she added.

"I bet you've just had your birthday."

Alicia nodded again. "What's in the bowl?" she asked. "What are you talking to?" She stepped closer to Stacey.

Stacey grinned. "I think you'll be surprised. Want to see?"

"Okay." Alicia peered into the bowl.

Stacey pulled back the flannels. There was Bobby.

"Aaghhh!" shrieked Alicia. She burst into tears.

"What's the matter?" exclaimed Stacey.

"I don't like that thing! Why do you have it with you?"

Stacey paused, trying to work out what to tell Alicia. Before she had a chance to speak, the front door opened, then closed. "Bobby!" cried Alicia.

Bobby Gianelli hurtled into the kitchen and flung his school bag on the floor. "I'm home!" he announced. "Hi, Alicia. Hi, babysitter."

Alicia was still crying. "Bobby, look in that bowl," she said, pointing.

Bobby took a look at Bobby. "Weird," he said. He opened the fridge and removed a carton of milk. "Whose is it?"

"It's mine," Stacey answered. And then she explained about the Modern Living project. "And you'll never guess what," she said finally.

"What?" asked Bobby. He and Alicia were sitting at the table, facing Stacey. They looked at her seriously.

"His name is Bobby."

"That *egg's* name is Bobby?" said Bobby. Stacey nodded. "Well, remember, I'm supposed to pretend it's my baby, not just an egg. And if he were my baby, I would have named him."

"Right," said Bobby. He put his empty glass in the sink.

"So, Bobby, what do you want to do today?" asked Stacey.

Bobby opened a cupboard and looked inside. He closed the cupboard. Then he knelt down and opened his school bag.

"Bobby?" said Stacey again. (No answer.) "Bobby?"

"Are you talking to me?" asked Bobby. Stacey nodded. "Oh, sorry. I thought you were talking to your egg. What do I want to do today? I don't know. Play football, I suppose, if the other kids will play. I'd better change into my kit." Bobby left the kitchen. From halfway up the stairs to the second floor he called, "Can I bring Bobby with me?"

"You *are* Bobby!" replied Alicia.

"I think he means this Bobby," Stacey said, tapping the mixing bowl. "I'll see!" she called back. (She was thinking, No way.)

"Oh, good. Let Bobby take that egg,"

said Alicia, who was sitting as far from the bowl as possible, her eyebrows knitted.

"Don't you like Bobby?" asked Stacey.

"He's my brother!" replied Alicia.

"I mean the egg. Are you afraid of Bobby the egg?"

"Yes."

"Are you afraid of all eggs?"

"No."

"Then why are you afraid of Bobby?"

"I'm not. He's my—"

"Bobby the *egg*!"

"I never saw an egg in bed before."

"Pretend he's a baby, not an egg."

At that moment, Bobby the boy returned to the kitchen in his football kit, which turned out to be a sweatshirt, a pair of jeans, and a bicycle helmet. "Okay, I'm ready," he said. "Is the egg?"

"*Is Bobby*," Alicia corrected him.

"What?" said Bobby.

"What?" said Stacey.

"Never mind," said Alicia.

"I'm ready to play football with the egg," said Bobby.

Yikes, thought Stacey. "Bobby," she said, "*I* have to look after the egg. He belongs to me. Do you understand?"

"Sort of." Bobby left then, saying he would be over the road.

"Okay, Alicia, what do you want to do?" asked Stacey.

"Walk to the stream. But not with Bobby."

Stacey sighed. Then she saw that Alicia was truly frightened, so she called Austin Bentley and asked him to come and pick up Bobby early. Luckily, he was at home. Later, after he and Bobby left, Stacey and Alicia walked down the street to the little stream. Alicia sat on a sunny rock and tossed pebbles into the water. Stacey sat on a patch of dry grass and thought. What if Bobby had been her real child and she had no husband to call on for help? she wondered. What did you do if you were a single parent and you were at work and your child got ill and the nurse phoned and said he should come home from school? What if you couldn't leave your job? Or what if you were at home and something happened to you and you simply needed help?

"I bet my mum is scared sometimes," Stacey said over the phone to me that night. "I bet she wonders about the "what ifs". Like what if she got a job and she was at work and I was at school and I went into a diabetic coma? Or what if something happened to *Mum* and no one could get in touch with my dad? I bet Mum worries a lot, Mary Anne."

"I think all parents do," I replied.

"But they probably feel a little safer if they aren't *single* parents."

"Mm. Maybe. Stace? Are you worried

because you're the daughter of a divorced mum? And your dad doesn't live nearby? That would be okay. I used to worry more when my dad was single."

"Yeah. I worry sometimes." Stacey paused. "You know, this afternoon was kind of funny with two Bobbies, and Alicia afraid of the egg and everything. But I decided something. I am going to wait until I'm really old before I have a human baby."

10th CHAPTER

Ever since we had our baby, Logan and I had spent very little time alone together. We hadn't been out – just the two of us – for ages. How many places can you easily take a baby to? I suppose we *could* have taken Sammie to Pizza Express or the diner or the coffee shop, but it just didn't seem like a great idea. Anyway, Logan and I would have been busy feeding Sammie, holding her, and doing all those things you have to do to occupy a baby, and that would have sort of defeated the purpose.

But one Friday, at the end of Modern Living class, Logan said to me, "Mary Anne, I'd really like us to go out tonight. I hate to leave Sammie behind, but . . . I don't know. I just want to go to the cinema or something."

Considering how attached Logan had become to our daughter, this seemed like an especially nice idea. I think he was taking our class project a little more seriously than anyone, except maybe Alan and Kristy. If I hadn't known better, I might have thought he cared more about Sammie than he did about me. So a film sounded like a terrific idea, and I told him so. "Oh, Logan, great!" I exclaimed. "I can't wait. And don't worry about Sammie. I'll take care of everything."

"Great. I'll come to your house at six-thirty."

Ding-dong.

That evening, our doorbell rang promptly at six-thirty. Dad and Sharon were upstairs getting ready to go out to dinner. Dawn was babysitting for Haley and Matt Braddock.

I was standing at the front door holding Sammie in her basket.

When I let Logan inside, the first words out of his mouth were, "What's Sammie doing?" He took the basket from me.

"Sleeping?" I suggested.

"I mean, what's she doing *here*?"

"Coming with us," I answered. "We can't leave her alone."

"Didn't you get a babysitter?"

I shook my head. "Dad and Sharon are going out. Dawn's babysitting at the Braddocks'. I didn't want to ask any of them to look after Sammie."

86

"Well, what about someone else? Claudia or someone?"

"Oh, Logan. Can't we just bring Sammie with us? We don't have time to find a sitter now. We'll miss the beginning of the film."

"Bring a baby to the cinema? No way."

But in the end, that was what we did.

I checked Sammie to make sure the identifying marks on her shell still showed up. Then I added a large scrap of flannel to her basket, since our cinema starts using the air-conditioning around the middle of March, in order to keep the temperature at a pretty steady 45° all year-round.

"When's she due for her next feed?" Logan asked me, as we stood in the queue, that was stretching down the pavement.

"Right in the middle of the film," I answered. "But that'll be okay. One of us will be holding her anyway."

"Yeah. One of us will."

Something in Logan's tone of voice made me glance at him and wonder exactly how our evening was going to go. But just then the doors opened, and we filed inside along with the rest of the crowd. I got distracted juggling Sammie, my purse and the extra sweaters I'd brought along. I forgot what Logan had said. And how he'd said it.

"Are you hungry?" Logan asked me, as we walked through the lobby.

"Sort of. Are you"

"Starving. I didn't eat dinner. What do you want?"

"A small popcorn and a small diet Coke."

"Okay." Logan went up to the counter and said to the woman, "One small popcorn, one giant popcorn, one small diet Coke, one large diet Coke, and a large box of Peanut M&M's, please."

Well, not only did all that food cost a fortune, but the two of us couldn't carry it. Not with Sammie and the sweaters. We had to get one of those cardboard boxes like you get on trains, and then sort of hobble into the auditorium and down a darkened aisle.

"If we were really married and really on a budget," I said to Logan, as we looked for seats, "we could probably have paid our electricity bill with the money we spent on food and cinema tickets tonight."

"I know."

"Just think if we had to pay a babysitter, too."

"I suppose you have to splurge sometime," said Logan, but he looked as if he weren't sure he meant that.

The auditorium was getting crowded. Even so, I whispered to Logan, "I think we're going to need three seats tonight. We have so much stuff."

Luckily we found a row consisting of

three empty seats. It was right over on the side of the auditorium and quite close to the front, but at least we'd found what we needed. I eased myself into the middle seat, and Logan sat on the aisle. I put Sammie in the third seat, the one by the wall. But she didn't weigh enough to hold the seat down.

It flipped back up, trapping Sammie and her basket between the seat and the seat back, "Yikes!" I cried.

Logan saw what had happened, but he was holding that flimsy box full of spilly drinks and popcorn. He needed both hands to carry it. Even so, he nearly dropped it. "Mary Anne!" he hissed.

"I'm *sorry*," I said crossly. I dropped my armload of sweaters and grabbed the handle of Sammie's basket with one hand and the seat with the other. I pushed the seat down and gingerly lifted the basket.

Sammie was safe inside.

"She's okay," I said to Logan.

"I knew this wasn't a good idea," he replied. "Okay. Now *hold* Sammie."

"I can't. I mean, I can't hold her *and* the popcorn *and* my drink. Just a sec." I pulled down the seat again and put the sweaters on it. "Do you want to give me your coat?" I asked Logan. (He actually likes the temperature in the auditorium.)

Logan put the tray of food on the floor, took off his coat, handed it to me, and picked up the food. Then I put Sammie on Logan's coat, and he handed me my popcorn and drink. At last we were settled.

"Excuse me, is that seat taken?"

Logan and I glanced up. Standing at Logan's elbow was a tall man in a suit. He was looking at Sammie's seat with raised eyebrows.

"Well," said Logan.

"Well," I said.

The man checked his watch. "The film is going to begin any minute now, and the auditorium is packed," he pointed out.

I thought about what might happen if I told the man the seat was occupied by an egg. The outcome didn't look good.

Logan must have been thinking the same thing, because he sighed and said, "No, it's not taken."

I gave Logan back his coat, which he sat on.

I put on one of the sweaters.

I sat on the others.

Then I put Sammie on my lap.

"Logan," I whispered as the lights began to dim, "I can't hold Sammie and eat, too." (My food was on the floor.)

"Neither can I," Logan replied. "Anyway I've got more food than you."

"All right. I'm going to put Sammie's basket on the floor until I've finished eating. She'll be okay there."

"Shhh!" hissed the man on the other

side of me. He was the first person I've ever known who wanted to pay attention to the cartoon about not dropping litter in the auditorium, and buying fresh popcorn at the concession stand, and how to find the exits in case of fire.

"Sorry," I replied.

"You can't put Sammie on the floor!" Logan whispered loudly.

"SHHH!"

"Sorry."

I put Sammie on the floor anyway. "She's right between my feet," I said to Logan. "If anyone takes her basket, I'll know about it."

"Excuse me," said the man, "are you two going to talk through the *entire* film, or just this first part?"

"Sorry," I said again.

But Logan said, "I think just this first part." Only he said it so softly the man didn't hear him.

The film turned out to be really good. It was funny and exciting. I was glad of that. During the first half of the picture, Logan kept turning to me and grinning. He was relaxing. So was I.

Except for my right foot. It had gone numb from being held in the same position for so long. Sammie or no Sammie, I had to shift my legs. So I did. Then I reached down to check on her. I felt around inside the basket.

Sammie had gone.

I gasped.

"What's the matter?" asked Logan.

"Sammie's not in the basket," I said. My heart was pounding. Logan grabbed up the basket. Then *he* felt around inside it. "She must have fallen out!" he exclaimed, trying to whisper. "You let her fall out. You lost our daughter!"

"I did not!"

"You did too. I bet she's rolling around in the aisle somewhere."

Logan was half right. Sammie was rolling around, but she wasn't in the aisle. She was just under my seat. Except we didn't discover that until after Logan had panicked and called over an usher to shine his torch on the floor. I thought the man in the third seat would kill us.

When Sammie was nestled safely in her basket again, Logan said stiffly, "Maybe we should hard-boil her." Then he tugged at my elbow. "Come on. We're going now, Mary Anne."

"Fine," I replied.

"Good," said the man.

Logan and I carried our stuff to the lobby, threw away our rubbish, and struggled into our coats. Logan picked up Sammie's basket.

"*I'm* supposed to have her tonight!" I cried.

"No way. You almost lost her," said

Logan. "Not that I really want to take care of her *again*. I'm always taking her."

"You mean you're always *taking* her. You never let me have her."

"Okay, then *you* take her tonight."

"Oh, no. You don't trust me. You just said so."

Logan didn't answer. He grabbed Sammie's basket. Then he went off to call his parents for a lift home, and I called my dad, and Logan and I went off in a huff.

11th CHAPTER

Tuesday

Well, my brothers and sisters did it again.

I don't know why that surprises you anymore, Mal.

I don't know why, either. But really... it's a good thing my parents are so tolerant. They'll have to buy another dozen eggs tomorrow.

Yeah. The kids were nice to Skip, though. I think they liked him.

Lucky for him.

What's that supposed to mean?

Nothing. Never mind. Come on, Dawn, we're way off track. We'd better finish this notebook entry. We have a meeting tomorrow.

On Tuesday night Mr and Mrs Pike went to Parents' Evening at Stoneybrook Elementary School. Imagine what the evening is like for them. *Seven* of their kids are pupils at the school: Claire at nursery school, Margo in the second grade, Nicky in the third, Vanessa in the fourth and the triplets in the fifth. No wonder they stay for the full three hours the school is open. (When I went to SES, my dad could do Parents' Evening in under an hour.)

While the Pikes visited SES, Mal and Dawn sat for Mal's younger brothers and sisters. Dawn left our house shortly after six-thirty. She left with her child, an egg named Skip. Skip lived in an empty Kleenex box, standard size. Dawn and her husband, this boy called Aaron Albright, whom Dawn didn't like very much, hadn't prepared the box except to line it with some paper towels to prevent Skip from injuring himself. (For the record, Dawn did *not* name Skip. Aaron did. Dawn said if she'd had her way, she would have named her son Douglas. She said Douglas is a good, strong name, and that Skip is what you'd name some little cartoon character, like maybe a young chicken wearing trainers and a cap.)

Dawn and Skip arrived at Mallory's just as Mr and Mrs Pike were getting ready to leave. Mal was trying to get the triplets to help her clear up the kitchen after dinner.

"Washing dishes is girls' work," Dawn heard Adam say.

"Adam," Mal replied, "there is no such thing as girls' work. But if there were, it would be called women's work."

"There *is* girls' work," said Adam.

"Is there boys' work?" Mal asked him.

"Of course."

"What is it?"

"Shovelling snow."

"I can do that," said Mal.

"Mowing lawns."

"I can do that, too."

"Cleaning gutters."

"And I can do that."

Adam turned away from his sister, looking pained. He couldn't win the argument, and he knew it. Luckily, when he turned round, he found a distraction. Dawn and the Kleenex box.

"Hi, everybody," said Dawn.

The youngest kids were still sitting at the kitchen table, dawdling over bowls of ice cream. Vanessa was sitting there, too, but a pad of paper lay in front of her. She was scribbling on it, probably composing a new poem. Mal was at the sink, and the triplets were hovering around the doorway, trying to escape the cleaning-up process.

Adam spotted Skip's box immediately. "What's that?" he asked.

"What's what?" answered Dawn, which

only goes to show how accustomed my friends and I had grown to lugging around mixing bowls and Kleenex boxes and stuff.

"That box," said Adam.

"Yeah, what is it? It's too small to be a Kid-Kit," added Margo.

"Oh, it's Skip, my egg," said Dawn wearily. "I'm supposed to pretend he's my baby. You know, feed him and everything."

"Feed an *egg*?" asked Jordan.

"Well, not really." Dawn described the Modern Living experiment with a little help from Mallory.

The Pike kids were so interested that they hardly noticed when their parents left for the elementary school. "Bye," they called vaguely.

"Dawn? How long will you be married to Aaron?" asked Vanessa.

"Hey, is your name Dawn Albright now?" Claire wanted to know.

"Yeah, do we have to call you Mrs Albright?" Nicky giggled.

"Oh, I hope not," said Dawn, but she was smiling. "Even if we had really, really, *really* got married, I wouldn't have changed my name. I like my name. I will always be Dawn Schafer."

Byron was looking into the tissue box for about the ninety-fifth time. "Your baby is naked," he commented.

"Yeah, he isn't even wearing a nappy," chimed Vanessa.

"I wish I were married and had an egg-baby," said Margo.

"Me, too," said Vanessa. She looked hopefully at Byron.

Byron sighed. "Okay. I'll be your husband," he said. "But only for tonight."

"Who will be my husband?" asked Margo.

"Not me," said Adam defiantly. "I am never, *ever* getting married."

"Jordan?" said Margo.

"Oh, all right."

Surprisingly, Nicky agreed to be Claire's husband.

"Okay, let's adopt babies," cried Vanessa.

"Adopt them from where?" asked Mal, even though she thought she knew what the answer would be.

"From the fridge, of course." Vanessa removed a half-empty carton of eggs from the bottom shelf of the fridge. She put it on the table and opened the lid carefully. "Ah, aren't they sweet?" she said.

"It's the egg nursery," added Nicky.

"Hey, there are enough here for each couple to adopt *two* children," Byron pointed out. "And Mum will still have one left over for tomorrow. Mal, can we? Adopt the eggs, I mean?"

"I suppose so," Mallory replied.

Several hands reached for the carton. They were stopped in mid-air by Jordan. "Wait! Where are you going to put them?

We'd better prepare rooms or something for them."

"*My* children are not going to live in any tissue box," said Margo. "*My* children are going to live in a house. Come on, Jordan." Margo took two eggs and led her brother to the recreation room, where she succeeded in talking him into arranging up the doll's house for their children.

Meanwhile, Vanessa and Byron arranged their eggs in a shopping bag, and Claire and Nicky put theirs in eggcups.

"That's what eggcups are *for*," said Claire.

"And, now they're dressed," added Nicky. (Each eggcup was in the shape of a pair of crossed legs wearing blue trousers. On the feet were polka-dotted socks and big red clown shoes.)

"We'd better dress *our* babies," said Vanessa. "I don't want them to go around naked, like Skip."

"How are we going to dress them?" asked Byron. "I'm not sewing anything. I'll be these eggs' father, but not their tailor."

"Oh, we don't have time to sew clothes," Vanessa replied. "We'll just colour their outfits on with crayons." She fetched a box of crayons from a shelf in the recreation room. "Here we go." Vanessa aimed a yellow crayon at one egg. "A nice bright shirt for you. . . Hey, this hardly shows up at all." Vanessa pressed down harder.

The egg broke.

"Oh! Oh, no! I've killed him!" shrieked Vanessa. "I've killed little – I've killed poor little, um, little—"

"We didn't even name him," said Byron sadly. "Poor egg."

"Poor, poor nameless killed egg," added Vanessa. She was holding the yellow crayon in one hand and the broken egg in the other. The yoke was sliming through her fingers and dripping on to the floor.

Dawn and Mallory both rushed forward – not to comfort Vanessa, but to cup their hands under the egg goo in an attempt to catch it.

"You stay here," Mal said to Dawn. "I'll go for the paper towels."

"The paper towels?!" wailed Vanessa. "Is that all you care about? The rug? Our egg has just been in a terrible accident. If *I* were in a terrible accident, would you run around trying to clean up my blood, or would you—"

"Vanessa! For heaven's sake, it's an egg," Mal reminded her.

"And you've only *known* the egg for a couple of minutes," said Dawn.

"I had grown attached," Vanessa replied stiffly.

Mal didn't answer. She ran off, then returned with a roll of paper towels and a plastic dustbin bag (bio-degradable). While she and Dawn cleared up the mess, Vanessa watched sadly. She looked around the recreation room at Margo and Jordan, who were putting their eggs to bed in the doll's house, and at Nicky and Claire, who had loaded their eggs (in the cups) into a doll's buggy and were taking them for a walk to the garage door. Then she looked at Byron, who was lowering their remaining son into the paper bag.

"Mallory, may we please have that last egg?" she asked in a small voice.

"What – the one in the fridge?"

"Yes."

"Then we won't have *any* eggs." (Mallory had a sneaking suspicion that a few more accidents might occur.)

"But . . . but. . ." Vanessa's lower lip k trembled. "My *baby*!"

"Maybe you should let her have it," Dawn whispered to Mal.

Mal sighed. "Okay. I don't think one egg is worth all this trouble." She turned to her sister. "Vanessa, you can have the egg."

"Oh, thank you! We'll be really careful this time, won't we, Byron? We won't try to dress either egg. They can be naked."

"Hey, you lot!" called Nicky. "We're taking our eggs out to dinner at a restaurant. Want to come with us?"

"Sure," agreed the other kids. And before long, the Pikes had returned to the kitchen and arranged the eggs around the table.

Nicky stood to the side, a dish towel over one arm. "Here are the specials *du jour*," he announced. "Eggs over easy, eggs Benedict, egg salad—"

"Nicky!" cried Claire and Margo.

Mal and Dawn began to laugh. The Pike kids could make anything fun.

12th CHAPTER

"I want a divorce."

"I beg your pardon?" said Mrs Boyden.

"I want to divorce Miles."

It was Shawna Riverson who was speaking, and she wasn't kidding. Our Modern Living class had just got under way, and I had a feeling it wasn't going to be a typical class. What was typical about a class in which the pupils got married and had to care for egg-babies?

When we had settled ourselves at our desks that morning, Mrs Boyden had moved in front of her desk. Usually she sits behind it in a teacher-y sort of way. But on that day, she was wearing jeans and a casual top, and she perched herself *on* her desk.

"Okay, kids, let's talk," she had said. "Tell me how you're doing as couples. Tell me how each of you is doing as half of a couple."

That was when Shawna had said she wanted a divorce.

"Shawna, what's going on?" asked Mrs Boyden.

"It's just not working out, that's all," she said.

A couple of kids sniggered. Shawna sounds as if she were speaking lines from a soap opera. Logan and I looked at each other. *We* weren't sniggering. We hadn't laughed much since the night at the cinema. If something was wrong between Shawna and Miles, I could understand that. These things happened.

Mrs Boyden didn't laugh, of course. She gazed solemnly at Shawna. "Tell me what's happening," she said.

"I have to take complete charge of the – of our baby." (Apparently, Shawna and Miles had not named their child.) "Miles hardly ever takes care of it. I lug it around school. I do everything."

Mrs Boyden didn't so much as glance at Miles. She never turned her attention away from Shawna. "Have you asked him to help?" she wanted to know. "Or do you just expect him to?"

"She just expects me to!" Miles burst out. "She never talks to me. She acts as if I'm a mind reader. As if I'm supposed to know everything she thinks or everything she wants."

"Hold on, Miles," Mrs Boyden interrupted. "Let Shawna finish speaking. Then you can have a turn. Shawna?"

"Well, I shouldn't have to ask him to do everything."

"Has he ever taken care of a baby before?" asked Mrs Boyden.

"I don't know."

"No, I haven't!" exclaimed Miles.

"But the point is, I have this egg all the time," said Shawna. "Yesterday I missed half of my gym class moving the – the baby around, trying to keep it out of the sun. And I was late for school this morning because I left the egg at home and had to go back for it."

"I see," said Mrs Boyden. "Miles?"

While Miles spoke, I thought. Shawna and Miles hadn't named their egg. They didn't want to be bothered with it. As far as Shawna was concerned, having a baby was a pain in the neck. Yet Shawna did treat the egg as her baby. If she'd been totally disinterested, she could have left her baby at home that morning when she realized what she'd done. But she went back for it. I was amazed by how real our children had become to us. On some level, my classmates and I felt as if we were actually married and as if we were actually parents. Mrs Boyden was pretty clever. Maybe she was a little unconventional, but she was becoming one of my favourite teachers.

"I don't really have time for the egg or for this experiment," Miles was saying, "but I wouldn't, you know, abandon a kid. I'd take care of the egg, if Shawna would ever give it to me."

"Why haven't you ever asked for it?" exploded Shawna. Her eyes had filled with tears. By then, the room was absolutely silent. No one was sniggering. No one was even smiling.

Miles looked at his hands, which were folded on his desk. His mumbled answer to Shawna was, "I don't know."

Shawna didn't reply. She turned her head away in disgust.

That was when Logan poked me. I leaned towards him, thinking he was going to whisper something about Shawna. Instead, he pointed across the room to two kids I didn't know very well, Angela and Kevin. They were holding hands and Angela was crying. In the emptiness that seemed to follow Miles's statement, Angela put up her hand (the one that wasn't clinging to Kevin).

"Yes, Angela?" said Mrs Boyden. She handed Angela a box of Kleenex but didn't tell her to stop crying or anything.

I was completely unprepared for what Angela said. I'd thought she was crying because of what had gone on between Shawna and Miles. Maybe they reminded her of her own parents. But when Angela said, "Um, Kevin and I lost our baby," I nearly died.

"What do you mean?" asked Mrs Boyden.

"We lost her."

"We lost the *egg*," Kevin spoke up. "It happened yesterday afternoon. We were at the park. Cathy was with us. She's our egg. I mean, she was our egg. And she was in the box we always kept her in."

"The yellow biscuit tin," Angela added.

"Right," said Kevin. "Cathy was with us when we left school, and she was with us when we reached the park. We checked. But when we were leaving the park, we checked again, and the box was empty."

"We tried to retrace our steps," said Angela. "We walked around everywhere. But we couldn't find her."

"We don't know how she got out of the box."

"I feel terrible," said Angela. "Honestly. I mean, if she really had been our kid. . . How could we have been so irresponsible?" Angela was crying again.

The room was silent. I suppose everyone was thinking similar thoughts. That in the blink of an eye, anything can happen to a child. You turn around and she's gone – lost or maybe even kidnapped. Or she's eaten something poisonous. Or she's fallen, or been hit by a car. Those things happen every day to all kinds of families.

Angela and Kevin were the first kids in our Modern Living class to lose their baby, and it wasn't funny.

"Are you worried about the grade you'll get on your project now?" asked Mrs Boyden, which seemed a little insensitive.

"No!" cried Angela. (She shouted it, actually.)

At the same time, Kevin said, "Yeah, I suppose so."

Angela gave him a hard look, then softened. "All right, I suppose I am a little worried, but that wasn't the first thing I thought about when I looked in the box and discovered it empty."

Mrs Boyden nodded. "I understand. Listen, don't worry about your grade. You still owe me a paper, and you can complete it despite what has happened, but some aspects of your project will now change. See me after class, okay?"

"Okay," answered Kevin and Angela.

Mrs Boyden turned her attention to the rest of the class. "What else?" she asked. She propped her feet on an empty chair. "Anyone? No one. . .? So things are perfect for the rest of you?"

At that point, I nearly put up my hand. No, things were not just fine between Logan and me. We had nearly lost our own child. We had discovered we didn't quite trust one another as parents.

"Mrs Boyden?" said a quiet voice.

I turned round. The voice belonged to a boy who was new at school. He'd been paired up with this girl called Zoe.

"Yes, Tarik?" said Mrs Boyden.

Tarik couldn't look at our teacher. He couldn't look at Zoe or anyone else, either. He stared straight ahead and sort of spoke to the blackboard. "Maybe I should talk to you about this after class, but I – I can't complete the project. I've never had to say that to a teacher before, but it's the truth. I can't do this."

"Why not?" asked Mrs Boyden gently.

"It's just . . . too much. I mean, Zoe – she's doing her part. But, see, I play two sports and I'm in the choir and I have an after-school job, and my parents are getting divorced and my mum needs a lot of help and I can't do this egg thing, too."

"You mean, caring for a child is more than you can handle at this point in your life? You're overwhelmed?"

"Well, yeah."

"That's okay. Put that in your paper. There is no expected outcome for this project, nothing right or wrong that can be said in your papers. But I'd like to talk to you after class, too. Zoe as well. We'll work something out. Okay. Anyone else?"

★

Whew! What a class. When it was over, Logan and I just sat in our chairs. Logan doodled. I looked at Sammie, safe in her basket on Logan's desk, protected by more padding than ever.

"I suppose we aren't the only ones having problems," I said.

"I suppose not," replied Logan. "In fact, I think we're doing pretty well."

"I bet most parents argue about how to bring up their kids."

"Not to mention other things. Like money. My parents had a big loud talk about money last night. That's what they call arguments – loud talks. And they had the loud talk at about two A.M."

"Scary," I commented.

"Yeah." Logan got to his feet. He picked up Sammie's basket."

"I thought you had baseball practice for gym today," I said.

"I do."

"So let me take Sammie."

"Well—"

"You still don't trust me, do you? Just because I lost her for five seconds. Logan, accidents happen. Look at Kevin and Angela."

"I know." Logan didn't let go of Sammie, though.

My eyes filled with tears. "I'll see you later," I whispered, and ran out of the room without Sammie.

"Mary Anne!" called Logan.

I didn't answer.

Logan and I had a long way to go before we could reconcile our differences.

13th
CHAPTER

Not long after that memorable Modern Living class, I found myself babysitting for Ricky and Rose again. For some reason, I wasn't looking forward to the job. I wasn't dreading it; I just wasn't approaching it with glee. I wasn't jumping up and down, singing, "Oh, boy, babies! I get to take care of babies again!"

Luckily, Sammie didn't come along on the job with me. Logan had taken her home with him.

"This will make the afternoon much easier," I said to Kristy, as we left school that day. "Just *two* babies."

"Yeah. Piece of cake. Sitting for the Rodowsky boys could be much harder. The Walking Disaster and his two brothers. Think what could happen at the Rodowskys' in an afternoon."

I rolled my eyes. "Mayhem," I said.

"Chaos. Anarchy."

Kristy smiled. "Oh, there's my bus!" she cried. "I've got to go. Have fun this afternoon, Mary Anne."

"Thanks!" I said. "I'll talk to you tonight."

I walked to the Salems' house, dawdling a little. The weather was absolutely gorgeous, warmer than usual, with a wonderful smell of damp earth and new leaves in the air. Perfect baby-walking weather.

I rang the Salems' bell and was greeted by Mrs Salem, who looked pretty worn out. Her eyes were red, and she seemed limp.

"Hi, Mary Anne," she said. "Whew! I'm exhausted. The last thing I want to do is go to this meeting, but I'm on the board of the Small Animal Rescue League, so I have to attend."

I hesitated. I wanted to ask Mrs Salem if everything was okay, but I wasn't sure I should. I mean, adults always ask kids that question, but should a kid ask an adult? I didn't want Mrs Salem to think I was being nosy. However, *she* had said she was exhausted, so I went ahead and asked.

"Oh, I'm fine," Mrs Salem replied. "Just tired. The babies seem to be changing their routine. I never know what to expect. They were sleeping through the night just fine, and now, well, they're not and they didn't go down for their naps this afternoon until later than usual. So they should sleep longer. You'll probably have a chance to get some homework done this afternoon."

"Great. I was going to take Rose and Ricky for a walk, but I *do* have a lot of work."

Mrs Salem wrote down the number of the Small Animal Rescue league and reminded me where the emergency numbers could be found. Then she left. I watched her back her car down the drive. She was yawning.

I settled myself at the kitchen table with a glass of orange juice and a bran muffin. I opened the book of short stories we were reading for English class.

"The Tell-tale Heart," by Edgar Allan Poe," I murmured.

The story was scary. I don't know why I was surprised. Poe's stories are all scary. I was reading along, and my heart was beginning to pound, when something squeaked.

I yelped and knocked over the glass of orange juice.

"Drat!" I cried, as the juice spread across the Salems' table and dripped down one of the legs and on to the floor.

I mopped it up with paper towels and forgot about the squeak until. . .

"WAHH!"

I jumped, jerking my hands up and knocking the book across the kitchen to a work surface, where it landed on this bowl of fruit.

"WAHH!" I heard again. It was Ricky. I could tell his cry from Rose's. I could also tell that his cry was going to become a scream.

I ran upstairs and into the twins' room. Ricky was sitting in his cot. His face was red and tearstained.

"Hey, Ricky. What's the matter?" I said soothingly as I lifted him into my arms. "Your mum said you just went off to sleep. Why are you up so soon? Are you wet? Or hungry?"

Ricky's answer was a shriek, so I hurried him out of the room before he could wake his sister.

I carried Ricky to the kitchen.

I felt his nappy. Dry.

I offered him a bottle. He fussed and turned his head away.

"What is it? What can I do for you?" I asked.

Ricky drooled and cried.

From upstairs, I thought I heard a whimper, although it was hard to hear over the noise Ricky was making.

"Come on," I said to him. "We'd better check on Rose."

I carried Ricky back upstairs. With every step, his wails seemed to grow louder.

"Shh, shh," I said soothingly. "Calm down."

But he didn't. By the time we had reached the bedroom, he was throwing his head back and screaming so hard I thought he would choke.

Rose stirred in the cot. Her eyelids fluttered. She was waking up.

I fled downstairs. "Ricky, Rose needs her sleep. Can't you calm down?" I said. I walked him around the ground floor of the house, making a circle from the kitchen to the dining room to the living room, through the hall, and back into the kitchen As long as I kept moving, Ricky confined his crying to loud whimpers. If I slowed down, the screaming started. I knew what he needed. He needed a walk in the buggy. I was pretty sure that (and only that) would calm him down. But what about Rose? I couldn't wake her up just because her brother needed a walk. I also couldn't check on her while her brother was crying. If I brought him with me, he'd disturb her. If I left him strapped into his high chair or his baby chair, he would begin the awful earshattering, choking screaming.

I was desperate.

I phoned my sister.

"Dawn, can you come over to the Salems' straight away?" I asked shakily.

"Of course. What's wrong?"

I explained as quickly as I could. "So the

thing is," I finished up, "I can't be in two places at the same time. Someone has to take Ricky outside. I've never heard such screaming. Or seen such drooling."

"I bet he's teething," said Dawn. "Give him one of those hard crackers. I'll be over as soon as I can."

"Thank you. You've saved my life," I said seriously.

Fifteen minutes later, Dawn arrived at the Salems', sweaty from having ridden her bicycle in such a hurry. I was still walking Ricky in circles around the ground floor. He was gumming madly on a teething biscuit I'd found in the kitchen cupboard. The biscuit had calmed him down slightly – as long as we kept moving.

"Do you mind taking Ricky?" I asked Dawn. I circled from the dining room into the living room, Dawn at my heels. "I'd take him, but I think I'd better stay here in case Mrs Salem comes home. It would probably be better if she found the same babysitter who was here when she left the house."

"I don't mind taking him," Dawn replied. "It's so nice out. Where's the buggy? We'll leave straight away."

"It's in the garage. Can you wheel it to the front door? I don't want to stop moving until I can put Ricky straight into the buggy."

Dawn found the buggy while I circled with Ricky. As soon as she was waiting outside, I made one last circle, but when I reached the hall, I turned right instead of left, walked through the front door, which Dawn was holding open, and plopped Ricky in the buggy. Dawn was pushing him down the walk before he knew what was happening. Immediately, his cries began to fade.

I went back inside and checked on Rose, who was (miraculously) still sleeping. Then I collapsed in an armchair in the living room.

I was just reclining there, enjoying the peace when. . .

"WAHH!"

Oh, no. Not again.

I ran upstairs.

Now Rose was awake, sitting up in her cot, screaming and drooling.

"I suppose you're teething, too," I said wearily, understanding why Mrs Salem looked so haggard. "At least I know what to do now. You need a biscuit and a walk."

I found a teething biscuit for Rose – and then realized that in order to take her for a walk, I needed the buggy, of course. I ran to the front door and looked up and down the street. Dawn and Ricky had already disappeared. Double drat. So I picked up Crying Baby Number Two and began making the circle. Kitchen to dining room to living room to hall and back to kitchen.

I was still walking Rose when Dawn returned, and Dawn and I were still walking both babies when Mrs Salem returned.

"Do I *have* to write about that job in the notebook?" I asked Dawn that evening. "I would really rather forget the entire incident."

14th CHAPTER

Ordinarily, when the phone rings at our house, everyone runs for it as if we were going to win a prize for being the first one to answer. On the evening after my latest disaster with Ricky and Rose, the phone rang, and *no one* dived for it.

We were all tired.

I was tired from my taxing afternoon. Dawn was tired for the same reason. And Dad and Sharon were tired because they'd each had a difficult day at work. Every member of my family was worn out in a different room.

Ring . . . ring . . . ring.

The phone rang three times before I realized what was happening.

"Dawn, can you get that?" I called from my bedroom.

"Why?" she called from *her* bedroom.

"Because it's *ring*ing."

"Mum'll get it."

"No she won't!" Sharon yelled from downstairs. "She's too tired."

Ring . . . ring.

"Will someone please answer the phone?" said Dad.

"Mary Anne will!" shouted Dawn.

"I will not! I can't move!"

The phone stopped ringing.

"Did someone answer that?" called Sharon.

"No!" replied Dad and Dawn and I.

"You know, that could have been an important call," said Dawn. "Maybe someone died and left us an island or something."

"A tropical island?" I asked.

"Yes, with palm trees and beautiful seashells."

The phone rang again.

I sprinted into Dad and Sharon's room. So did Dawn. We grabbed the receiver at the same time. "Hello?" we said.

"Hello?" said Dad and Sharon on the other extension.

"Hello," said a fifth voice.

"Logan?" I asked.

"Mary Anne?"

"Okay, everyone can get off the phone," I said. "We haven't inherited an island. This is just Logan calling."

"*Just* Logan?" he repeated. "Thanks a lot."

"Don't be insulted," I told him, giggling, as the rest of my family went back to being tired. "It's just that – Oh, never mind. It's a long story."

"Oh, well, I was phoning because. . . You won't believe this, but good news! Sammie is walking, and I captured the event on video-tape."

I began to laugh again. "A Kodak moment?" I suggested.

"Definitely." Logan was laughing, too.

I knew he was phoning so we could talk things over, so we could make up once and for all. "How is Sammie really?" I asked.

"She's fine. How were the twins this afternoon?"

"A mess. They're teething. I'm glad you were looking after Sammie today. I could *never* have handled her *and* the twins. As it was, Dawn had to come over and help me."

"Wow! I hardly ever hear you say you can't handle a sitting job."

"Sitting is different when babies are involved."

"Yeah. Mary Anne? I'm sorry we've been arguing."

"Me, too," I answered. "It's Sammie and Modern Living. That's why we're arguing. Mrs Boyden is asking us to do something really difficult – be adults, be married, have babies, and at the same time be kids at school. I'm glad she didn't give us *real* babies. Can you imagine what a state we'd be in now?"

"For one thing, we'd be broke. Dad took Hunter to the doctor for a check-up the other day, and you know what that visit cost? Seventy-five dollars! Seventy-five dollars when nothing was wrong with him in the first place. And we still haven't got the bill from the lab for the tests they're doing. Who knows how much that will be for? I don't know how my parents can afford to look after three children. Kerry and Hunter and I are ex*pen*sive!"

"Well, we already know we can't afford even an egg right now, but I didn't expect us to argue so much. I thought that when two people got married they just moved into a nice little place and began hanging curtains and planting flower beds."

"You mean they played house?"

"I suppose so. I never thought about stuff like what to do if you can't find a babysitter. Or if you and your husband couldn't agree on how to bring up a baby."

"Maybe when you're older you can work those things out more easily."

"Maybe. I don't think that being older solves everything, though. Look at Dawn's mother and father. Or Kristy's mother and father. Or Stacey's mother and father."

"Yeah. But I bet you have a better *chance* at a relationship if you wait a while. Until after college or something."

"Probably."

"I mean, we couldn't get married now," said Logan.

"We? You and *I*? Get married *now*?" I squeaked. "I'll say we couldn't. I want to enjoy the rest of the eighth grade first. I want to enjoy being thirteen and not have to worry about all those things I'll have plenty of time to worry about when I'm twenty two or something."

"Yeah. I would like to play baseball without first having to think of who's going to watch Sammie. That would be a luxury. I'm not ready for so many complications."

"Me, neither. Logan, I really like you. I hope you know that."

"I do."

"But I'm not ready to be your wife, or anyone's else's wife."

"That's cool. I'm not ready to be a husband."

"Do you think this is the kind of material Mrs Boyden wants us to include in our report? What we learned about ourselves?"

"Probably. I think she wants us to consider ourselves as couples and also as the single parts of couples. Remember the questions she asked at the beginning of class one day? The day Shawna said she wanted to divorce Miles?"

"Yeah. And we've learned some things about loyalty and trust and independence and responsibility. Maybe we should divide our paper into two sections. In one, we'll describe what we've learned about ourselves. In the other, we'll describe what we've learned about relationships; about the aspects of relationships."

"That's a great idea," agreed Logan. He sighed.

"What's wrong?" I asked.

"Nothing. I'm just sitting here looking at Sammie. When this project is over, I'll miss her."

"Me, too."

"But not *too* much."

"No, not *too* much." I paused. "I wonder what Mrs Boyden will do with our babies when we don't need them any more."

"I don't even want to think about it."

"Neither do I. I think I should go now, Logan. I haven't started my homework yet. But I'll see you and Sammie at school tomorrow."

"Okay. Bye, Mary Anne. Love you."

"Love you, too."

We hung up. I was heading for my room but detoured down the hall to Dawn's room instead. I walked in and sat in her armchair.

"What did Logan want?" asked Dawn. She was sitting at her desk, writing up a lab report for science class, but she stopped and looked at me. She stuck her pencil in the pencil jar.

"To talk about Sammie. Nothing special, though. You know what I've been thinking, Dawn?"

"What?"

"About the Kumbel catalogue. You can throw it away."

"I can? How come?"

"Well, what's *your* opinion about my dad and your mum having a baby now? I mean, what's your opinion since you spent the afternoon with a fussing, teething baby?"

"Oh." Dawn looked sheepish.

"Because *I* was thinking," I went on, "that maybe it isn't a very good idea after all. Not that *we* couldn't take care of a baby properly. We *are* professional babysitters. But a new baby might be rough on our parents at their age. Not that they're old—"

"Of course not," interrupted Dawn. "But they might not be strong enough to go through teething."

"Or to toilet train a kid."

"Anyhow, they need their sleep now. How could they get up every three hours during the night to feed a newborn?"

"They couldn't. And in about ten years the kid would want to go to Disney World. Do you think Dad would ride Space Mountain with our brother or sister?"

"No way. Mum probably wouldn't, either."

"And you and I would be out of college

and living on our own by then," I pointed out. "So we wouldn't be any help."

"That's right."

"Where *is* the Kumbel catalogue?" I asked.

Dawn found it in her wardrobe. We opened it to the baby pages we had marked, and we gazed at the pictures.

"Not having a baby will save a lot of money, too," I said, looking at the prices. Baby equipment was not cheap.

"But that little lamp is awfully cute," said Dawn wistfully.

"Well, save your pennies," I said. "Maybe one day you can buy it for your own room." Dawn closed the catalogue. I stood up. "I'm still curious to know what our baby brother or sister would have looked like."

"And I think it would have been great if our parents had had a baby of their own. A little Schafer-Spier."

"But I suppose it wasn't meant to be."

"I suppose not."

15th CHAPTER

It was the last session of our Modern Living class. The following week we would begin a new course – Health. No one was very interested in it, but we had to take it, so complaining was no good. (Miles tried to look on the bright side. "Isn't sex education part of Health?" I heard him say. Logan laughed. I blushed.)

Logan and I walked into Mrs Boyden's class together. I was carrying Sammie in her basket. Logan was holding our precious term paper. It was 32 pages long, typed, single-spaced. Well, actually, word-processed, not typed. Logan had printed it out on his home computer.

We took our seats, and I put Sammie on my desk. Logan and I watched the room fill up with our classmates and their eggs. Mrs Boyden was at her desk, thumbing through her lesson book. When the bell rang, she closed the book and stood up.

"Well," she began, smiling, "you've made it. You survived."

"*We* didn't," said Angela. "Kevin and I lost Cathy. We—"

"I meant you survived as married couples," Mrs Boyden replied gently. "And I'm proud of all of you. Some very heavy issues have been discussed in this class, along with some very personal feelings. Your honesty is what made the class a success. Also, your ability to suspend disbelief. If you hadn't been able to pretend your eggs were babies, you wouldn't have learned so much.

"Today," Mrs Boyden went on, "I would like each husband and wife to pair up and write a short composition, which will be handed in with your final papers. The subject of the composition is saying goodbye to your children. The time is now twenty-one years in the future. Your babies have grown up, become adults, and finished their schooling. They are ready to leave you and lead lives of their own."

"Logan," I whispered, feeling tearful, "Sammie doesn't need us any more. She's going to leave us!"

"At the end of the class," said Mrs Boyden, "you will leave your eggs behind. They will no longer be your responsibility."

"What are you going to do with them?" asked Shawna.

"Do you really want to know?"

Shawna shook her head. "I don't think so."

"Okay. Break up into your pairs, then."

I slid my desk over to Logan's desk, bringing Sammie with me.

"So?" said Logan. "Where's Sammie going?"

"Off to her first important job," I answered. "In New York." (New York is where I hope to land *my* first important job.)

"We're going to let our baby move to big, dangerous New York City?"

"Dear, she's not a baby any more," I reminded my husband. "She's an adult. She's twenty-one. And she's been offered a position in a publishing house. She will be an editorial assistant. We can't hold her back."

"You're right," agreed Logan.

We wrote our composition and added it to our paper.

After we had handed in our work, I looked at Sammie and said, "I suppose this is goodbye. You've been a real—"

"A real good egg?" Logan interrupted.

I made a face at him. But I didn't say anything. I knew he was joking around because he didn't want to get sentimental in class, where everyone could see him.

Some men have such a hard time dealing with their emotions.

That afternoon our BSC meeting was attended by seven humans and no eggs. Although earlier I had been sad about letting Sammie go off to New York, I was now feeling quite free. I wasn't the only one.

Stacey bounced into club headquarters crying, "Freedom at last!" She sounded the way most kids do on the day the summer holidays start. "No more mixing bowl," she went on, "but I *do* miss Bobby . . . sort of. Well, just a teensy bit."

At 5:28, Jessie ran into the room, the last club member to arrive. As she settled onto the floor next to Mallory, she looked around, then asked, "Where are your babies?"

"Gone," said Kristy sadly.

"They grew up," added Dawn.

"Mine went to New York to start a career," I said.

Jessi and Mal didn't know *what* we were talking about, so we described our last Modem Living class to them.

"Cool. What are the rest of your children doing?" asked Mallory.

"Bobby is going to teach high school history," said Stacey.

"Izzy became a car mechanic," said

Kristy. "He opened a garage in Stamford. I made him promise to visit every Sunday."

"My baby is going to become a famous artist," said Claud. "Naturally."

"Mine's at medical school," said Dawn.

The phone rang then, and we arranged a job for Claudia with the Newtons.

"You know what I think?" I spoke up after a break in the conversation. "I suppose if I absolutely *had* to, I could bring up a child of my own. But I wouldn't want to. I'm too young."

"Also, your dad isn't ready to be a grandfather," said Stacey.

"No, I'm serious, Stace. I'm not kidding around. Do you think you could be a parent right now? I mean, if you'd just given birth?"

Stacey frowned. "No. I really don't. How would I support a baby? Anyway, I don't *want* to be a parent. Not yet."

"You're right," I agreed. "I could only bring up a baby if I lived at home and Dawn and Dad and Sharon helped me. I couldn't do it by myself."

"I do want to have kids one day though," said Dawn.

"Definitely!" agreed the rest of us.

"But maybe when I'm older," she went on. "When I'm twenty-five. Maybe even thirty. You know, now lots of women are having their first baby when they're *forty*. Or older. I'm not in any hurry."

"Me, neither," I said, "but I don't want

to wait until I'm forty. Twenty-five sounds like a good age."

"I'm going to have eight children, like my mum did," commented Mal.

"It's a good thing you won't have them all at once," replied Stacey. "You might want to stop after one or two."

"Maybe. Anyway, I don't have to decide now."

"And in two years you'll take Modern Living," said Kristy, "and you can have a trial run with just one egg-baby."

"I hope my first baby is a girl," said Jessi dreamily. "I will call her Mary Rose. I've always wanted a daughter named Mary Rose."

The phone rang again then, and our meeting became busy with BSC stuff. No one mentioned the eggs again.

When Dawn and I got home that evening, we received a call from Sharon, saying she and Dad would be about half an hour late and asking us to start dinner. So we did. As we took things out of the fridge and put them on the kitchen table, Dawn said, "Mary Anne, do you think you'll ever be able to eat eggs again?"

I shook my head. "Not for a long, *long* time."

"I know what you mean."

My sister and I began chopping vegetables for a salad. "I certainly am glad," I said, slicing a carrot, "that we didn't say anything more to our parents about having a baby."

"Whew! I'll say," agreed Dawn.

"Can you imagine if we had convinced them and your mum had got pregnant straight away and then we had finished Modern Living and had changed our minds?"

"We would have been a little late."

"Yeah, just a little."

"Is being a little late like being a little pregnant?" Dawn asked.

I laughed. "I suppose so. Either you are or you aren't."

Dad and Sharon entered the kitchen just in time to hear that last part of our conversation.

"Who's having a baby?" asked Dad suspiciously.

"No one, thank goodness," I answered. "No one we know of."

"How's dinner coming along, girls?" asked Sharon.

"It's ready," I said.

"Let's eat," said Dawn.

"Let's eat in the dining room," added Sharon.

"Ooh, special occasion?" I asked.

Sharon shrugged. "Maybe, maybe not."

We sat at the dining room table and passed around the salad and this Chinese vegetable dish Sharon makes and brown

134

bread and these vegetable patties that are supposed to look like hamburgers but don't.

When our plates were full, Sharon looked at Dawn, then at me, and smiled. "Girls," she said, "Richard and I have been thinking about your wish for a baby. You haven't mentioned it for a while, but we know that doesn't mean you aren't still thinking about it"

I know my face turned pale then. I felt faint. Across the table from me, Dawn's eyes widened to the size of basketballs, and her hands began to shake. Oh, *no*. Why couldn't parents just forget things once in a while? Why did they have to remember everything?

"Um," I said.

"Um," said Dawn.

"You see, the thing is, Dawn and I talked about it and we realized we shouldn't have. . ." My voice trailed off.

"Don't worry," said Sharon. "It's okay. Richard and I have discussed everything and we decided if you really want something to care for, you may get another pet. Tigger might like some company."

I let out the breath I was holding. Oh, a *pet*. I managed a grin at Dawn, who grinned back. "Do you want a pet?" I asked her.

"Do you?" Dawn countered.

"Not really. Tigger's enough."

"That's how I feel. . . But thanks, Mum. Thanks, Richard."

"Yeah, thanks," I said.

Dad looked surprised. "We thought you'd jump at the chance to get another pet."

"We might have, if it weren't for Modern Living," I replied.

"Modern Living?"

"Yeah. Dad," I said, "you have no idea how hard it is to be a parent."

KRISTY FOR PRESIDENT

The author gratefully acknowledges
Nola Thacker
for her help in
preparing this manuscript

1st
CHAPTER

Friday. Finally. And was I ever glad. It's too bad you can't organize the weeks so that Fridays come round more often. Or so that you have extra ones to use every once in a while, when you need them – like those cards in Monopoly to Get Out of Jail Free. Not that I think of Stoneybrook Middle School as jail.

But if Friday had just come earlier this week, I would have missed a test in science on Wednesday, for example. I didn't fail it. But I wasn't ready for ten true-false questions about the similarities and differences between vertebrates and invertebrates.

At least it was Friday now. The tannoy system was just finishing crackling and garbling out announcements, which sounded like someone with his hand over his mouth practising ventriloquism. (Stacey McGill says it brings a little of New York City here to Stoneybrook, Connecticut, because that's how all the announcements on the underground sound.) After the announcements we'd be going to assembly.

Stacey is from New York originally. She's a little more sophisticated than the rest of us. The rest of us isn't all of Stoneybrook Middle School, although she often does seem older than everyone else at SMS. The "us" I'm talking about is the Babysitters Club. That's a business that my six friends and I operate. I'm the chairman and Stacey is the treasurer and – well – more about that later.

When the announcements were over, and the bell had rung, I picked up my books and headed for the assembly hall. Stacey and Claudia Kishi were going in just as I got there. Stacey and Claudia are best friends–they share a sort of city-cool sense of style, for one thing – and Claud is also vice chairman of the BSC.

"Friday at last," said Claudia, as if she'd been reading my mind. Claudia is not too fond of school. In fact, you could probably say school is not her best subject, although she is bright and very creative.

"Does anybody know what this assembly is about?" I asked.

"Maybe," Claudia said, "they're going to cancel school for the rest of the day."

"Good idea," I replied.

"In your dreams," said Stacey, shaking

her head. Claudia and I grinned at each other and followed Stacey into the assembly hall.

Mary Anne Spier and Dawn Schafer were saving us seats.

I plopped down next to Mary Anne. "Whew! This week has been too long."

Mary Anne looked at me sympathetically. She knew about that science test. "I couldn't do everything you do, Kristy," she said. "It's amazing."

I thought about that and felt better: babysitting, coaching the Krushers, which is what you might call a well-rounded softball team (the youngest player is only two and a half and the oldest is eight), being chairman of the Babysitters Club, and keeping up with school is a pretty tough schedule. I raised my eyebrows and said, in a snobby tone, *"Organization.* If one is organized, one can do anything."

Mary Anne made a face, then suddenly lifted her arm and waved. Mallory Pike and Jessi Ramsey, who are sixth-graders and junior officers in the BSC, hurried to join us. Jessi was giggling and Mal was rolling her eyes, but before we could talk any more, the assembly was called to order.

It was not the most interesting assembly in the history of the school. In fact, it was more like having the tannoy announcements read clearly and in person. About five minutes after it started I looked down the row of seats and saw:

Stacey, staring into space, fiddling with one of her earrings (a small silver replica of the Eiffel Tower). Claudia, her head bent, her long black hair, which was swept up and over to one side, falling forward over her cheeks as she drew something in her notebook. Dawn, doing some quick catch-up homework. Mal, just plain reading – probably a horse story. Jessi, sitting very upright, one leg raised, flexing her ankle. Mary Anne, not doing anything quite so obvious to show she was bored, but glancing around – very casually, of course. Probably looking for Logan Bruno, who is her boyfriend.

I sneaked a quick look around myself, wishing Bart Taylor went to our school. I sort of have a crush on Bart. Only – I have a giant crush on him. Then I noticed the Special Needs kids. Like the BSC, they were all sitting together. But then they do everything together, even staying in the same classroom although the other pupils change classes.

Sometimes the other pupils – the "normal" ones – make fun of the Special Needs kids. I couldn't help wondering whether if we saw more of them, it would happen less. I mean, I know the world isn't perfect, and you can't change everybody. But you have to try, right?

What would I do, I wondered, remembering Susan, a girl who is autistic. I'd babysat for her not too long ago. That job – and Susan – had taught me to look at the Special Needs kids almost as if I were seeing them for the first time, which in a way I suppose I was. "Learning different". That was a phrase I'd heard used. They learned different things differently – the way Stacey was a whiz at maths and Claudia saw the world full of possibilities for creating new sculptures and drawings and paintings.

Susan was locked up in her own world, as if the world outside didn't exist at all. She was away now at a school that probably had the best possible chance of helping her. But these kids were right here. What if—

"Kristy?"

Mary Anne was poking me, and I realized the assembly was over.

Then I realized it wasn't over at all. It was a fire drill.

"Just in time," said Stacey. She nodded towards the stage, where the head teacher was thumping on the microphone, so it gave out one of those EEEEE-NNNNNNN sounds, like fingernails on the blackboard with the volume right up.

Mary Anne clapped her hands over her ears and made a face, and we all stood up obediently.

The head teacher was saying something, but you couldn't understand it. Fortunately, there had been so many fire drills lately that we were pretty experienced at handling them. There was a lot of shuffling and giggling and teachers clapping and making signals like traffic police. I heard a shriek and whipped round. Maybe the school really was on fire. But then I saw Cokie Mason, her face red. She was rubbing her shoulder and glaring at Alan Gray. He'd obviously just given her one of his stupid knuckle punches.

Alan Gray is such a goon sometimes.

"I bet that hurt," said Mary Anne, *almost* sympathetically. That's Mary Anne. She can be sympathetic to the most rotten people. And considering some of the tricks Cokie Mason has pulled on her (and on me, for that matter), Cokie should be at the top of Mary Anne's rotten-people list.

Thinking about that, I decided maybe, just this once, Alan wasn't being such a goon. "Probably another false alarm," I said.

"Yeah," said Claudia. "I like missing lessons, but this is a little *extreme*."

Everyone got outside pretty quickly. Since we had all been in the same place this was easier than usual. I noticed that some of the kids seemed to be drifting away, towards the pavement. I looked back at the school, half expecting to see smoke pouring out and teachers motioning us further away to safety. But SMS just stood there stolidly, the same as always.

I looked back and more kids were following. I couldn't believe it. Then one of the substitute teachers, Mr Zorzi, walked quickly by. A minute later we saw him at the head of the group of kids, his arms held up.

The mass exit from the school grounds stopped.

Claud started to laugh. "I don't believe it," she said. "Alan and the other boys just started walking and everyone followed."

She was right. Another teacher had gone out to join Mr Zorzi and they came back, leading Alan Gray, Justin Forbes and Kelsey Bauman. Alan and his friends looked sort of sheepish, but you could tell by the way they were glancing sideways at people and grinning a little that they were pleased with themselves, too.

Stacey shook her head. "Would you follow those boys anywhere?"

"No way," said Dawn.

"Not a trusty leader," agreed Claudia.

After an assembly (well, half an assembly) and a fire alarm, the rest of the morning went by pretty quickly. And despite all the variations in our morning routine, what was being served up for lunch looked just the same.

"What is that stuff?" I asked Claudia.

Claudia peered down at her plate. "I like to think of it as art," she said loftily.

"Splatter art," I agreed. "You know, like in those horror films. . ."

"Ugh! Kristy!"

"Don't worry, Stacey," I said soothingly. "You didn't get the hot lunch."

Dawn, who was placidly opening a carton of yoghurt to go with her bean salad, said, "I believe that is called meat loaf."

Mary Anne picked up her fork and started to cut the meat loaf. Just as she cut it, I shrieked.

Mary Anne gave a little shriek herself and dropped the fork. I lowered my voice mysteriously. "I think it's still alive."

Everyone cracked up, except Mary Anne, who was looking a little green. She gave me a Look, and I said, "Okay, okay."

I picked up my own fork and took another look at the meat loaf. It was grey, and the tomato sauce was pale red and watery. The mashed potatoes next to it had a sort of oozy quality. And I wasn't so sure I liked the colour of the broccoli. It looked like something that had been attacked by Bunnicula, the vampire rabbit.

I sniffed at my lunch. "This does not smell great," I said.

"No," said Dawn, who is totally into healthy food.

"I can't believe they keep serving us stuff like this. It can't be good for you."

"No," repeated Dawn.

"You know, Kristy," said Stacey, who also brings her own lunch, "why don't you do something about it? Class presidential elections are coming up. Run for class president."

"Maybe." I gave the broccoli a poke, decided it was safe even if Bunnicula had got there first, and started to eat. I had forgotten it was almost time for class elections. It was probably one of the things that was going to be talked about in the assembly. The requirements weren't any big deal. The main one was that you had to have a B average.

That part, at least, would be no sweat.

"You could, you know," said Stacey, polishing off the apple she'd brought for dessert. She pointed to the soggy piece of angel food cake on my tray, which was beginning to look a little too much like the mashed potatoes. "Your motto could be, "Let us eat cake."

Everyone cracked up.

2nd
CHAPTER

If Friday was wild and crazy, Saturday was pretty normal, too – wild and crazy.

Nannie and I ate breakfast to the sound of live music. Nannie is my – our – grandmother. Not too long ago, Mum got married again. (Our dad left when I was a little kid. He lives in California, and we never really hear from him.) Mum named Watson Brewer, and we had to move into Watson's house. Okay, it's actually a mansion, and moving wasn't so bad, although I hated to leave because I lived right next door to Mary Anne and across the road from Claudia.

But life in a mansion is okay. Before this, Sam and Charlie, my two older brothers who are at Stoneybrook High School, had to share a room. And David Michael, who is a second-grader, practically lived in a cupboard. Now we all have our own rooms. But we're filling the mansion up pretty fast. Watson's two kids, Karen, who's seven like David Michael, and Andrew, who is almost five, spend every other weekend with us and two weeks during the summer. And then there's Emily Michelle. She's our adopted sister. She's from Vietnam and is two and a half.

And that's where Nannie comes in. Watson and Mum both have demanding jobs, and so Mum asked her mother to come and live with us and help while everyone is at work or at school. And she did.

So that's Nannie.

Breakfast was toasted muffins with peanut butter and strawberry jam for me and plum jam for Nannie.

The music was Karen and David Michael singing in the study. They'd made up this game to the tune of "Do-Re-Mi". Except instead of singing "do-re-mi" they were singing nonsense rhymes. Andrew, who is shy and quiet, was sitting at the table with us, methodically eating his cereal.

"What's happening today?" I asked Nannie.

"Boo!" (Karen) "Ooh!" (David Michael) "Foo!"

"Bowling," said Nannie, eyeing the plum jam for seconds.

"It's good for bowling," I said helpfully.

"My thoughts exactly," she replied,

149

reaching for it again. "What are you doing today?"

"Babysitting for David Michael and Karen and Andrew and Emily Michelle this morning. This afternoon I'm looking after Jamie and Lucy Newton."

"Sounds like a busy day," said Nannie.

"Noooo," said David Michael, and it didn't rhyme, and it didn't sound very happy.

I got up and gave my plate a quick rinse and put it in the dishwasher. "Sounds like I'd better get started."

In the study I found David Michael and Karen staring at one another. They'd stopped singing. They were standing eyeball to eyeball.

"Kristy?" That was Mum. I took another quick look at David Michael and Karen. They weren't moving or blinking, so I stepped into the hall.

Mum and Watson were on their way out. "We'll be back at midday," said Mum. "Emily Michelle is just waking up."

"I'll go and get her."

"Thanks, dear." Mum and Watson hurried out of the door. For a moment it was quiet. I knew Charlie and Sam had left early. That just left the six of us in the house, all peaceful and calm.

"You blinked!" shrieked Karen.

At about the same time I heard Emily Michelle. "Hiiiii?"

I stuck my head into the study. "Start again," I said to Karen and David Michael.

"He blinked first!"

"Did not!"

"Did too!"

"Listen," I suggested. "Close your eyes, and see if you can catch each other peeping."

"That's silly," said David Michael.

"Lilly!" sang Karen.

David Michael grinned and took a deep breath. I took one of my own, checked on Andrew (still struggling with his cereal), and ran upstairs to get Emily Michelle.

After that, the morning went a bit more smoothly. Emily Michelle doesn't talk a lot yet, but she's learning. She was very definite about how I made her peanut butter muffin, for example, but in a nice, positive way. "Yes!" she crowed when I started making it. "Oh-oh!" she said, sounding very alarmed when I reached for the plum jam. Then when I swapped to the Marmite she beamed. "Yes!" she said again, happily.

The sun was shining outside, so after Emily had eaten, we all took Shannon out into the back garden.

Shannon's great. She's a Bernese mountain dog puppy, and she's enthusiastic about everything. She's still in her clumsy puppy stage, but she's very clever. And it's funny, she seems to understand that Emily Michelle is littler and more vulnerable than

151

David Michael or Karen or Andrew. She's always much calmer with Emily.

Karen picked up a leaf as soon as we got outside and stuck it under her headband. "I'm a leaf collector," she said.

"Me, too," said David Michael.

"I'm the *chief* leaf collector. You are the executive vice-president in choosing colours."

"Red," said David Michael instantly. They bent over and started searching for red leaves. Shannon and Andrew joined in, not sure what they were doing, but glad to help out.

"You want to make a leaf collection, Emily?" I asked.

Emily squatted down and peered at a leaf. She picked it up and looked it over with a serious expression. Then she put it back down exactly where she'd found it.

"No?" I asked.

She looked at me solemnly.

"We can write messages on the green leaves. Would you like to do that?" I pulled a couple of green leaves off a tree and brought them back. I picked up a twig and wrote a big E on one. "See," I said. "That's an E. It's what your name begins with."

I handed it to her. She inspected it, then put it down precisely, and looked at me expectantly.

"As leaf chief," said Karen, "I now

declare we have the red leaves in the whole garden."

"Hi," said a voice behind me just then and I looked up. "Shannon," I said. "Hi! Can you stay for a while?"

Shannon Kilbourne lives opposite us. When I first moved into the neighbourhood I thought she was an awful snob. But she's turned out to be a good friend, even though we don't get to see that much of each other. (Shannon goes to a private school.)

"Not right now," said Shannon. "Astrid and I are going for a walk, and we came to see if you wanted to come."

Just then Shannon the puppy saw her mother and frisked over to her. (Shannon gave us one of Astrid's puppies when our collie, Louie, died. We'll never forget Louie, but it's nice having a puppy around, too. And yes, David Michael named Shannon the puppy after Shannon the person.) The two dogs touched noses, tails wagging furiously.

"I wish I could go with you two," I said, "but I'm babysitting."

"Yeah . . . I could put it off. What about this afternoon?"

"I have another job this afternoon," I said regretfully.

"Oh. Well, listen. Maybe tomorrow. Astrid needs the exercise. She's gaining weight, and that's not good."

"Her daughter could always use some company."

"Okay. See you tomorrow maybe. Come on, Astrid." She pulled gently on Astrid's leash, and Astrid went along easily.

"See that?" I asked Shannon the puppy.

By the time the morning was over, we had collected a pile of yellow leaves, a pile of red leaves, a pile of red and yellow leaves, a pile of orange leaves and a pile of brown ones. And I had helped Emily Michael spell out her name in leaves.

"Now," said Karen. "We will do the leaf dance." She raised her hands and began skipping in and out among the piles. David Michael started doing a sort of bunny hop of his own after her.

"Leaf," he shrieked.

"Chief," sang Karen.

"Beef," sang David Michael.

Then Shannon got in on the act. Woofing happily, she plunged after them. Only she didn't dance in and out among the piles of leaves. She jumped *into* the piles. The leaves went flying everywhere.

"Oh, no!" cried David Michael.

"Good grief," I muttered. Karen put her hands on her hips and frowned at Shannon. Shannon jumped up, trying to catch a leaf.

Then David Michael said, "It's a real leaf dance."

The frown left Karen's face. "It is. It is!"

She and David Michael followed Shannon, throwing leaves everywhere.

It really was a leaf dance, and fun to watch. David Michael and Karen and Andrew and Shannon were jumping and weaving around in all the colours.

"Come on," I said to Emily Michelle. "We've got time for just one dance before lunch."

"Yes," replied Emily. She reached down and picked up her leaves in her fist. Then she and I walked over to the leaf dance.

David Michael was spinning in circles now, making himself dizzy. Karen joined in. Emily studied them for a moment, then smiled. She drew back her arm and threw her fist of leaves into the middle of the dance.

"Oh-oh," she said.

"Yes-yes," I said. "Let's dance." I danced Emily around in the leaves until she started to laugh. Then I felt someone watching. I looked up. It was Bart Taylor, sitting on his bike.

"Come on," I called to him.

Bart parked his bike and stepped to the edge of the leaf dance.

"Hi," I said. I indicated swirls of leaves and the children. "Leaf dance," I explained.

"Looks like fun," he said, and I knew he

meant it. He didn't act as if it was childish or weird to find me covered with leaves. It's one of the things I like about Bart – in addition to his deep, deep brown eyes and nice smile and . . . anyway.

"It is fun," I said. "Want to join us?"

"I just stopped by to say hello," he said. "I'm on my way to a Bashers practice in a little while."

"How're they doing?" I asked.

He raised his eyebrows at me. "Want to come along?" he asked.

"Maybe later," I said. "I've got another job this afternoon."

"Okay," he answered. We watched the leaf dance for a little while longer; then Bart had to go. "Come over if you can," he said. I waved as he cycled away. I knew I probably wouldn't be able to make it. I had homework, for one thing – especially some serious science studying to do.

Mum and Watson came home not very much later, and we ate lunch. Karen kept her chief's leaf on, and at lunch Emily Michelle looked up, then said, distinctly, "Leaf."

"Good for you," said Watson.

"Next time," said Karen, "you can be leaf chief, Emily. I will be. . ."

But I didn't get to hear what she'd be.

"Oh, my lord," I exclaimed. "I've got to get over to the Newtons'. See you later."

I got to the Newtons' just in time. Jamie,

who is four going on five, answered the door, with his mother.

"Hi, Jamie. Hi, Mrs Newton."

"Kristy, come on in." Babysitting for the Newtons is one of my favourite jobs, not just because Jamie is fun and funny, or because his baby sister, Lucy, is adorable. Mrs Newton is also very well organized. She had written down where she would be for the next couple of hours, and had left snacks for Jamie in the fridge.

"You know where everything is," she said as she was going out. "Lucy should sleep. I'll be back by five.'"

Jamie and I waved to her, and then Jamie led me into the living room. He stood by the window and stared out.

"Jamie?" I said. It wasn't like him to get upset when his mother left. He usually liked having me babysit for him.

He didn't answer. "Jamie, she'll be back at five o'clock. Now, let's see what we—"

"Look," breathed Jamie.

I looked. A group of boys of Jamie's age and a little older were pedalling their bicycles frantically down the pavement. "Do you want to go out and ride your trike with them?"

But Jamie shook his head vigorously. Then he looked at me, his eyes shining. "Not yet, Kristy," he said.

He waited, so I asked him, "When, then?"

"When I get my bike." He started hopping up and down, he was so excited. "Guess what, guess what, guess what," he sang.

It looked like it was my day for singing babysitting charges.

"What?" I asked.

"I'm getting a real bicycle."

"Wow . . . a real bicycle."

"NOT a tricycle. A bicycle."

"That's great, Jamie."

"And I'll be able to go fast and faster and faster!"

I put my hand on his shoulder and spoke slowly before he went any faster. "That really is good news, Jamie. I remember when I got my first bicycle."

"You do? Was learning to ride hard?"

I thought about it. I didn't remember it being hard, but I didn't want to tell Jamie it was too easy, in case he didn't pick it up straight away.

"Not hard, exactly," I said. "Besides, it's just like playing softball for the Krushers. With practice, you can do it."

"I'm going to practise and practise and practise."

"How about if we do something else now?"

"Can we read a book?"

"You choose one and we will. First let me go and check on Lucy." Jamie headed for his room, and I went to Lucy's.

She was sleeping like a baby. I wanted to pick her up, she's so soft and sweet smelling (most of the time, anyway) and fun to hold. But I knew if I woke her up and she didn't go back to sleep it would mean she might be grumpy later on. And I didn't think Mrs Newton would be happy with a sitter who left grumpy babies in her wake.

"Kristy!" called Jamie.

I went to his room and settled down on the bed next to him. "Okay, what book did you choose?"

"It's a new one," he said. He held it up and I read the title: *The Bicycle Rider.*

Those bicycle wheels must have still been spinning in my head when Stacey phoned that night after I finally settled down to doing some homework.

"Listen, Kristy, I've been thinking," she said.

"And I've been trying to," I said. "But vertebrates are *not* something my brain likes to dwell on."

"Well, what about this, then? Have you made up your mind about running for class president?"

"You think it's a good idea?" I asked.

This was much more interesting than science homework.

"Who's more organized than you are?" asked Stacey. "And you're the chairman of the Babysitters Club, so you have experience of being in charge. Somebody needs to do something about the school, and not just the lunches."

"We-e-ll," I said. "Let me think about it a little more."

"You might think about this too," said Stacey. "I heard Grace Blume is running." (She's one of Cokie's cronies.)

"I'll let you know on Monday."

"Good," replied Stacey.

And that's what I thought about for the rest of the weekend – when I had the time.

3rd
CHAPTER

The first thing Claudia said when I reached her house for the meeting on Monday afternoon was, "Have you made up your mind yet?" So I knew she and Stacey had been talking it over. I'd been talking it over too, sort of – with myself. But I still wanted to talk about it a little more with the others.

I shook my head and settled into the director's chair, pulling the visor I usually wear down low. "Okay," said Claudia cheerfully. She began rummaging behind her chest of drawers, and I knew she was looking for something to eat.

Claudia is a junk-food fanatic, and she keeps goodies stashed all over her room in places she doesn't even remember, sometimes. Her room is sort of a secret junk-food collage, if you think about it. She's very creative about collecting junk food, hiding it and finding it.

161

Her ambition is to be an artist, and she is really good. She once got an honourable mention in a show at a local art gallery for a work in progress (she would have got first place if the piece had been finished). But she doesn't like school very much. She's a terrible speller, for example.

Maybe part of it is that her sister, Janine, is a real genius. She's still at high school, but she's already taking college courses, and when she talks, she's very formal. She's a conservative dresser, too. Not at all like Claudia.

Today, for instance, Claudia was wearing lime green cycling shorts, a long, long bright pink shirt and a cropped lime green striped shirt over that. She was also wearing black hightop leather trainers with pink butterfly hairslides clipped to the laces. She had two feather earrings in one ear (lime green, of course), and a tiny pink heart in the other. Claudia's gorgeous – she has perfect skin and she's Japanese-American, with dark eyes and shining black hair (today it was pulled up on top of her head and fell down to one side). But even so, not many gorgeous people could get away with some of the outfits Claudia pulls together. But that's how she always looks. Pulled together and gorgeous.

Claudia is the vice-chairman of the

Babysitters Club because we meet in her room three times a week on Monday, Wednesday and Friday, from 5:30 until 6:00. Claudia has her own private phone line, the only one of us who does. This is good because when we use the phone, we don't tie it up for the other people in her family.

I'm the chairman since I thought of the idea for the BSC. I got it one night while I was listening to my mother phoning around, trying to find a babysitter for David Michael. Suddenly it came to me. What if Mum could make one phone call and reach several different babysitters at once? Actually, I thought, reach three babysitters at once, since Mary Anne and Claudia and I were already doing a lot of babysitting. But we agreed that three might not be enough, so Claudia suggested that Stacey join us. Stacey had just moved to Stoneybrook and was starting to be friends with Claudia.

She said yes. So with Mary Anne as secretary and Stacey as treasurer, we were all set. We advertised and worked hard, and we got good recommendations. Soon we had all the babysitting jobs we could handle.

That's when Mary Anne suggested we ask Dawn, who'd just moved to Stoneybrook from California, if she'd like to be a member of the club, too. Dawn agreed, and she became our alternate officer. Then Stacey had to move back to New York (it turned out to be temporary), and we still had as much business as before, if not more, so Jessi Ramsey and Mallory Pike joined us as junior officers. In fact, everybody in the club is an officer except Logan and Shannon, who are associate members. They help us out when we need extra babysitters.

Mary Anne, who is my best friend, and Dawn, who is Mary Anne's other best friend, arrived at the meeting next. They came in the door, just as Claudia shrieked, "Aha!"

Mary Anne stopped, looking a little flustered. Then she saw the sweet 'n' sour gummy bears Claudia was holding up and smiled.

"Catch," Claudia said, and tossed the bag to Mary Anne. Then she got down on her knees and started running her hand between the mattress and the box springs of her bed.

"Thank you," said Mary Anne. She sat cross-legged on the bed, opened the club notebook, and put the gummy bears beside her. Dawn sat down opposite her in Claud's desk chair.

I suppose the fact that Mary Anne and I are best friends proves that opposites attract. We do look sort of alike. We both have brown hair and brown eyes and are short. Actually, I'm the shortest person in our class. But where I have a big mouth and sometimes say things without thinking, Mary Anne is quiet and shy. She even dressed like a shy kid, until she convinced her father to let her grow up a little.

Her father couldn't help being strict. Mary Anne's mother had died when Mary Anne was very young, and Mr Spier wanted to make sure he brought Mary Anne up properly. But he was very hard on her. Now she pays more attention to clothes, although her style is very different from Claudia's or Stacey's, and she wears her hair in distinctive styles. That's another way in which Mary Anne and I are different. I'm happy just wearing jeans and a T-shirt or a poloneck, and trainers. In cold weather, I just add a sweater and sometimes a baseball cap. My best baseball cap has a collie on it. That's in memory of Louie. He got very ill and we had to have him put to sleep. (It was Louie, in a way, who helped Shannon and me to become friends.) I like my hair to look neat too.

Mary Anne is also very sensitive and romantic. Maybe because of that, she's the first one of us to have a real boyfriend. That's Logan Bruno. He's a Southerner, and Mary Anne thinks he looks just like Cam Geary, her favourite filmstar. And even though I'm not interested in boys much (except for Bart Taylor), Logan *is* cute.

Anyway, Mary Anne's father not only started letting Mary Anne make some changes, he did some major changing himself. He got *married*. He married Dawn's mother, Mrs Schafer! Only she's Mrs Spier, now. They'd known each other at high school here in Stoneybrook, when Dawn's mum was Sharon Porter. But things hadn't worked out and Dawn's mother moved to California and married Dawn's dad. The Schafers had Dawn and Dawn's brother, Jeff, but then they got divorced. And Mrs Schafer ended up back in Stoneybrook. That's how Mary Anne went from being an only child, except for her kitten, Tigger, to having a good-sized family. The Schafers and Spiers live in Dawn's house, now, since it's bigger. And Dawn is now not only Mary Anne's other best friend, but her sister, too.

Once you see Dawn, you never forget her. She is striking looking. She has long, long, pale, pale blonde hair, blue eyes, and is tall and slender. And she definitely has her own personal style – like the two holes pierced in each earlobe. Also, she will *not* eat junk food. Or red meat. But she will eat tofu. And real, *live* fruit. I mean an apple is okay, but it's not my first choice.

Other than that Dawn is very easygoing. She does her own thing, and lets people do theirs. It's hard to ruffle Dawn, although she does get hurt. She's been through some tough times, too. Not only did her parents get divorced and her mother move back to Stoneybrook (and away from the warm California sun), but in the end, Dawn's little brother, Jeff, decided to move back to California to live with his father. Dawn had thought about living in California, too, once, but fortunately for us she decided to stay. And now, after adjusting to her new life with Richard (Mr Spier) and Mary Anne, I think Dawn's perfectly happy in Stoneybrook.

Oh, yes. Dawn loves ghost stories. And the old farmhouse she lives in *might be haunted*. We've never been able to prove it. But we've never been able to prove it isn't, either. At least there's a secret passage in it that might be haunted.

"Aha!" said Claudia again. She tossed a bag of Twiglets to Dawn, and propped herself against the headboard of the bed, holding a bag of M&Ms.

Stacey, Jessi and Mal were the last to arrive at the meeting.

You already know a little about Stacey. What you don't know is that in addition to being New York sharp (and cool), Stacey is also a diabetic. That's a disease in which your pancreas doesn't make enough insulin, which means your blood sugar level can get out of control. When that happens you could faint, or even get really ill. So Stacey has to give herself injections of insulin every day and watch what she eats very strictly. Absolutely no sugar. In a way she has the same problem with her parents that Mary Anne had with her father. Stacey's an only child, too, and when her parents found out she was diabetic, they started being super, super cautious and careful with her. They also started taking her to all different kinds of doctors, even when Stacey finally felt that she was coping with things and had a doctor she liked and knew was doing a good job. Stacey had to talk pretty firmly to he parents, too, but at last they understood.

Anyway, Anastasia Elizabeth McGill (that's Stacey's real name, but don't call her that!) moved to Stoneybrook in the seventh grade when her father's company transferred him to Stamford. Then, just a year later, they transferred him back to New York. So Stacey returned to the town she was born and raised in – but not for long. Stacey's parents got divorced, and her mother moved back to Stonybrook. And Stacey chose to come back to Connecticut, too.

Stacey is boy-crazy (just like Claudia). She is also a really cool dresser. Like that Monday, she was wearing a black skirt and tights that were two colours: one leg was red and the other was black. And her shoes were shiny black and laced up to the ankles. She was also wearing this enormous black poloneck sweater with red flecks in it, and one round red earring and one square black one. her hair, which was in a mid-perm state around her face, was pulled back with this silver lamé band.

She looked great.

Jessi Ramsey and Mallory Pike are both eleven years old, in the sixth grade and best friends. Mal used to be one of our babysitting charges. She's from a family of eight kids (she has four brothers, three of them identical triplets, and three sisters), so she's had a lot of experience with children. It was only natural that she "graduate" to being a member of the BSC herself. And Jessi is sort of connected to Stacey. when Stacey moved back to New York, Jessi's family moved into Stacey's old house.

Jessi and Mallory are two very different best friends (like me and Mary Anne) who also have a lot in common. They're both the oldest in their families, and their families still treat them like babies (at least, that's the way Mal and Jessi feel). But they did manage to get pierced ears, and they both love horse stories. Oh, yes – they both have pet hamsters.

Mal wears glasses and has a brace and red hair. She likes to draw and write and

169

would like to be a childrens' writer and illustrator one day.

Jessi's family is a good bit smaller than Mal's – average size, with her parents, her Aunt Cecelia, an eight-year-old sister named Becca and a baby brother called Squirt. And her passion is ballet. She's good, too. She takes special classes at a dance school in Stamford where you have to audition just to get in. She's already danced lead roles in performances before hundreds of people.

Another difference is that Jessi doesn't have a brace or glasses or red hair. She is black, with black hair and brown eyes. This doesn't matter to Mal or to any of us, but some people in Stoneybrook, I am ashamed to say, were bothered. The Ramseys' neighbours gave them a hard time in the beginning. Luckily, they've settled down now.

And that's the Babysitters Club. I looked around at everyone and cleared my throat. It was exactly 5:30. "The meeting will come to order," I said.

"See? You even talk like a class president," Stacey pointed out.

Just then the phone rang. I picked it up. "Hello, Babysitters Club."

It was Mrs Newton. I took down the information about the sitter she needed and told her I'd call her straight back.

"Mrs Newton needs someone next

Monday from three-thirty until five. She's taking Lucy to the clinic for a check-up."

Mary Anne flipped the club notebook open.

"Stacey, you're already scheduled for the Marshalls. And Mal, you and Jessi are down for—"

"I know. My family." Mal's mother always wants more than one babysitter because those seven kids are definitely a handful.

"I've got an art class," Claudia said.

"Krushers practice," I said, reluctantly. Jamie is one of my favourite babysitting charges, and we're all crazy about Lucy, too.

"That leaves Dawn and me," said Mary Anne. "Dawn, if you'd rather—"

"No. You take it, Mary Anne. I need some free time, and a Monday is good for that.

"Don't forget our BSC meeting," I pointed out.

Dawn flashed a smile at me. "How could I forget?"

The phone rang again, and Mary Anne picked it up. It was the Papadakises, who live in my neighbourhood. After we'd arranged for a sitter – Dawn this time – we had a lull.

"Did you see the notice about the class play?" asked Claud. She was alternately eating Jaffa cakes and sweet 'n' sour gummy bears. It made me go all pucker-mouthed just to watch.

"*Mary Poppins*," I said. "Disgusting."

"I used to love *Mary Poppins*," said Mary Anne diplomatically.

"Used to is the operative phrase here. I can't believe it! I think we should so something real."

"Definitely," said Dawn. "*Mary Poppins* is a little babyish. Now if it was *A Raisin in the Sun*. . ."

"Or what about *Our Town*? Or *The Glass Menagerie*? I mean, why don't we have any say in this? School is supposed to be challenging! Not . . . not Mary Poppinsish!" I said.

"Well, I just want to work on the scenery. Maybe you could do it, too, Mal?" Claudia put in.

"You know," I said, really working up steam. "The play committee could use the talent we have at SMS, too. Like Jessi—"

Jessi laughed. "This sounds like a speech, Kristy."

"Yeah," said Stacey. "A candidate's speech."

I stopped. "You honestly think I should run?"

"You should so what you *want* to do," Mary Anne said firmly.

Was Mary Anne trying to tell me something? If she was, I wasn't listening. At least not then.

I looked around the room. If I ran, I would have a head start. I had Team Kristy right there – the Babysitters Club. I knew I could count on my friends.

"I'll do it," I said. "I hearby officially announce my candidacy for class president."

"All right!" cried Stacey.

"Awesome," said Dawn.

"That's great, Kristy," sad Mal.

"Subs and treasurer's report, please," I said suddenly to Stacey, switching back to the BSC meeting. I'd had so much to think about, I'd almost forgotten.

We all groaned, but we each handed over a dollar. "That makes us seven dollars richer," reported Stacey. "We *were* getting low," she said after giving us the grand total.

The phone rang. As Mary Anne answered, Mal looked around at us. "I was thinking of running for office too," said Mal. "For secretary of the sixth grade."

"Way to go," I said, but I have to admit, I was thinking more about my own campaign.

Mal went on. "I don't know. Maybe not. Probably no one would vote for me."

"You have my vote," said Jessi.

"You'll do great, Mal," said Mary Anne, loyally.

Mal blushed a little, but she didn't look entirely convinced.

I glanced at my watch. It was 6:00. "Uh-oh. Time to go. Charlie will be here any minute to pick me up." (We pay him out of our subs to drive me to and from BSC meetings.)

"Kristy for president!" sang out Claudia. I had to admit, it sounded pretty good.

4th CHAPTER

Jamie was excited. And that's an understatement.

"Can you see anything?" he asked me for about the thousandth time.

"Not yet," I said.

Today was the day his bike was being delivered. There was a good chance it would arrive before his mother returned from her meeting. I hoped so. Jamie's enthusiasm was contagious. I was excited myself.

Jamie went down to the end of the drive and peered both ways. He came back. "I can't see anything yet."

"A watched pot never boils, Jamie."

Jamie wrinkled his nose. "What does that mean?"

That stopped me. I'd heard it all my life, but I'd never explained it to anyone. "It means, well, it means that if you keep looking for something to happen, it's not going to. Like if you were watching a pot of water, waiting for it to boil, it would never boil. Or it would *seem* like it was never going to, because all you were doing was standing there watching it."

Jamie looked even more confused than I sounded. Luckily, just then I heard Lucy through the open front door of the house.

"Come on," I said.

Jamie followed me reluctantly into the house, looking back over his shoulder every step of the way. I would have let him stay outside, but I didn't want him racing out to the street to watch for the bike while I wasn't with him.

"We'll go back outside," I promised. "You can help choose a toy for Lucy to play with."

"She likes anything," said Jamie. But he came along behind me.

Lucy is the best baby ever. She is *so* cute. And bright. She'd just let out one little experimental sort of wail, to get my attention. When I got to her room she was making urgley-smiling sounds.

"Urgley-urgley to you." I smiled at her and reached down and picked her up to check if she needed changing. Fortunately, she didn't.

Jamie picked up a soft bright cloth bunny with embroidered eyes and long embroidered eyelashes.

"Hurry," he said.

We'd just reached the front hall when we heard the sound of the van pulling up.

"My bike's here!" Jamie screeched, and he took off.

Sure enough, the delivery man was lifting a big box out of the back of the truck.

"Newtons'?" he asked.

"I'm Jamie Newton," Jamie told him. "That's my bike."

I signed for the bike and settled Lucy in her playpen in the garden while Jamie wrestled with the cardboard.

We peeled the bike free and stepped back to admire it. Only it almost fell over.

Jamie's face fell. "It's supposed to have stabilizers."

"Wait a minute. It does. Look, here they are, wrapped separately." I studied the sheet of instructions that had come with the bike. "It looks like all you have to do is screw them on."

Jamie didn't seem any happier. "I don't know *how*."

"Neither do I, but we can try. You have some tools in that drawer in the kitchen, remember? Go in and get a screwdriver and a pair of pliers. Okay?"

"Please," Jamie reminded me.

"Please," I added, and ran towards the kitchen. While he was gone, I stuffed the cardboard packaging into the recycling bin and took another look at the instructions. No problem. I hoped.

And it wasn't. Maybe I should take mechanics or something, because the wheels went on as easy as could be. There was even a little tube of grease for the wheels and the chain.

"All set. Ready to roll, Jamie?"

Jamie was so excited he'd stopped talking. He just nodded vigorously.

"Okay. Up you go." I gave him a boost and rolled the bicycle across the patch of grass on to the drive.

But when I looked at Jamie again, he wasn't smiling. He was just staring down at the ground.

"Jamie? Ready for your first real bike trip?"

Jamie didn't nod. Instead he shook his head, still looking at the ground.

"What's wrong?" I asked.

He looked up then. "I'm going to fall off," he wailed. "I'm going to fall over and it's going to hurt!" He stared back down at the ground.

"Oh, Jamie." I put an arm behind him. "No you won't. You have the extra wheels. You're all balanced. You won't fall. I'll stay right with you." Jamie didn't answer. But I could feel how tense he was. "We could wait. Just a little while, you know. Until you got used to the idea."

"NO."

I waited, anyway. This was a new one. I tried to think what to do, tried to remember learning to ride a bike myself and come to think of it I *did* remember falling. But that was after the stabilizers, wasn't it?

While we were standing, frozen, in the drive, Claudia showed up. "Claudia!" Was I ever relieved. Two heads would be better than one, for certain.

"Hi, Kristy. Hi, Jamie. Great bike!"

Jamie smiled and looked up (just for a second). "It's mine."

"I know. You look great." Jamie nodded slightly.

"So, Claudia. Why don't you get on the other side and we'll walk alongside Jamie and hold on to him and the bike for his first ride," I suggested. "Sort of like human stabilizers."

Claud understood straight away. "Great." She put her arm around Jamie and gave him a little squeeze. "Let's just take a couple of steps, for practice, okay?"

Jamie nodded a little more, so that's what we did. Two steps, stop, then two more steps, stop, then two more.

"Don't you have art class today?" I asked Claud.

"Got out early. Mary Anne said you were here today, so I came over." We reached the end of the drive and made a big wide semicircle turn and started back. Jamie was frowning with concentration.

"Because," Claudia went on, "I have some ideas for your campaign."

"The campaign? Oh – great!" I hadn't forgotten about it. I mean, who could, when you'd had to register and fill in forms and all that at school. But I'd sort of put it off, because no one could officially start campaigning till the following week.

Which wasn't that far away now.

"What I thought is, you need a theme. And a striking design. But something simple, too. That's the key to good design, you know. Simplicity. A shape the eye can instantly recognize as symbolic of what, or who, it represents." Claudia may not like school, but she knows all about art.

We reached the top of the drive and waited while Claudia flipped through her art notebook. "Here," she said, holding something out to me.

On a piece of paper was the letter "K", a really bold drawing of it. By the top of it was a + sign. "See," Claudia explained. "It can mean K+ like a super grade in school. And what we do is we put this everywhere. You could just go around putting the word *Okay* everywhere, but with your brandname K+ in it."

"That's how you really spell it, isn't it?" I teased, and Claudia, who is a world-class creative speller – which unfortunately means she doesn't always spell words the way the dictionary does – grinned.

I grinned, too. "It looks great, Claudia."

I was really getting enthusiastic now. "We can make badges and all kinds of slogans—"

"Like A+ = K+."

"Or *Extra*-special K."

"Or Kristy for K+ President," said Claudia, writing it out quickly in her notebook.

"It's definitely time to get organized. Maybe we could get together after the club meets this Friday. I don't have a sitting job that night, and we can check with Mary Anne and see who does—"

"Even if they do, we could have pizza and just go to our jobs from my house."

"Good idea. Claudia, you're a genius."

Claudia looked pleased.

Jamie, meanwhile, did not. "More," he said. "I need to practise more."

I checked on Lucy, who was still being the perfect baby, crawling contentedly around the playpen. "Hi, Lucy," I said.

She sat up and waved her hands around, making a sound that could have meant "Hi, Kristy."

"Kristy!"

"Coming, Jamie!" I patted Lucy gently, then went back and took up my position by the bike.

As we turned and headed down the drive again, Claudia said, "Oh, I almost forgot. Mal's decided to go ahead and run for secretary of the sixth grade. Jessi's going to manage her campaign."

"She'll do a great job," I said. "Will you be my campaign manager?

"We-e-ell," said Claudia, pretending to think. "Since I *am* an artistic genius, I suppose I can."

"Super. Super-plus," I said.

"Kristy for president." Claudia flung up her free hand and pretended she was waving to a crowd.

"Babysitters rule," I answered, laughing.

We pushed Jamie up and down the drive about a hundred more times until his mother came home. I thought he was getting better, but I couldn't be sure. At least we weren't stopping every two steps. I was glad I hadn't told him that learning to ride a bike was easy. Right now it looked as if Jamie was going to have to work pretty hard at it, even with stabilizers.

But I knew he would, too. That's one of the things I like about Jamie, that we all like. He's definitely not a quitter.

5th CHAPTER

At the end of our meeting on Friday, as Mal and Jessi were heading down the stairs to go and sit for Mal's brothers and sisters, I got out of the director's chair and indicated that Claud should sit in it.

"You're the campaign manager," I said.

"Speech, speech," teased Stacey.

Claudia held up the bag of tortilla chips she'd been devouring and said, "I hereby declare as my first official act as Kristy's campaign manager that we order pizza."

"We *do* have to keep our strength up," Dawn put in. "Good nutrition is a key ingredient to a successful campaign. . . I vote for mushrooms."

"Onions," said Stacey.

"Double cheese," Mary Anne said.

"Pepperoni?" I asked. "On half," I added as Dawn wrinkled her nose.

Claudia pulled the phone towards her

and placed the order, while Mary Anne turned to me. "Do you want me to collect money from everyone, or. . ."

Like a good babysitter – and a good candidate for class president – I was prepared. "We can't use the BSC money, of course. So this is on me. Think of it as campaign expenses."

"I can see you know how to campaign," said Dawn solemnly.

"I also know how to shake hands, and I'm very good at kissing babies."

Stacey said, "You've got to win, Kristy. Look at the other candidates. Alan Gray. . ."

"Yeah, but he nominated himself," said Dawn reasonably. "He's probably not going to get all that many votes."

"Besides, Alan Gray would probably shake babies and kiss hands," I said, choking. The thought of Alan Gray kissing *anybody* made me shudder.

"And then Grace," said Dawn. "She definitely got nominated."

Grace Blume wasn't a much better candidate in my opinion. After all, she, like Cokie, has pulled some nasty tricks on me and the others in the BSC. Still, she's popular, which is probably why she's running. For Grace, being elected to class president means winning a popularity contest, and that's about it. She'd probably just rest on her laurels – after she'd got a rule passed against members of the Babysitters Club attending Stoneybrook Middle School!

"Pete Black got nominated, too. He's not so bad," Mary Anne said.

I wrinkled my nose. I didn't want to contradict Mary Anne, but I think Pete can be really immature.

Mary Anne saw me and smiled. "But you're definitely the best, Kristy."

"Right on," said Dawn.

"Right on?" asked Stacey.

"I think it's an old hippy expression."

"Oh. Like far out."

"Like right." Dawn shook back her blonde hair, which she had arranged in little plaits around her face.

"The pizza won't be here for at last twenty minutes, so let's get started," said Claudia, hanging up the phone. She flipped open her art notebook. She'd done a new, more detailed drawing of some of the K+ designs. They really stood out.

"I thought we'd use this design for our handouts, and we can try other designs for the posters. Mary Anne, did you bring poster paper?"

"Didn't you see me bring it in?" Mary Anne motioned to where a huge bag of poster paper was propped against the foot of the bed.

"Right," said Claudia, very officially. "Now, we can also make badges, like this. . ." She flashed another design ". . . or this."

Mary Anne reached out for the designs and studied them thoughtfully. "I like them both."

Claudia nodded. "Well, we could use them both. . ."

"Whichever we choose, we can't do that straight away," said Stacey, being practical. "To make badges we need dozens and dozens of the same design."

"You're right, Stace. I need to make a whole sheet of designs, and then we can do colour photocopies of the sheet and cut the designs out. That'll save time."

"And meanwhile we can start on the posters. And if we don't finish them this afternoon, I can ask David Michael to help me finish them at home."

Claudia started pulling out newspapers to spread around on the floor, and paint and Magic Markers, and soon we were making posters while Claud concentrated on the sheet of badge designs.

We worked for a while, and just as I was beginning to think seriously about pizza, there was a knock on the door. Claudia opened it to find her sister, Janine.

Standing next to each other, Claudia and Janine couldn't have looked more different, even though that day Claud was dressed fairly conservatively: white jeans, red shoes with big bows, a tropical jungle shirt with each button shaped like a piece of fruit, and her hair pulled to one side of

186

her shoulder with a banana hairslide. But Janine, with her short hair and fringe, pullover, plain skirt and loafers, made Claudia look extremely exotic.

"I believe you would be glad to know that a pizza delivery has just been effected," said Janine. She talks like that all the time. It's part of being a genius.

"Right," said Claudia. I got up, pulling the money out of my pocket, and ran downstairs with her.

When we got back upstairs, carrying the pizza and balancing napkins and plates and Diet Cokes, Janine had stepped into the room and was studying the posters we'd finished and propped against one wall to dry.

"You've chosen a logo, I see." She peered over her glasses more closely at one of them. "It's quite a good one. Simple, but striking. That's extremely important in product identification. The consumer has to be able to make the association readily between the identifying symbol and what it represents."

Normally, Janine's encyclopaedia act, even though she doesn't mean to sound so formal, can be a little trying. But this time I just stopped and stared. "You know what, Janine? That's exactly, or *almost* exactly what Claudia said!"

Claudia and Janine looked at each other, and then we all burst out laughing.

"Well," said Janine, turning to go, "I can see your campaign is in excellent hands, Kristy. I wish you the best of luck."

"You said it!" I gave Janine the two thumbs-up sign.

"Thanks, Janine," said Claudia, sounding a little surprised. It's hard to admit, because older siblings can be a pain sometimes, but getting a compliment from them is extra special. And Janine is not someone to just throw compliments around.

Which made me more sure than ever that I had the best possible campaign manager. And team. But would that mean I would win the election?

Chewing on a slice of pepperoni pizza, I looked around. Stacey, as cool as ever, eating a slice of double cheese, pepperoni, onion and mushroom pizza; Claudia, who was absently picking up the mushrooms off her slice and studying her art notebook; Dawn, laughing and trying to catch the strings of cheese with her fingers; and Mary Anne, carefully taking small bites of her pizza and grinning at Dawn. I grinned myself. With the Babysitters Club behind me, how could I lose?

But then I remembered Grace the Snob, who probably thought a good class president was one who was the leader of a very select group of total snobs; and Alan, the Pest of All the World (whose principle qualification for leadership, as far as I could tell, had been leading half the school off into the distance during the fire drill); and that Nerd Pete, and I stopped grinning. I had to win, I *had* to. I wasn't being arrogant. I simply knew how important it was for me to be elected. Because if I wasn't, look at the remaining choices.

I had to run, and I had to win, and I had to do it to save the eighth grade.

6th CHAPTER

Friday

Well, Kristy and Claudia had told us how excited Jamie Newton is about his new bicycle. They'd also told us he seemed a little unsure of himself. That's not surprising. I remember I was, too. (I can really remember that, as well as the first time I rode without my father helping. It was great.) But I don't know how we're going to get Jamie sure enough of himself to take that first big step. Or pedal....

When Mary Anne arrived at Jamie's that afternoon, Jamie, Mrs Newton and Lucy met her.

"Terrific," said Mrs Newton. "Right on time, as always."

Mary Anne thought that this was a good beginning, even though Jamie shot past Mary Anne without even saying hello.

"Hi, Mrs Newton. Hi, Lucy. Hi, Jamie," Mary Anne replied politely.

Mrs Newton picked up her bag and Lucy's baby supplies bag, and headed towards her car. Mary Anne put down the Kid-Kit she'd brought along (not that she was going to get to use it!) and followed Mrs Newton and Lucy. "Lucy's doctor is very good about not keeping her patients waiting, so we shouldn't be gone more than an hour and a half. Jamie can have a snack in an hour, but not any later than that. I don't want him to spoil his appetite."

"Good luck," said Mary Anne.

"Come on!" That was Jamie, shouting from the drive, where he'd wheeled his bicycle out of the garage.

"It's just a routine check-up," Mrs Newton reassured Mary Anne, putting Lucy into her car seat. After they'd backed out of the driveway and driven away, Mary Anne trotted over to Jamie, who was still holding on to the handlebars of his bicycle.

"It's a beautiful bicycle, Jamie. Did you choose the colour yourself?"

"Yes," said Jamie. Mary Anne could tell how preoccupied he was, because normally he would have told her all about why he'd chosen red with white racing stripes and at least a dozen other wonderful things about whatever it was that interested him – which in this case, of course, was his bike.

But he wasn't interested in talking about his bike that day. He was interested in riding it.

"Hold on," he commanded.

"Hold on, please," said Mary Anne.

"Please," repeated Jamie shortly, and he began climbing on to the bike as Mary Anne held on to the handlebars.

"Are you going to show me how you ride?" she asked.

"No!" said Jamie. "I've just got my bicycle. I don't know how to ride it yet."

"Of course. Let's practise, then, okay?"

Since that was exactly what Jamie wanted, he didn't wait for an answer. He just started pedalling determinedly. When they reached the foot of the drive, he slowed down almost to a stop. Mary Anne looked at him and saw that his face was red and he was biting his lower lip.

"You're doing a great job, Jamie," she said, half worried he was going to bite a hole in his lip.

They inched around the corner of the drive and on to the pavement and Jamie didn't answer.

"Jamie?" said Mary Anne.

"Uh," grunted Jamie, but at least he stopped biting his lip. Mary Anne was surprised. She'd never seen Jamie quite like this. He's stubborn, but he's not obsessive or anything.

She was in for a bigger surprise when Jamie pedalled on to the pavement. He slowed down almost to a standstill for *every* crack. And when they reached the corner and had to turn round, Jamie slid off the bike.

"Are you tired?" asked Mary Anne.

"I'm turning round," replied Jamie, as if that should be obvious to anyone.

So Mary Anne helped Jamie turn the bike around and waited for him to climb back on, and they started down the pavement. They inched along in front of his house towards the corner at the other end of the block. Suddenly, Jamie came to a dead stop.

Mary Anne didn't ask if he was tired this time. She was learning. "What is it, Jamie?"

He pointed and shook his head violently. "That stick!"

Mary Anne looked and almost asked, "What stick?" but, fortunately, she saw the skinny little stick lying on the pavement just in time.

"Do you want it?" she asked, and then realized the answer just as Jamie said, "It has to move!" If the cracks in the pavement scared him, then the stick probably seemed like a major obstacle.

But when Mary Anne let go of the bicycle to get the stick, Jamie howled, "DON'T!"

She waited for a moment for him to calm down, and then she said, "But, Jamie, how am I going to get the stick?"

He shook his head again without answering.

"Listen, Jamie," said Mary Anne patiently. "If you don't pedal and you don't move, you'll be fine. And I'll move the stick really fast. It'll only take a second. I promise."

Jamie hesitated, then said, "You *promise* promise?"

"Promise, promise, promise with a capital P," answered Mary Anne.

So Jamie made himself very rigid and straight and said, "Okay." Mary Anne grabbed the stick, threw it on the grass, and went back to Jamie.

He relaxed as she took hold of the bicycle again.

"See," said Mary Anne. "You did great. Wasn't that easy?" They started forward again and she said, "You know, you *have* made progress, Jamie. Didn't you need both Kristy and Claudia to help you ride the first day you got your bicycle?"

"Uh-huh," said Jamie. they came to the

corner and he got off and turned the bike round and got back on.

Cheerfully, Mary Anne kept up a flow of encouraging conversation. "You know, everything gets easier with practice. You learned that from playing for the Krushers. Remember how hard it was for you when you started playing? Now Kristy and the Krushers wouldn't know what to do without you."

"Yeah," said Jamie, and he didn't sound quite so fearful. But he continued to slow down at every crack.

Encouraged, Mary Anne went on. "You know, it's like they say. If you're riding a horse and you fall off, the important thing is to get right back on."

Big mistake. Jamie's face turned bright red, and he practically screamed, "I'm not going to fall!"

By the time Mary Anne had calmed him down, they'd reached the foot of the driveway. "This is a lot of practice," she said. "Sometimes you can practise better if you take a break. Why don't we go and get the Kid-Kit, and—"

"No."

"No, *thank you*," said Mary Anne, suppressing a sigh. The Kid-Kits are something all the kids love, because what kid doesn't like reading books that aren't his own, and playing with toys that aren't the same old ones? So we take our Kid-Kits to some of our jobs (not to all of them, because then they'd be ordinary, and not a treat) and replenish them with new toys and books and colouring books out of our subs from time to time.

Anyway, when Jamie said no to the Kid-Kit, Mary Anne knew she was in for a really long afternoon with the bicycle.

"No, thank you," repeated Jamie, and then he stopped so abruptly that Mary Anne almost fell herself.

"You're good with the brakes," she said, but Jamie didn't hear her. He was staring at the pavement.

Mary Anne looked. All she saw was a leaf.

"The leaf?" she asked.

Jamie nodded.

She moved the leaf and they crept forward.

Every time she suggested they stop, Jamie refused. He didn't even want his snack. At least after they'd been up and down the pavement half a dozen times it was clean – not a twig or a leaf or a pebble in sight.

However, it didn't help that the other kids in the neighbourhood kept riding by. They weren't teasing Jamie or anything. A lot of them waved and said "Hi!" and "Nice bike". But they were zipping along, riding with just one hand, or even (well, maybe those boys were showing off a little) with no hands at all, and there was Jamie, red-faced and struggling along.

Finally, Mary Anne convinced Jamie to stop – by convincing him that she needed to rest. And she did. She made iced tea for both of them (it was too late for Jamie's snack by then) and she and Jamie sat on the front step, with the bicycle propped carefully next to it.

The neighbourhood kids kept whizzing by on their bikes. Jamie's face, watching them, was sad and annoyed at the same time.

Mary Anne racked her brains, trying to think of something to say to make Jamie feel better. Finally, she remembered the campaign for class president.

"Listen, Jamie," she said. "Kristy's running for president of our class at school. Do you want to help her?"

"How?" he asked.

"We can think up campaign slogans. You know, good things about Kristy and why people should vote for her, like they do on adverts when they want you to remember to buy what they're advertising."

Jamie perked up a little at that. "Kristy for pres, she's the bes," he said straight away. He is a clever kid. (Which may be why he's having so much trouble learning to ride his bicycle. He hasn't fallen off yet – but he can imagine falling off. And because he's clever, he can imagine it vividly and clearly.)

Laughing, Mary Anne said, "Wait a minute. I'll get pencils and paper and we'll write these down."

She and Jamie came up with some silly slogans, some funny ones, and some good ones, too: "Choose Kristy or else" (that was Jamie's). "You can't miss with Kristy" (Mary Anne). And a terrific one: "Kristy for president of the class – make some changes and make them last" (both of them together).

It was fun, and Jamie seemed to forget about his bicycle woes for a while. But Mary Anne didn't. Even after Mrs Newton came back (Lucy's doctor said she was just perfect, which we all knew, of course) and Mary Anne was heading home, she was trying to think of a way for Jamie to overcome his fear of falling off his bicycle.

It wasn't going to be easy.

7th
CHAPTER

When the campaign for class president started, everything seemed to move into top gear. Suddenly the halls were full of posters. Lots of SMS pupils started wearing badges and rosettes.

Stacey had had a really good idea. Instead of making only posters, we'd also made lots and lots of photocopies of our "Kristy for president" slogan with the big K+ symbol beneath it. Claudia also designed a handout showing only the symbol, and we photocopied that and plastered dozens and dozens of them everywhere around the school, like on fences by building sites and things. According to Stacey, that was the way people in New York advertise things, especially rock concerts.

Of course, before we K-plussed everything, we asked permission. At SMS we had rules (naturally) about where you could put campaign material, but out of school, you couldn't be sure. Some people said no to the handouts and some said yes, and some seemed sort of surprised that we asked at all and just shrugged. As every babysitter and little kid knows, a shrug is like a maybe – it means yes. We ended up with more yeses than nos, so it hadn't hurt to ask.

And we used recycled paper and wrote at the bottom: "recycled paper/please recycle". That was Dawn's idea.

Mary Anne suggested that we keep moving posters around, and putting up new ones (we made all the posters reversible, too) so the campaign would stay interesting, and kids wouldn't see the same posters over and over again. We took turns going to school early to do that, but I tried to go early every morning since I was the candidate.

When I couldn't help in the mornings, I'd do the poster switch after school, which is what I was doing when I realized I was going to be late for a meeting.

The meeting was for the candidates. As I dashed downstairs I wondered what on earth we could possibly have left to discuss. The candidates had already attended several meetings. The door was closed when I got to the room, but the meeting hadn't started yet. Mallory had saved me a seat, and I slid into it in my best Krusher team style.

"Safe," I muttered.

Mal grinned. "You didn't miss anything," she whispered.

"Tell me about it," I whispered back.

Mr Kingbridge, the deputy head teacher, went over the rules of the campaign again, and I tried to use the time (subtly, of course) to look over some class notes. I have very good concentration, so it took Mal's elbow against my ribs to tell me that Mr Kingbridge was saying something new about the school elections.

"As you know," he was going on when I looked up, "we want the candidates and the pupils to have every chance to interact in a meaningful way prior to the elections. Therefore, I am pleased to announce that in addition to a Campaign Day next week before the election, when candidates will be setting up booths in the school cafeteria and spending two hours in the morning campaigning. . ."

Including shaking hands, I thought. But not kissing babies!

". . .in addition to that," Mr Kingbridge repeated, "we are going to give the candidates the opportunity to debate and to make two speeches."

Several hands shot up then, but Pete's was first. He stood up. "Excuse me, but when you say opportunity, do you mean it is a requirement?"

"It is, yes, going to be part of the campaign experience," said Mr Kingbridge.

I groaned. I wasn't the only one.

From somewhere in the chorus of groans behind me I heard the phrase "dress to wear" (Grace, I thought, who else?) and that jerk Alan intoning, "Friends, Romans, countrymen, lend me your ears, your eyes, your noses. . ."

Beside me, Mallory wasn't groaning, though. She was absolutely frozen, her eyes enormous behind her glasses.

"Mal?" I said.

She turned to look at me and blurted out, in a panic, "A *debate?* Me? I've never done that before. This is awful!"

"You can do it, Mal," I said. "Don't worry." However, I was worried. Not because I had never taken part in a debate before. (I hadn't.) I just didn't know how I was going to find the time to do it.

Mr Kingbridge answered a few more questions and then dismissed us.

"Oh, Kristy. A debate!"

Poor Mal. I tried to say something that would comfort her.

"Just think of this as reasoning with a much larger, older group of babysitting charges," I suggested.

"Somehow," said Mal, "that doesn't help."

I gave a strangled cry and Mal jumped.

Of course, it was Alan the Pest. He'd pinched me on the arm.

"You do that again, Alan, and you'll be sorry!" I glared at him, but it didn't do any good. He just turned round and walked backwards in front of us.

"You and I are going to debate, Kristy. What do you think?"

I thought if he kept walking backwards, he was going to bump into the pole behind him, but I didn't say anything.

Alan crashed into the pole and slid to the floor. But the way he did it made me suspect he knew all along it was there. Mal giggled as he threw his arms out and pretended to be injured.

"Good grief," I said, stepping over his writhing body.

"A debate is an exchange of dialogue, Kristy!" Alan propped himself up on his elbow to call after us. "Somehow, I don't think you want to exchange dialogue with me."

"Brilliant, Alan," I said crossly. "Talk about someone who needs a babysitter," I went on to Mal.

"Or a keeper," suggested Mal. "A handler, an Alan-tamer."

"Now there's a thought. . . See, Mal? You're a fast thinker. You come from a big family where you automatically have to speak up for yourself. You're a great babysitter. . ."

Mal blushed and shoved her glasses back

up on her nose. "So you'll be fine in a debate."

"Thanks, Kristy." Mal turned towards her locker. "I know you'll do a super job. See, you're already convincing me. Sort of."

"Good. . ."

"See you tomorrow."

"Bye," I said absent-mindedly.

Things will fall into place, I told myself as I opened the locker door. I caught my science book before it fell out – just the book I was looking for – and smiled. They *will* fall into place, I repeated to myself. Just like my locker. I can't get *every*thing done.

Things did seem to fall into place over the next few days. I even found time to make a special campaign badge for Jamie that said, "Kris for pres, 'cause she's the bes", with "by Jamie Newton" on the bottom of it, to take to him the next time I sat for him.

But then another meeting was announced one morning over the loud-speaker. It was for that same day, right after school. Great, I thought. I had an appointment then with my English teacher, Mrs Simon. How was I supposed to go to the meeting *and* the appointment? It just proved why I was needed as class president. This lack of organization was typical of SMS!

I was still fuming as I dashed out of Mrs

Simon's room that afternoon, after agreeing to rewrite a report. "I know you can do better, Kristy," she kept saying. "I've seen what you do when you work up to your full potential." I thanked her, because I'd hate to get a low grade in English, but I didn't see when I was going to have time to rewrite a report.

I was ten minutes late to the candidates' meeting. Grace looked over her shoulder as I came in, then whispered something to the person sitting next to her, and they both sniggered.

Ignoring them, I slid into a seat at the back of the room and tried to look intelligent as Mr Kingbridge glanced over at me. He kept talking, but also handed a piece of paper to a person in the first row, and gestured to him to pass it back to me. So then everybody turned round and knew I was late. Mal, who was sitting at the end of a row, gave me a sympathetic look.

The handout was about Campaign Day. It also listed the campaign rules in writing. Mr Kingbridge read them aloud, then said, "Any questions?" and looked at me.

Even if I'd had any I wouldn't have asked! I jammed the paper in my notebook and shot out of there as soon as we were dismissed.

I had to get to the library, and fast. Charlie was going to pick me up in an hour, and I wanted some time to work on my latest science homework. I *had* to get that done. It was due in the next day, and I was babysitting for the Kormans that night. which was, I'd decided, going to be the perfect time to do some of my homework.

Was I ever wrong!

I was almost late getting to the Kormans'. (Have you ever noticed that? How when a day starts getting crazy and hectic, it just keeps getting crazier and more hectic? And if you're late, you keep running later. . .?) Luckily, I wasn't *really* late. which is good, because it is very important for members of the BSC to show how responsible they are, and being on time is a big part of being a responsible babysitter.

So I was a responsible babysitter – just in the nick of time. Skylar, who is a year and a half old, had already started crying because she knew, probably by the way her mother and father were rushing for the door, that they were Going Out and Leaving Her.

Melody, who is seven, was standing in the hall watching her parents in an abstracted sort of way, as if they were people in a film. Bill, Mrs Korman told me, was upstairs doing his homework

"We'll be back by ten," Mrs Korman told me. "Everyone has had dinner, but Bill and Melody can have dessert in a little while – it's ice cream. You know where everything is, of course."

"Have a good time," I said.

"Bye," said Melody.

"Waaah," said Skylar from her playpen.

I picked Skylar up. "Wah, waah," I said softy. "Is that any way to say hello?"

"WAAAAAH," howled Skylar, struggling in my arms. I changed her nappy. No problem there.

"Maybe she's sleepy," suggested Melody. "You could read to her."

"Good idea, Melody." I shifted Skylar and headed up the stairs. "Why don't you choose a book and we can read to Skylar until she gets sleepy."

Melody ran ahead of me into her room. "Skylar has books, but they don't have enough words," she told me.

By then Skylar's wails had become the long babbling sounds of unhappy protest that babies make. She was winding down. Good, I thought. A couple of pages and she'll be asleep like a baby!

But Skylar is a real individualist. I took the book Melody gave me, *Bedtime for Frances,* and started reading. Skylar kept complaining. I read to the end, with Melody standing at my shoulder, looking at Skylar and at the book, and Skylar kept complaining.

"Another book?" asked Melody.

"Okay," I said. I wondered if I could read my history homework assignment to Skylar. That would definitely put her to sleep.

We read *Goodnight Moon* and *Runaway Bunny*. Skylar's complaints were in the whimper range now, but they were still there.

"Let me try," said Melody. So I handed the books over to her. She picked up *Goodnight Moon* and began to read in a singsong voice.

And it worked! As Melody turned the last page, Skylar sighed and burrowed into sleep.

"Good work, Melody," I whispered. We crept into the hall. Now I could start on my homework.

But Melody had other ideas. "I'll help you with the ice cream," she said.

"Ice cream?"

"Dessert," she reminded me.

"Okay," I answered. "You tell Bill and we'll rendezvous in the kitchen. Let's coordinate our watches."

Melody looked puzzled and held up her bare wrist. "Aha," I said. "When the big freckle gets past the wrist bone, then you'll know it's time for ice cream."

"Silly," said Melody.

A few minutes later Bill followed Melody into the kitchen saying, "there's no such thing as freckle ice cream."

"Freckle ice cream time," said Melody, holding up her wrist. "And I bet there is freckle ice cream."

"Yes . . . vanilla. It has those little freckle flecks," I teased.

208

"See," said Melody.

"What about Macadamia Nut? Big freckle ice cream." Bill made a gagging noise.

"Or Rocky Road – freckle and marshmallow melting skin ice cream! Ooooh!" shrieked Melody.

"Or with raisins – freckles and wart ice cream," added Bill.

"Oooh, oooh, oooh!" Melody cried.

"Whoa, whoa, whoa," I said. "What we have is Chocolate Chip."

"Yuck," said Bill. "Ice cream with moles."

"Double yuck," said Melody.

I put the dishes in front of them. "Okay, you two, they're just chocolate chips. Not moles."

"I don't want any moles in my ice cream," said Melody.

"Me neither," said Bill.

Great. I'd created another monster. For a long time, Melody and Bill had believed a monster lived in their toilet. Now they believed, or liked to believe they believed, that chocolate chip ice cream was full of moles.

I took a bite of my ice cream. "See? Just chocolate."

Melody stared at me. "Yuck, Kristy."

"Okay, then pick the chocolate chips out."

Melody bent her head over the bowl and

carefully began picking out the chocolate chips with her spoon and lining them up on the table.

"They look like chocolate chips to me," I said.

"Moles," said Melody.

"Kristy, can you help me with my homework?" asked Bill.

I sighed. I needed help with *mine*. But I said, "Okay. After you finish your ice cream."

"Grrreat. Stupendous," said Bill. He started picking the chips out of his ice cream, too.

I looked down at my own ice cream, which was melting into a vanilla and chocolate chip puddle. I wasn't going to pick out the moles – er, chips. I was going to eat it all. Because I wasn't going to get to my homework that night. That was clear.

I took a big bite of the ice cream. "Ugh!" said Melody. "Yumm," I said, smiling. If I couldn't get to my homework, I wasn't going to worry about it. I'd think about it in the morning.

8th
CHAPTER

Have you ever noticed how fast tomorrow always comes? Like when you have homework to do? (I did finish my homework after babysitting for the Kormans. I got up extra early that next morning, and *just* managed it.) Or when you have to be at school early?

We – the candidates – had to be at Stoneybrook Middle School half an hour early on Campaign Day to set up our booths. Claudia and Mary Anne also got up early. Then they came round to help me carry stuff into school (Charlie had agreed drive us) and to give me some tips about dressing.

"Why can't I just wear jeans and a nice shirt?" I asked.

"A light blue shirt would be good," said Claudia. "I read somewhere that light blue looks best on television."

"This is not television, Claud. Just the SMS cafeteria. But I *do* have a light blue sweatshirt."

"Kristy. No sweatshirt," said Claudia firmly.

"Why don't you wear your black trousers?" asked Mary Anne. "They look good."

"Okay," I said, digging through the wardrobe.

Claudia was doing some digging, too. "Here. Why don't you ever wear this?"

"This" was an enormous sweater of a sort of creamy brown, with little black and green stripes running across it. I shrugged.

"Try it on," said Claudia.

At last I emerged in my black sweater, and loafers. "I still look preppie," I complained. But I really didn't look too bad.

"Kristy!" a voice called.

"That's Charlie – come on." We gathered the stuff together, staggered down the stairs, and headed for school.

The cafeteria rang with people talking, shouting, pushing tables, and jockeying for the best place.

"Here," said Mary Anne. "Not too close to the end."

"And not too close to Alan," put in Claudia.

We set up the booth, which Claudia had designed. My logo appeared on red posters, over and over again. We had badges, rosettes and a handout that told all about me and what I wanted to do. Claudia had designed that, too. It looked like a report card. Beside each point was the column for the grades, and in every column it just said "K+". It looked pretty cool. It was concise, effective and distinctive. And serious. I wanted to convey how serious I was.

Which some people didn't. Alan, for example, had dressed in balloons. He looked like a big bunch of grapes. Everyone who took a badge and put it on got to pop one of the balloons.

You could tell right away he was going to be a big, noisy hit.

Mal, looking nervous, was sitting at her booth with Jessi. Behind her was a big drawing of a clock, and written across it was "Time to let Mal keep the minutes!"

"That's great, Mal," I said.

"Have a clock," said Jessi. She handed me a badge designed like a clock with the slogan on it.

"This really is great," said Mary Anne. "Oh, Mal, you're sure to win. I wish we could all vote for you."

"You can, when Mal runs for student council president," said Jessi.

"No way," said Mal, and we all laughed.

"Uh-oh," said Mary Anne. "Speaking of time, here comes everybody."

We headed back for my booth. Campaign Day had started at SMS.

The next two hours were a blur, but a very distinct blur. Alan, who'd chosen a spot near mine (so much for planning), came to visit me almost straight away.

"Go on, Kristy," he said. "Stick a pin in me."

"Don't tempt me," I answered. "What are you trying to say, Alan?"

"It doesn't matter what you say, Kristy. It's whether people remember you. First principle of advertising."

"This is a campaign for class president, Alan. You're not trying to sell breakfast cereal or something."

Alan flapped his arms and made the balloons flutter. "Are we having a debate?"

"No!"

Just then someone said to me, "What *is* your platform?"

At last! A real question. Someone who was interested in the issues. A voter who wanted to become an *informed* voter.

I picked up my report card. "If you'll look at this card, you'll see the issues I am addressing. For example, I think we need to do something about our assemblies. They could be a lot more interesting. We could poll the pupils and find out what type of people they might like to see at the assemblies—"

"Nobody's going to listen to pupils."

"They will if you show them you care. And you can show them you care by voting for me."

Just then someone popped several of Alan's balloons at once. Amid shrieks and laughter, people began to drift away.

"Wait a minute," I said.

"They'll be back," said Mary Anne. "There's a lot to see."

Claudia reappeared.

"Where have you been?"

"Grace," said Claudia glumly.

"What?" I cried.

"Go and see."

"I'll be right back." I headed in the direction Claudia had pointed, and then wished I hadn't.

Gruesome Grace and Creepy Cokie were in a booth set up to look like a studio. Cokie had slung a video camera over her shoulder. A monitor was perched on the table. Beneath a huge, glittering banner that said, "Meet THE candidate for class president", sat Grace. Her make-up was about three feet thick, and she was wearing a pale blue sweater, matching ski-pants, and a ton of jewellery. Grace was sitting and talking to people from our class, one by one. While she talked, Cokie taped them, and the event was being shown live an the monitor.

Kids were standing three-deep around, trying to watch. And if that wasn't bad enough, Cokie was also taking their photos with a Polaroid while they sat with Grace beneath her banner. They got to keep the pictures.

"I don't believe this," I said to myself, I also instantly thought of another idea for my campaign. From now on, there had to be a limit to how much money anyone campaigning for office could spend.

"This must have cost a fortune," muttered someone at my elbow.

"No kidding," I answered, turning before I realized who it was. "Pete!"

"Hi, Kristy."

"Hi," I said.

"Not the best place for a booth, is it?" He nodded towards his own booth, directly opposite Cokie's.

"Hmm," I said. I was surprised, a little. Pete's booth was serious, too. He had handouts and had badges that said "Pete for President" and "Vote for Pete, for SMS's sake!" Basic, but also serious.

"I have to get back," I said.

"Good luck," said Pete.

"Oh! Uh, good luck," I answered.

"I hope Alan runs out of balloons soon," said Mary Anne when I returned. When I didn't answer, she asked, "How bad is it?"

"Remember when Claudia was talking about television?" I asked. "And I said this wasn't television?"

Mary Anne nodded. Claudia smiled.

"It *is* television. Only it's Grace's TV show. She and Cokie have a video camera here."

"Wow. I can't believe her parents let her take their video camera."

"You know what?" said Claudia. "I bet it doesn't matter. I bet plenty of candidates have been elected without major media campaigns."

"Major media campaigns?"

"You know, we did a media blitz of our own. The whole school knows the K+ symbol."

"Media blitz?"

"And I have more ideas, too." Claudia picked up one of the badges and examined it intently.

"You'll win," said Mary Anne. "We just have to work extra hard."

"Extra hard," I repeated. "You're right, Mary Anne." I picked up a poster and a badge, and said to a crowd of pupils passing by, "Excuse me. I'd like to show you a very interesting report card. . ."

The bell finally rang and the candidates began to clear up. We had gathered almost everything together when a nastily familiar voice said, "How are you feeling about it?" Grace and Cokie were standing behind me. Cokie had trained the video camera on me.

"How about, 'Underdog bites back'?" I suggested, stepping up close to the camera. "Are you getting that Cokie?"

Cokie backed away a little but kept the camera rolling.

"You are so immature," said Grace.

I bit back the retort that it takes one to know one. Instead I shrugged. "You're entitled to your opinion, Grace. Or anybody else's, since I doubt you ever have any of your own."

"What do you mean?"

"It's a difficult concept, Grace. . . Are you getting this Cokie?"

"Turn it off, Cokie. Let's go." Grace glared at me. "The best man will win."

"Grace," I said. "The best woman – and the best candidate – is going to win. So why don't you just go somewhere and get some more practice at being a loser?"

I couldn't believe I'd said that. I heard Mary Anne gasp behind me, and knew she couldn't believe it, either. Good grief, this campaign *was* making me crazy.

I almost said I was sorry (apologizing to Grace – double good grief!), but she turned and flounced away, with Cokie behind her.

Bending over, I picked up a piece of purple balloon.

"A+, Kristy," I muttered to myself disgustedly.

I had planned on spending the rest of the day resting, sort of with my eyes open, at my desk. That plan got scorched in science when we were reminded of the major, major test coming up the next day.

And I had Krusher practice.

A short practice, a quick dinner, homework, and then cramming for the test?

I glance at the science book and my notes. No.

Could I skip the homework? No.

I could try to skip dinner, but somehow, I didn't think that would go down very well with Mum and Watson.

That left the Krushers.

The first thing I did when I got home was call the Krushers and cancel practice. I hated doing it. And I hated telling everyone it was cancelled.

"Practice is *important*," Jamie kept insisting when I told him, and I knew he was thinking about his bicycle, too.

"It is, Jamie. We'll have a practice soon."

But I couldn't say how soon. I wasn't going to make any more promises that I couldn't keep.

9th CHAPTER

Tuesday

You lot told me about Jamie Newton's NEW BICYCLE. But I still didn't quite get it. Until I arrived at the Newtons' this afternoon and discovered that my baby-sitting job had turned into a bike-sitting job. Or maybe a bike-holding job...

"Have you seen my new bike?" That was Jamie Newton's first question.

Dawn was prepared. She laughed and said, "I haven't seen it, but I've heard about it. I've heard it's beautiful."

Jamie said, "It's exactly perfect."

Mrs Newton had just left. It was a perfect afternoon. Lucy was lying on her back in the playpen on the porch, making pedalling motions with her legs and having an urgley-talk conversation with herself, with gurgles of laughter in between the urgley-words. Jamie was pulling on Dawn's hand, trying to steer her in the direction of his bicycle.

"First, why don't I make something like lemonade or iced tea, Jamie? We can let it chill while we're practising, okay?"

Jamie didn't look too thrilled, but he followed Dawn into the kitchen. She found some lemons and sugar, and gave Jamie the job of squeezing the lemons (after she'd cut them).

He seemed to enjoy it for a while, concentrating so ferociously that Dawn had to smile.

"That's a lemon-face." Jamie kept his face scrunched up while he juiced another lemon.

"It's the face you make when you squeeze lemons. See?" Dawn picked up half of a lemon and demonstrated, making a scrunched-up face of her own. Jamie laughed and made an even worse face.

After that, he invented six more lemon faces to go with the six lemon halves left that needed squeezing, and Dawn made lemon faces back while she stirred the lemonade. when it was made, Jamie did a taste test.

"Is that a lemon-face I see? Again?" asked Dawn.

"Sour," replied Jamie.

Dawn tasted it.

"Lemon-face!" crowed Jamie. He handed Dawn the sugar, and she spooned a little more in, even though it was white sugar, not even honey.

Tasting it again, Jamie made another face, a big goofy-grin face, watching Dawn carefully. She caught on. "A lemonade face?" she guessed.

Jamie shrieked with laughter, and Lucy, who now was sitting in her high chair, shrieked, too. Dawn put the lemonade in the fridge, picked up Lucy, and let Jamie lead her outside. she waited while he wheeled his bike out of the garage.

"It's a bea—, uh, a very cool, handsome, perfect bike, Jamie."

"I know," he answered solemnly. "Can we – may we – practise now?"

"Of course. Let me get Lucy settled first." Dawn took Lucy over to her playpen and put a bright purple cloth ball near her. Lucy turned her head sideways and stared at it, then began talking to it. Babies don't

222

know that everything doesn't answer. (Or maybe grown-ups don't know that things do. . .)

"Dawnnn!"

'Coming." She gave Lucy a quick pat and then went back to Jamie who was holding up his bike.

She stopped in surprise. "Jamie, where are your stabilizers?"

"I told Daddy to take them off," he answered. "Stabilizers are for babies."

"But—"

"Look." Sure enough, a group of older boys were swooping up and down the street.

"None of them have stabilizers."

"And you're ready to try riding your bike without stabilizers now, too?"

Jamie nodded emphatically. But his voice wasn't so emphatic when he added, "Yes. Now."

"Okay, what do we do?"

"Hold my bike while I get on."

That was easier said than done. Poor Jamie. He put one foot on the pedal and Dawn, who didn't quite realize how off balance it would make the bicycle, staggered back.

Jamie hopped off, quick as anything. His eyes were huge. "You dropped me!"

"No. I just wasn't ready."

"*You can't* drop me." Jamie's voice grew shrill.

223

"I won't. I promise. It's just that—" Dawn stopped. She was going to say, "It's just that without the stabilizers, your bike is really unsteady." But she didn't want to scare Jamie any more.

"It's just that I wasn't ready. That's all."

"Okay." Jamie got back into position, put his foot on the pedal, and waited. Dawn held the bike firm. Satisfied, Jamie grabbed her shoulder with one hand (which almost threw her off balance again), and swung up on to the bike seat.

"I'm ready to go," he announced.

Dawn held on to the seat and the handlebars to keep the bike upright. But even doing that, it was an extremely unsettling trip to the end of the drive. Jamie kept wrenching the handlebars, pulling Dawn sideways. She had to struggle to keep from falling over, bike, Jamie, and all.

It didn't take her long to realize, either, that Jamie wasn't pedalling hard enough to get any momentum going. She was not only holding him up, she was pushing him forward. And sure enough, when they reached the end of the drive, Jamie insisted on getting off, "helping" Dawn turn his bike round, and getting back on again.

Meanwhile, it seemed that every kid in the neighbourhood had decided to ride his bike down Jamie's street. Dawn saw Jamie glance at them from time to time with a sad expression. but most of the time he was wearing his bicycle variation of the lemon-face: eyes scrunched up, frowning, his lips pressed tightly together.

They headed up the drive and back down again. Dawn's arms were getting tired, her legs were aching, and her back was beginning to hurt.

"Jamie," she began.

"Watch out!"

"Wh-what?" Dawn swung round, half expecting to see a car bearing down on them – and then spent the next minute teetering precariously. Jamie didn't help. He was wrenching the handlebars around and flailing his legs wildly. One of his feet kicked Dawn in the stomach.

"Uhh!" It knocked the wind out of her, but it also knocked her backwards a little, and she was able to straighten the bike up.

"Jamie! What is it? Are you all right?"

"Stop, stop, stop!"

Dawn looked around wildly, and then gradually, remembering what she had read in the BSC notebook, it dawned on her. She looked down.

Sure enough, there in the drive was a branch from the maple tree, with a couple of leaves still attached to it.

"That branch?" she asked. but she knew the answer.

"We have to move it," declared Jamie.

This was twice as hard to do without the stabilizers. but Dawn finally managed to kick the branch out of the way with the toe of her trainer.

As they rode slowly up the drive, Dawn heard Lucy's voice. She wasn't talking to the purple ball or to herself any more. She sounded fretful.

"Jamie," Dawn began. But before she could suggest that he'd had enough practice for one afternoon, the front wheel wobbled, then turned completely sideways. Jamie, his bike, and Dawn all went down in a heap.

Dawn managed not to fall all the way, but she landed in a sort of tripod above the bike and Jamie. By the time she'd straightened up, Jamie had begun to cry.

Pulling the bike off Jamie, Dawn checked him for broken bones and for bumps. Fortunately, he'd just grazed his hands and one elbow.

"Come on," she said. she helped Jamie to his feet, being careful not to touch his skinned places, and led him into the house. She got the first aid kit out of the bathroom cabinet, then brought it and Jamie to the porch where she could keep an eye on Lucy.

As carefully as she could, Dawn wiped off Jamie's cuts and scrapes and put some ointment and plasters on them. By the time she'd finished, Jamie had stopped crying. But his face had gone from lemon to mule.

Frowning ferociously, he announced, "I'm never going to ride that stupid bicycle again."

"Jamie. . ." Just then Lucy began to cry in earnest. Dawn picked her up. She wasn't wet. Maybe, thought Dawn wryly as she gave her a little juice in a bottle, the purple ball had said something to her she didn't like.

She walked Lucy up and down, and Lucy gradually stopped crying. Her eyes closed.

"Jamie, I'm going to take Lucy to her cot. Stay on the porch. I'll be right back."

Jamie nodded, staring straight ahead and still scowling.

What am I going to tell him? Dawn worried the whole time she was putting Lucy down for her nap. In fact, she held an entire conversation with herself. She imagined saying to Jamie, The important thing is, after you fall, to get up and try again. But then herself said back, he needs those stabilizers. He's not ready to ride without them. But how, she asked herself, can I convince him to put them back on? And how, another part of herself asked, can I manage to walk up and down that drive, pulling that bike ONE more time?

Returning to the porch, Dawn took a deep breath. "Hey, listen," she started to say.

But Jamie wasn't listening to her at all.

He was watching the other kids flash by on their bicycles, their wheels spinning with silver flashes in the late afternoon sun. He was listening to the sounds of wheels on the pavement and the gears clicking and the whir of the wind as they flew by.

Gently, Dawn put her hand on his shoulder. Poor Jamie, she thought.

He turned.

"Dawn?" he said.

"Yes?"

"Dawn, can we practise on my bike some more?"

10th CHAPTER

I didn't believe it.

Quickly I flipped the test over, so no one could see it.

Not that anyone was trying to copy me or anything. No way. Not even if they'd wanted to.

Because I'd just *failed* the test. There was a big red 60 at the top. Which was not surprising when you saw how many red X's there were by my answers.

I don't know why I couldn't believe it, but I just couldn't. I mean, I don't get 60s. Generally, I'm a good pupil, even in subjects I'm not crazy about. Like science.

But I wasn't a good pupil any more. Part of me had to admit that, looking at those big (enormous) red numbers. Part of me said I should have been able to guess the right answers, just this once. And part of me was mortified.

I thought of Claudia, too. She's not good at school, and she doesn't get great grades. I wondered if she was actually used to seeing these kinds of numbers at the tops of her tests. Somehow I didn't think it was something anyone could get used to.

Except maybe Alan.

The bell rang and gratefully I shoved the awful test into my notebook, then shoved that deep into my rucksack. I told myself I didn't have time to think about it. I told myself to concentrate on what I was really good at. Just by stepping out of this room, I knew I'd see the signs: K+ – KRISTY FOR PRESIDENT.

Uh-oh. Would this mean I couldn't run? No. It was just one test. All I had to do was study and—

"Kristy?"

I jerked to a stop. It was Miss Griswold. She smiled.

"You know, Kristy, everybody has bad days."

"I suppose so."

"I think you're having a bad one now."

I smiled a little. What an understatement. "That's a fact," I said.

She smiled, too. "A scientific fact. Another fact is that you are a good pupil, generally. I have to say, your grade surprised me."

"Me, too."

"Did you revise?"

I shifted my weight. I wanted to lie and say that I had. But I hadn't. The test was telling the truth.

"No. I suppose I . . . I suppose I deserved that grade."

The answer seemed to satisfy Miss Griswold. She nodded slowly. Then she said, "Kristy, I know you're running for class president. I know you are the chairman of a thriving business. I don't usually do this, but under these circumstances, I want you to retake this test."

Who would ever think anyone could be so excited by the words "retake this test"?

Miss Griswold pulled her lesson book towards her and turned the page. "How about tomorrow at lunch?"

I thought quickly. No BSC meeting this afternoon, and no babysitting job, either. How had I finished up with a whole free afternoon? Never mind. I'd have plenty of time to study. Maybe I could really do well in the test.

"Great!" I said. "Thank you, Miss Griswold."

"You're welcome. Don't be late to class, now."

"I won't. And thank you again!" I hurried out.

I kept on hurrying for the rest of the day. I spent lunch in the library, doing homework that was due in that afternoon. I spent every spare minute between classes checking on posters. (Was it my imagination or had someone been knocking all of mine askew. Someone called, say, Grace?) Study hour was spent on more catching up.

This afternoon, I was definitely going to study science. Big time.

But I got home after school and met . . . David Michael, wearing his Krushers hat and T-shirt.

Krushers practice! I'd forgotten I'd rescheduled it.

"Are you ready, Kristy?"

"Uh, David Michael. . ."

"We need to practise. You said so."

"Yes. You are absolutely right. I was just going to say give me a minute to get myself changed."

"Okay." David Michael sat down at the kitchen table and stared at the clock. He really *was* going to give me only a minute.

I couldn't help but smile. As I walked by him I gave the peak of his hat a little yank.

"Hey!" he said.

"Maybe a few minutes," I said, and raced to my room to change.

It was a perfect day for softball. Everyone else seemed to think so, too. Most of the Krushers were already waiting for us when we arrived at the field.

"Plaaay ball," shouted Karen as we walked up.

"First we should practice some basics, okay?"

"Plaaay basics." Karen went into fits of laughter and about half the team went with her.

I waited a minute to give them a chance to giggle themselves out. After all, the Krushers are not your usual softball team. For example, the average age of the Krusher team member is 5.8. And one of the youngest players, Gabbie Perkins, is two and a half and doesn't quite understand the game yet. We throw Gabbie a tennis ball and stand very close to her when it's her turn to bat.

But age doesn't mean everyone doesn't try hard, and isn't good at *something* – even though not all of them are home run hitters, or fielders with rifle throws to first.

The giggling lessened and I held up my hands.

Then I looked over at Matt Braddock, who is just about our best player and who is also deaf. He was laughing, too. A lot of the kids know some sign language now (especially when it comes to playing softball), so they can talk to Matt. Someone had told him the joke, too. And I realized also that his sister, Haley, who can use sign language at top speed, was there to translate, in case.

But holding up your hands is universal, I suppose, for BE QUIET. (I mean, look at how many teachers use it.) Anyway Matt got quiet, too, although he kept this huge grin on his face.

"We're going to practise fielding grounders, okay?"

"What's a grounder?" asked Karen.

"I know, I know," said Jackie Rodowsky. "It's a ball that is hit along the ground."

"Good, Jackie." Jackie looked extremely pleased. He's sort of a, well, a walking disaster. Wherever Jackie goes, look out! The sound of something crashing or breaking or being bumped into is not far behind. But he's probably one of our toughest players. He never gives up.

"Does everyone understand? Okay. Now, what you do is, you get your body behind the ball. You don't bend over with your legs apart because then the ball would go right through them. And you put the tip of your glove all the way to the ground. That way the ball doesn't roll underneath it. But even if it did, your body would be there to stop it. Right?"

I looked at the circle of suddenly serious faces.

"Okay, Matt – why don't you just come and roll a ball to me and I'll demonstrate catching a grounder."

After we'd tried a few, I divided everyone up into twos and let them practise.

I stared off into the outfield.

It's funny how, when you have so much to do, and so much to think and worry about, your mind can just start thinking of nothing at all. I mean, it goes on a mini mind holiday without warning.

At least that's what was happening to me. The big, puffy clouds drifted overhead, the sun shone, and I drifted along with them, basking mindlessly in – mindlessness.

I don't know how long I hovered there. But suddenly I realized that someone was standing next to me, staring.

I looked down. It was Karen. Her hands were on her hips. The one with the baseball glove on it made her look as if she was growing a wing.

"Uh, yes?"

"Have we practised enough?"

I glanced around. David Michael and Linny were sitting on the ground, rolling the ball to each other. Matt and Nicky Pike were using bats like golf clubs to hit the ball back and forth, pretending they were playing golf (or croquet, maybe). Jackie was wandering around in right field, looking for something. (The ball?) The team wasn't practising much of anything.

I gave myself a mental shake, raised the whistle, and blew. Everyone looked up instantly.

"Come on in," I called. They trotted eagerly up to me. The poor Krushers. While I'd been watching the clouds, they'd been getting bored. It really wasn't the same, practising when the coach wasn't paying attention and helping you out.

"Okay, let's play a game. And we'll concentrate on making really good catches. They don't have to be perfect. Just do your best and remember what I told you."

I divided the teams up and sent them out. Since they were uneven, I went out to right field (which is traditionally where you put your least experienced player. Not much happens in right field because most batters are right handed and they hit to left field). I thumped my glove and shouted, "Play ball!"

Claire Pike, who is five and prone to tantrums, was up first. She swung and missed. She swung and missed again.

"Keep your eye on the ball," called Karen. (One thing about coaching Karen – she never forgets anything you tell her!)

Claire stared hard at Matt, who was pitching. She leaned over a little, squinting, watching the ball.

Matt threw a fast pitch. Claire swung – and hit it! The ball klunked down, rolled about a metre, and stopped.

She stood looking at it.

"Run!" screamed Karen.

Claire wrinkled up her brow. Then she started towards first base. She kept looking back at the ball.

Good grief! Was she still keeping her eye on the ball?

"Don't look *now*! RUN!" I shouted.

Both Matt and the catcher dived for the ball. It disappeared between them, and Claire stopped watching it. She ran as hard as she could to first base.

Safe!

"Good work, Claire," I said.

She frowned suspiciously. "You're on the other team," she said, and turned her back on me.

I couldn't help but laugh.

It felt good to laugh. It seemed as if I hadn't laughed for a long, long time. Not much to laugh about right now, I reflected. The big fat red 60 on my science test loomed before my eyes. I *had* to study tonight. I *had* to. . .

"Kristy!" shrieked David Michael.

I came down to earth abruptly. Jackie Rodowsky, the Walking Disaster, was running at top speed towards first base. Claire, still stealing anxious glances at the ball, was on her way to second. And the ball was streaking across the grass towards me.

Everything happened at once. One minute I was staring at the ball open mouthed, trying to gather my wits. The next minute, in a kind of super slow motion, I was stretching my glove down towards it.

Too late. The ball took a sharp, wicked hop and smacked me hard on the shin.

"OWWW!" I grabbed my leg, hopped once, lost my balance, and fell over.

"Get the ball," someone shouted. There was a mad scramble around me, then Matt held the ball up.

"Time out," called Karen.

I sat up, holding my throbbing shin, just as Claire touched home base.

"I made it!" she cried.

"No, you didn't." Karen trotted past her, on her way out to right field.

"I did!"

"It was already time out," said Karen. "Kristy fell down."

Claire's face scrunched up. She took a deep breath, turned bright red, and began to throw a tantrum. "Nofe-air! Nofe-air!"

We're all pretty used to Claire's tantrums by now, so, keeping my eye on her, I stood up and tested my leg.

I looked at the circle of anxious faces.

"It's all right. Okay, listen up. This was a *key* lesson. Pay attention!"

"You stopped the ball," said David Michael diplomatically.

"Yeah," several people murmured.

I looked at their face. They'd started to smile. The Krushers were a great team, no doubt about it.

"Um, let's play ball," I said. "But I'm going to coach from the sidelines."

I walked gingerly back towards the third

base line with Claire, who had stopped tantruming.

"Does it hurt?" she said.

"Only when I laugh. . . Okay, Claire, you go back to third, okay?"

Her face started to scrunch up again, and I added quickly, "That way, you get to run home again."

She thought about for a moment, let her breath out, and trotted back along the baseline.

I leaned over, pulled my cap down, put one hand on each knee, and called, "Play ball!"

For the rest of the practice, I made myself pay attention.

Making yourself pay attention is exhausting. After practice that afternoon, I felt pretty tired. And by the time dinner was over and I'd disappeared upstairs to study for my science test, I was wiped out. But I had to do it. Miss Griswold was giving me a second chance not to fail.

I opened my notebook, picked up my highlighter . . . and the phone rang.

"Kristy?" It was Claudia.

"Hey, Claud. Listen, I've got to study."

"Yeah. Don't you hate it? Unless it's art, but that's not work. That's art."

"I'm not any good at art," I said. "Or science, either, at least not right now."

"You're a good pupil, Kristy. And science is very organized. At least that's what my teacher always says. So you should be good at science because you're so organized."

I sighed. "I wish it worked that way."

Claudia went on, "So, have you written your speech yet?"

"Speech?" I gasped. I looked over at my calendar. Sure enough, there it was. Tomorrow the class assemblies were going to be held for the first round of speeches.

"Oh, no!" I cried.

"You haven't?" asked Claudia.

"I'm about to. Right now. Listen, Claudia, you saved my life. I gotta go."

"Good luck," said Claudia.

"Goodbye," I said.

When I sat down at my desk again, I pushed the science book out of my line of vision. Tomorrow morning I'd get up early tomorrow morning and study. And between classes. And maybe during the assembly.

But first I had to write a speech. A really, really good speech. I closed my eyes, imagined myself at the podium.

Ladies and gentlemen? No. Fellow pupils? No.

I pulled my notebook towards me, turned to a blank sheet, and began to write.

11th CHAPTER

"Thank you," I said to the mirror. I was practising my speech.

Someone tapped on the door to my room.

"Kristy?" It was my mum.

"Come in," I said.

She stuck her head around the door. "It's late."

"I know. I've almost finished."

"Anything I can help with?"

For a moment I was tempted. But what could she do? I could tell her how overwhelmed I felt, but that wouldn't make the feeling go away. I took a deep breath and shook my head. "Thanks, but I'm just in a panic right now.'

"Well. . ."

"So much work, so little time," I explained.

My mother smiled. "Don't forget to sleep," she said.

"I won't. 'Night."

"Goodnight, Kristy."

After she'd closed the door, I turned back to the speech. It was an okay speech. It *sounded* okay. At least I thought it did. I looked at the clock. Too late to call Mary Anne and read it to her. Her father has got a lot more lenient these days, but I don't think *anybody's* parents would appreciate a phone call at this hour.

It *could* be a better speech. Maybe tomorrow, if I had time . . . no, I'd forgotten about the science test. I looked over at my bed, then back at the pages of the speech, then at the science book. I got up and put the science book under my pillow and climbed into bed. I didn't really believe the knowledge would seep into my brain during the night, but I was desperate.

My eyes closed as soon as I turned out the light. I thought I'd worry so much I wouldn't be able to sleep. But sleep was no problem . . . then.

The problem came at about two a.m. I opened my eyes and stared into the darkness. Boom. One minute I'd been sound asleep (although not dreaming about science or science books) and the next minute I was wide awake.

And my mind was going a mile a minute. Speech. Babysitters Club meeting. Babysitting jobs – maybe I could let some of those slide for now. The Krushers (my shin gave a sympathetic throb). All the duties of being president of my class. At least I had experience at being a chairman; being chairman of the BSC had taught me just how many responsibilities a person in charge has.

Maybe I should temporarily resign from the BSC. Or go on inactive status. Would that work? The thought gave me a sharp pain in the stomach, but I reminded myself it would only be temporary.

Of course, with every thought, I had to turn over, or thump the pillow, or pull on the covers. It wasn't like being in bed at all. It was like swimming in choppy water, just trying to stay afloat.

I looked at the clock. Good grief. Almost an hour had passed. I had to get some sleep, or I'd be one of the walking dead the next day. Instead of Kristy Plus, my slogan would be Kristy, Rest in Peace.

Closing my eyes, I willed myself to stop thinking.

It worked for about a minute. Then I found myself staring into the dark, my mind going around and around, thinking the same things over and over again.

Finally I got up, very quietly, pulled my science book out, and took it to my desk. I turned on the lamp. I opened the book. If anything would put me to sleep, it would be studying science.

It was weird, studying in the middle of

the night. I mean, I'd heard my brothers complain about staying-up all night, but this was the closest I'd ever come. Turning the pages of the book seemed to make a lot of noise. And the house was so quiet. Staring at the pages, listening to the silence, I decided that big houses have a different kind of quiet from smaller houses, like the one we used to live in. Small houses were a noisier quiet. They creaked. Sounds didn't have so far to travel, maybe.

Maybe there was a scientific explanation. . . Science. I jerked my thoughts back to the book. I studied. I kept waiting to get sleepy.

But it was a long time before I did.

One thing about not getting enough sleep: You don't have enough energy to worry.

The next day for the first round of speeches, assemblies were held by grade in the assembly hall. The candidates had to sit in the front row. Just my luck, I got the seat next to Alan. He crossed his eyes. I ignored him.

Behind me, I could feel the whole eighth grade breathing down my neck. Don't be silly, I told myself.

Grace leaned across Alan towards me. "Is that your speech?"

I looked down at the paper-clipped pages in my hand.

"Yes. Why?" (That shows how out of it

I was. I *knew* better than to ask Grace anything.)

"No reason," said Grace. She leaned back and made a big point of opening a leather folder. Tucked inside was a thin stack of index cards, with typewritten words on them. Grace looked up and caught my eye. Satisfied, she smiled and closed the folder again.

Typical Grace, I thought. But typed index cards do not make a good speech.

Alan didn't seem to have any speech notes at all. I couldn't see Pete from where I was sitting. He was on the other side of Grace.

Our head teacher walked up to the podium and cleared his throat and waited. I glanced back. Mary Anne, a few seats behind me, caught my eye and nodded, holding up her thumb.

Where was everybody else? Before I could scan the assembly hall any more, the rustling and shuffling and whispering died away. Our head teacher smiled.

"We are here today for the preliminary round of speeches by our candidates for the offices of eighth-grade president, vice president, secretary and treasurer. Each candidate will have three minutes to present his or her platform. At the end of the speeches, if we have time, they will field questions. We'll begin with the candidates for secretary."

Good. I slid my science notes out under my speech notes and began to read over them. Somehow, all that reading in the middle of the night hadn't helped. The facts just wouldn't stick in my brain.

"Grace Blume," said Mr Taylor. Grace stood up, smoothed her hair, and walked calmly to the podium. She looked very pulled together up there, smiling at the assembly.

"When you choose your class president, you want to choose someone who can truly represent you," said Grace

She paused. She put one of the little white cards behind the other, then read the next one.

"I will be the leader you need." (Pause, change cards.) "We work hard." (Pause, change cards.) I'm going to leave out the rest of the pauses, but you get the idea.

Grace went on. "But you wouldn't have to work quite *so* hard if you had the right leader.

"As your leader, I would see to it that we didn't have to work so hard. We need to enjoy ourselves once in a while. For example, our football team has been winning! Isn't it time we celebrated that? And what about dances?"

And so on. I rolled my eyes, not caring if Grace saw me. I knew she was shallow, but this was ridiculous. She was making all kinds of impossible promises. But people

246

applauded when she had finished, as if they didn't know the difference.

Finally it was my turn. It was a long walk to the podium. I stood for a minute looking out at everyone. And everywhere I looked, I saw a member of the BSC – Dawn in one corner, Mary Anne near the middle of the room, Logan a little further back, Claudia in another corner, Stacey in the front. For a moment I was disconcerted: We usually sat together.

Then as I glanced around the room again, meeting their smiles wherever I looked, I realized they'd split up on purpose.

Suddenly, I didn't feel so dim and sleepy. I smiled at the whole assembly.

"I'm not up here to make a lot of promises that I – or anyone – can't keep," I began. Grace's eyes narrowed. "What I am here for is to talk about responsibilities. We're expected to study, to participate in school activities, to go to classes, to follow certain rules. We do that pretty well, I think. So it seems to me that we should have more responsibility. I don't mean more rules to follow. But more of a chance to prove ourselves. For example, we have a class play every year. Who gets to choose which play we put on? We have no input to that decision. I think it is time we did. I think we should have a committee of people from our class to choose which play we perform. . ."

As I outlined my ideas about school lunches and the Special Needs classes, I saw people nodding. They were listening! They agreed with me. And I was sure the applause as I sat down was louder for me than it had been for Grace (she, of course wasn't applauding at all). Anyway, I heard Claudia whistle (I think it was Claudia).

Then Alan got up.

The worst.

He stepped behind the podium and said, "Okay, everybody stand up."

There was a pause, then a buzz of talk.

"Come on," said Alan. "Up!"

The buzz of talk grew louder, but everyone eventually got to their feet.

"Good," said Alan. "Now, sit down again."

"What is this," said someone, "Simon Says?"

Alan waited, his arms extended, until the sniggering, grumbling pupils sat down. Then he folded his arms across his chest.

"I've just proved to you what a good leader I am. You all did what I told you. So now I'm telling you to vote for me."

That was it! He left the podium and returned to his seat, raising his clasped hands over his head at the rest of the class talking and laughing behind him.

I couldn't believe it.

After Alan, Pete seemed unbelievably mature. I grimaced. Alan was such a pest.

Just his existence had made Pete look good. Although it hadn't hurt any of the rest of us, either.

"Every one of the candidates for class president has presented some good ideas," Pete began. "And when I'm president, I'll be glad to try to put some of those ideas into practice. I, too, believe that we should be part of the decision about what class play we perform each year. I'd also like to see greater editorial freedom extended to our school newspaper. . ."

I groaned. Boring.

"Assemblies could be better here at SMS, too. I'd like to be part of a committee to take suggestions for speakers – speakers *we* would be interested in – and to help get those speakers.

"At least some of those assemblies should be about sport. We have a great football team—"

Pete paused while people broke into cheers. (I didn't cheer. I thought it was extremely manipulative to encourage the audience to cheer by talking about the football team.)

"But we have some other great athletes, too. They also deserve sports assemblies."

I had to admit it, it was an interesting idea. But was it practical? Wouldn't that mean we'd be holding pep rallies practically every ten minutes, if we included every

team in the school? Like the fencing team?
It would take some organizing. . .

"And that's only the beginning. But I
need your help first – your help when you
vote. Vote for Pete Blake for president."

The applause was loud.

Okay ideas. Some of them.

I pulled out my science notes. I needed
to use every minute to study for the test
retake at lunch. And I did. I had to hurry
to get there on time.

Miss Griswold was waiting for me.

"Sorry I'm late," I said.

She looked surprised. "You're not late,
Kristy. Slow down."

"Oh. Well, anyway, I'm ready for the
test."

Miss Griswold smiled. "Good."

I slid into my seat, pulled out a pencil,
and took the test from her.

"Good luck, Kristy."

Luck wasn't enough. Some of the material I'd studied came back to me – or was
it just familiar from being in the test the last
time? Maybe I should have stayed up all
night. I went over and over and over the
questions, and the answers, but I didn't feel
good when I handed the test back to Miss
Griswold.

She took out her red pencil. It got a
real going over. Finally, just before the
bell rang signalling the end of lunch, she
finished.

She looked up. "I'm sorry, Kristy," was all she said.

Numbly, I stood up and took the test from her hand. I felt my face turn red. I'd failed. In fact I'd got an even lower grade.

"Thank you, Miss Griswold," I mumbled and walked out quickly, before she could say anything else, ask any questions. What would I tell her anyway? I, Kristy Thomas, world-class organized person, was turning into a klutz and a failure? And it seemed that the harder I tried, the worse I did. I felt tears sting the backs of my eyes, but I pushed them away.

Stop it, I told myself fiercely. You're just tired. It's no big deal. It's just one test.

But I never, ever, in my whole life would have thought I'd fail the same test – not once, but twice.

12th CHAPTER

Thrusday

Good greif. Jamie is a bicicle monster! Really! Big time. If only he hadnt taken those trainning wheels off! But something good did happene Jaymi was trying to do to much, to soon, and he finally saw that. Maybe he (and we) can finally start tamming the bicycle monster...

"*This is* a great outfit, Lucy," cooed Claudia, following Jamie outside. They were going to see Jamie's bike (what else?). Lucy, looking even more adorable than usual (if that's possible), was wearing lavender overalls with pink stars on them, a pink shirt, pink socks and little purple trainers with shoelaces that had stars and moons on them.

Jamie was wearing jeans, a long-sleeved T-shirt, trainers and a look of ferocious determination.

"Okay," he said, wheeling his bike out of the garage.

"Great bike, Jamie. See the bicycle, Lucy? One day, you'll be riding a bicycle just like your big brother."

"No!" said Jamie. "Not for a long time."

Uh-oh, thought Claudia. Sore subject. Aloud she said, "Of course not. Not for years. It takes a lot of hard work, Lucy, and don't you forget it!"

Lucy said something in urgley, grabbed Claudia's hair (which was in a fat plait with seven bows in different colours tied up and down it) and pulled. It didn't hurt, because Lucy is a baby. But it definitely said, "I'm here. Pay attention to *me*."

"Lucy, you are too much," said Claudia, carefully extracting the plait from Lucy's fingers.

"I want to practise riding my bike," said Jamie.

"Okay. Why don't I put Lucy in her buggy and you can get on your bike and we—"

"No. You have to help."

Claudia's pretty easygoing, but she almost got annoyed at Jamie's bossy tone. Then she remembered the trouble he'd been having with the bike and softened. "Okay, Jamie. I'll tell you what, Lucy, it's the playpen for you for a little while, okay?"

So Lucy returned to her playpen on the porch to watch Jamie practise riding his bike. Fortunately, Lucy isn't one of those babies who is picky about what she watches. Watching Jamie and Claud go up and down the drive seemed just fine with her.

Claudia knew what to expect from reading the BSC notebook. So she inspected the drive and made sure every single leaf, pebble and twig were gone. Then she stood on one side of the bicycle and held it while Jamie climbed up on the other side.

"You know, Jamie, Kristy told me how she put the stabilizers on. . ."

"They've gone now," Jamie replied.

They started down the drive. Claudia wasn't sure, but she thought Jamie was probably as shaky as ever. Even though they didn't run into any twigs or leaves, every time she let go the least little bit, Jamie wobbled like crazy.

And he fell more than once, in spite of

Claudia's help. The front wheel would go one way, Jamie would make a dive, and all three of them (Jamie, Claudia and the bike) would lose their balance. At least Jamie didn't cry. Claudia decided that he'd probably had a fair amount of practice at falling off and was getting used to it.

But the third time he fell, Claudia thought she heard wailing. Only it wasn't Jamie. It was Lucy.

"Hold on a minute, Jamie," said Claudia, extracting herself from the tangle of bike and boy and heading for the playpen. Lucy's face was red and crumpled. Somehow, she'd managed to push her teething ring out between the bars of the playpen.

Picking it up and putting it back inside, Claudia leaned over and tickled Lucy's stomach. Lucy grabbed the ring and stuffed it in her mouth.

"Umm, good," teased Claudia gently. The red, scrunched-up look left Lucy's face and she waved her feet.

"Claudia!" said Jamie.

"Jamie, Lucy needs to play, too."

"I'm not playing," answered Jamie.

"I know," said Claudia. "You're working hard. But why don't we take a break?"

Suddenly Jamie wailed, sounding not much older than Lucy. "I can't. I can't!"

He bent over and began to wrestle the bicycle upright.

What could Claudia do? She helped Jamie get back in the saddle, and they began to struggle and wobble their way down the drive.

Just then, one of the posse of bicycle riding kids on the street, whom Jamie had been watching with such envy, wheeled to a stop at the kerb. The others pulled up alongside him.

Jamie became stiffer and more red-faced. It didn't help. And all those kids standing there staring didn't make Claudia feel any calmer either.

But they turned out to be just what Jamie needed.

As Jamie reached the end of the drive, the first boy said, "You should slow down a little. What happened to your stabilizers?"

"Took them off," said Jamie.

"Why? You hardly got to use them. . ."

"Because," said Jamie.

"You know what? It's easier if you use them for a while first. You're trying to do too much. It's impossible."

Claudia held her breath, half expecting Jamie to jump in and start arguing, but he looked at the boy and said, "Really?" His tone of voice was so relieved, Claudia wanted to hug him.

Instead she asked, "Where *are* your stabilizers, Jamie?"

"In the garage," he replied.

"I'll tell you what," the boy said, "if you put them back on, I'll help you practise."

"You will?" Jamie slid off his bike and took the handlebars from Claudia. She stepped back.

"Why not? Rich helped *me* learn to ride." The boy jerked his head towards one of the other boys, who nodded. "I practised with two stabilizers, then with one. Didn't I?"

Rich nodded.

"Really?" asked Jamie again.

The boy grinned. "Yeah. One wheel at a time. That's all you can do anyway, you know. One thing at a time."

"Can we practise tomorrow? I'll ask my mum and dad tonight to put the stabilizers back on."

"Okay." The boy hopped on his bike and pushed off. "See you tomorrow, Jamie."

"Okay," Jamie called.

And just like that, the red-faced, stubborn, miserable bike monster was gone. Smiling sunnily, Jamie wheeled the bike round (with a little help from Claudia) and headed back up the drive.

"I'm going to learn to ride my bike," he told Claudia. "They're going to help."

"That's great, Jamie."

Jamie wheeled his bike into the garage and smiled up at Claudia. "Want to take Lucy for a walk?" he asked.

"You think you have time for that now?"

"Oh, yeah," said Jamie. "You can't practise all the time, you know." Hiding a smile, Claudia said solemnly, "I know."

13th CHAPTER

"Kristy? Kristy!"

I jumped about a mile. "Karen!"

"I scared you, didn't I?"

"You did," I agreed. "I think you made me grow some grey hair."

"Let me see." Karen marched over to the sofa I was sitting on and stared. "Nope."

"Too bad."

"Why does hair turn grey? Why doesn't it turn some other colour? Like green?" Karen wondered.

"I don't know."

"Mine's going to turn green *and* purple. I'll be a scientist and make it do that."

That reminded me of the science test. And the list I was making. Claudia's afternoon with Jamie kept coming back to me. *One wheel at a time.* You can only do one thing at a time. That was the trouble. I was trying to do about ten things at a time. And not doing any of them well.

"Can you?" asked Karen.

"What?"

"Come and decorate the pancakes. We're having a Sunday pancake lunch, and Nannie and Emily Michelle and David Michael and I are cutting up fruit and all this good stuff and we're going to make the pancakes into shapes and put faces on them."

"Can I just come and have some pancakes later?"

"Oh, no! That's not as much fun, Kristy."

I sighed. "I know. I just have so much to do. I have to finish this list."

Karen looked at me mournfully. With her glasses, she is very good at it. But I truly had to get organized. I looked mournfully back at her and shook my head.

"Silly billy," said Karen. "Goodbye."

"Goodbye," I replied, and sighed again. Then I heard myself. Two sighs in two minutes. Not good. I am not a person who sighs much.

But I was making a list. I was going to become the most organized person on earth. And as soon as that happened, I wouldn't be so, well, disorganized. Things would get done. Things would be fine.

But the best-laid plans of mice and men – and babysitters – go wrong. I knew my new organizational strategy was already in trouble by Monday afternoon, as I dashed up the stairs at Claudia's house, late for our meeting.

Claudia was on the phone, arranging a job. Mary Anne had opened the appointment book on her lap. Mallory and Dawn were throwing popcorn in the air, trying to catch it in their mouths. Stacey was leaning gracefully against the headboard of Claudia's bed, watching. Jessi was opening a bag of yoghurt raisins.

My chair was empty.

"Sorry," I cried, rushing in. "I finished at the Papadakises' and then I tried to start my homework and the next thing I knew, Charlie was calling me and I was late." I collapsed in my chair.

Everyone stared.

"Okay, okay," I said. I straightened up and took a deep breath.

Mary Anne, who sees a lot, asked quietly, "What's wrong, Kristy?"

"I'm fine," I said. I looked around at my friends' faces as Claudia hung up the phone. "Well, maybe not fine, exactly."

"Exactly what?" said Dawn.

"Miss Griswold called Mum and Watson about my science grade."

"Oh, no. The worst. Are you grounded?" asked Claudia knowingly.

"No. But they're going to 'monitor' my assignments – that's what they told Miss

Griswold – to make sure I complete my homework."

The phone rang and Claudia picked it up. I said quickly, "No jobs for me for a while. Unless it's absolutely necessary."

"Oh, Kristy! Did they say you couldn't babysit?" cried Mallory.

I shook my head. "No, I did. But it's only temporary. I've just decided to cut back a little."

After the details of the babysitting job had been worked out and Claudia had phoned the client back, Mary Anne said, "What about your campaign? Are you ready for the debate yet?"

"Well, I'm up to date with my homework," I answered evasively.

"Kristy! That debate is important!" exclaimed Stacey. "You have to get ready for it."

"*I will*." Uh-oh! Did I sound as grumpy as I thought I did just then? "Sorry, Stacey," I said quickly. "You're right. I'll get to work on it as soon as I get home. After all, I know what my position is. That's pretty clear-cut and simple. And Grace and Alan, lord knows, don't have a position. And Pete's not much better."

"Pete's okay," said Mary Anne.

"I didn't say he wasn't okay, Mary Anne. But his platform, his *reasons* for wanting to be president are not much better than Grace's or Alan's. . ."

"Whatever Alan's reasons are," muttered Claudia.

Mary Anne looked stubborn, but she didn't say anything.

"Are you ready, Mallory?" I asked. Mallory's face turned red.

"I suppose so," she said.

"Your opening speech was good," Jessi announced firmly.

Mallory threw Jessi a grateful look. "I had planned to do a little more work on it tonight, though."

"You know, what you should do is relax," Jessi told her. "I read about this relaxation technique for stress. You lie down, and you picture yourself doing whatever it is – like giving the speech – just perfectly once, from beginning to end. Then you go and do something nice for yourself."

"Like eat ice cream with chocolate sprinkles and butterscotch topping," put in Claudia.

Mallory laughed.

"Hold the ice cream. I'll get to work on the debate tonight," I promised. "Now, if the meeting has already come to order, what about subs?"

"Right," said Stacey. "Thanks for reminding me, Kristy."

"What are leaders for?" I asked sweetly. Everyone groaned.

That night, while Mallory was (maybe) practising relaxation, I was doing my homework in world-record time. By nine-thirty, I had finished. Whew!

I pulled out a new notebook and opened it. I picked up my pen.

I remembered one of the rules of giving a speech: Tell them what you're going to tell them, tell them, then tell them what you've told them.

Hmmm. Useful, maybe, but this was a debate. I had to be absolutely clear on what I thought the goals of our class should be. And I had to be absolutely clear on what I thought were the weaknesses of the other candidates' goals. My goals had to sound like the best. Not hard, I reasoned, since they *absolutely* were.

"Number 1," I wrote.

The phone rang.

"We," I wrote.

"Kristy, it's for you," my mother called.

When I picked up the receiver a voice said, "Hello, stranger."

"Bart!" *Stranger?* Oh, lord. Was I going to have to add Bart to my list of things to worry about?

I was starting to worry about the list!

"Well, at least you recognized my voice," said Bart.

"Lucky guess," I teased.

Bart laughed, and I laughed, too. And I almost felt guilty about being on the phone, laughing! But I was glad he'd called.

Twenty minutes went by in no time at

all. Then I told Bart, reluctantly, that I had to ring off. "I have to get ready for the debate, you know."

"I wish I could be there," said Bart.

"Me, too," I replied, and we said good night.

I went back to my debate notes. "Number 1. We need to. . ." resolutely ignoring the ringing of the phone.

"Kristy." My mother's voice. "It's Jessi."

"Hello," I said, snatching up the receiver. "Listen, I'll have to talk to you tomorrow. I'm behind in my work."

"Honestly, Kristy. What if you win the election? If you don't have time to talk to me, how will you have time to be president of the whole class?"

Jessi's words hit home. "Oh." I sighed again. "You're right, Jessi. But what can I do? I can't drop out of the race."

"Maybe you should drop out of something else, then," said Jessi.

"Like the human race," I muttered. I felt awful.

"What?"

"Nothing. Listen, Jessi, I really am swamped."

"I know. I'll talk to you tomorrow."

She hung up pretty quickly. I sat and stared at my paper.

"Number 1. We need . . . a president who has time to be a president. . ." And it was time to find the time.

14th CHAPTER

The "Kristy for president" team had done a great job. Everywhere you went in SMS, the signs jumped out at you. The badges were a huge success, too. I saw them all over the place: on rucksacks and school bags, hooked on to lockers and taped to notebooks. "Good visual coverage," declared Stacey. We would vote the Friday after the debate. The campaign was becoming intense.

It seemed as if people were more involved, too. Which meant, I thought, that the issues were important to us. We *did* care about our school, and we *did* want some responsibilities (besides homework and going to lessons). Furthermore, I thought that with this kind of support just for the campaign, we were showing everyone we were serious and willing to work and handle our responsibilities.

Responsibilities.

Suppose Grace won? I doubted she was even capable of organizing a school dance. And I don't think she'd begun to think about all the work involved. Once she found out, that would be the end of Grace's participation. But what would we do? Impeach her? That would make a nice headline for the school newspaper.

Which reminded me of Pete and his campaign. He had one, or *maybe* two good ideas, but they were really only the sorts of things that would appeal to a minority of kids. Special interest groups. That was the phrase. Pete's campaign appealed to special interest groups.

Alan. Please.

It was my responsibility to run for president. Besides, so many people had worked so hard. Including me.

But not hard enough.

I thought about this over and over again. And I kept scrambling, squeezing in homework, a Krushers practice, a minimum of babysitting jobs.

You wouldn't think I would have a lot of time to think, but somehow I did. I was even catching up on my work a little bit. Part of the reason was I had simply put aside the campaign and my debate speech.

If Jamie had become a sort of bicycle monster for a little while, hadn't I become a sort of political monster?

I'd let down the Krushers, cancelling practice and then not being there mentally when we did have one. I'd got the worst grade I'd ever got in science – twice. I'd been late to meetings – BSC meetings, campaign meetings – and close to late for babysitting jobs. I'd had to give up babysitting jobs (and money!). I'd hardly seen Bart. And I'd practically bitten Jessi's head off for telling me the truth.

Added to that, now my mother and Watson had to monitor my homework as if I were a little kid.

All of those things were responsibilities, too. They were *my* responsibilities. And I wasn't living up to them.

It happened one night. I was sure I'd go straight to sleep, I was so tired. But instead, I lay in bed with my eyes open, thinking everything over one more time. Making my lists (again) of what I had to do (like homework, especially science), and what I wanted to do (like spend time with my friends and coach the Krushers and eat pancakes with faces on them).

But this time, when I finished my lists, I knew what I was going to do. The only way to do everything I wanted to do, and needed to do, and do it right, was not to run for class president. I was going to have to drop out of the race.

I said it aloud, for practice. "I have to drop out of the race."

It didn't sound so bad. It could have been worse.

I said it one more time. No. Not so bad at all.

Immediately I was sleepy, so sleepy that I didn't even know I'd fallen asleep until I woke up the next morning, ready to go, ready to do everything except be class president.

I wasn't sure quite how I was going to go about telling everyone what I had decided. Silly ideas – like going around to all the posters and writing K- – came to mind. Or going to the head teacher's office and making an announcement over the PA system (except, of course, no one would have understood it). Probably, I could have just told the rest of the BSC and they could have spread the word for me.

Although I cringed to think how my friends would feel about my dropping out of the race. After all that work. I almost talked to Mary Anne about it. I knew she'd be calm and sensible and supportive (at least, I was almost absolutely certain she would be supportive). But then I thought of another way of handling it.

Once I made that decision, it was easy to stop worrying about that along with everything else. It must have shown, too, because that very next morning, Mary Anne (she's calm, sensible, supportive *and* perceptive) said, as we walked into SMS together, "You must have finished preparing for the debate."

"I'm ready," I assured her. "Why?"

"You *look* ready. More pulled together."

I looked down. I was wearing jeans and a crewneck sweater, one of my standard uniforms.

"Kristy! I'm not talking about what you're wearing!"

"I know, I know."

We caught up with Stacey and Claudia then. They both looked great (I'd been so busy, I hadn't even *seen* anyone, it seemed like, even though I'd been seeing everyone almost every day. If that makes any sense.) Stacey had pulled her hair back into a plait with a silver hat pin stuck through it. She was wearing purple trousers, soft black flat ankle boots, black-and-white-striped socks, and a black-and-white-checked shirt, only the checks were all different sizes. She had square silver earrings in her ears.

Claud's hair was down, but she was wearing a hat. On the green hat ribbon was pinned a "Kristy+" badge. Her tights were orange and her dress was tie-dyed every colour you could think of. She was wearing her feather earrings, and she'd drawn a star on her face next to her right eye.

"It's *great* to see you all," I said.

Everyone looked a little surprised. "Right, Kristy," said Stacey.

"She's ready for the debate," Mary Anne explained, laughing.

"Ohhh. Good job, Kristy. Need any special art effects?"

I shook my head. "Thanks, Claudia, but I'm all set. Now I only have to worry about science."

Claudia made a face.

"Don't worry," said Mary Anne loyally.

"Yeah . . . be happy," added Stacey.

Thinking about the science homework, complete and all correct (at least I was pretty sure it was) I laughed. "I am," I said. "I am!"

The day of the assembly, I joined the other eighth-grade candidates in the front row of the assembly hall. After the head teacher explained the rules for the debate, he handed the podium over to the candidates so we could each make a one-minute opening statement.

This time, Grace didn't lean over to make snide remarks about my notes. She couldn't have, anyway, because I didn't have any. But she was busy shuffling through hers, looking worried. Alan was carrying a notebook stuffed full of papers, and a pen. Pete surprised me, though. He was holding one piece of paper, with typing on it. He looked like he knew what he was doing, and was pretty sure of himself.

"Now, Kristy Thomas, candidate for

eighth-grade class president," said the head teacher.

I took a deep breath, stood up, and walked slowly to the podium. I gripped the sides of it (I was a little nervous) and looked out at everybody.

My friends were sitting together this time, in the middle of the assembly hall. Mary Anne, Dawn, Stacey, Claudia and Logan. Mary Anne gave me a big smile.

I smiled back at her and at everybody.

"I'm Kristy Thomas, and I'm not a candidate for class president."

A buzz swept through the hall, so I did what the head teacher did. I kept quiet and waited. While I waited, I looked at my friends.

I don't know what I expected, but they didn't look upset. Mary Anne was nodding slowly, thoughtfully. Claudia looked surprised, and she and Stacey (who also looked surprised) were whispering to each other. Dawn looked as calm as ever. And Logan was frowning a little.

The buzzing died down, so I went on. "I've enjoyed running for office," I said. "I've learned a lot. One of the most important things I've learned is that a person shouldn't try to do too much. The office of president of the class is one with a lot of responsibility – especially if the new president wants to make changes. I think we need some changes, but I'm not the one to make them. I already have a lot of responsibilities. I want to do well at the things I am doing right now, and I want to have time to enjoy what I do. If I stayed in the race and won, I wouldn't be able to do the job right.

"I wish the candidates for president the best of luck. I know whoever is elected will do a terrific job. I'm sorry to withdraw from the race, but I think – I know – I am doing the right thing.

"I want to thank all of you for your support, and especially my friends." I looked down at the members of the BSC. They all seemed pretty calm now. Did they understand?

"Thank you," I said.

It was Mary Anne, I think, who started to applaud. Some of the other kids joined in. So the walk from the podium back to my seat wasn't so bad after all.

I'd done it! And it felt – okay. Even the smirk Grace gave me didn't change my mind. I listened to the rest of the debate in a daze.

When the assembly was over, Mary Anne was the first to reach me.

"Kristy!" she said, and hugged me.

The others were smiling. "Does this mean you're back in the babysitting business?" asked Dawn.

"Definitely," I said.

Claud held up her hand and I slapped it.

"I'm still going to wear this badge," said Claudia.

"A collector's item now," Stacey told her solemnly.

I grinned. Then my friends and I walked out of the assembly hall together.

15th
CHAPTER

I took down the last of Mallory's posters and put it on the pile.

"Whew," I said to Mary Anne.

"You can say that again. It's much easier putting *up* campaign posters."

"Yeah." We headed for Mallory's locker. She and Jessi had stacked a heap of posters beside it.

"What are you going to do with all the posters?" asked Mary Anne.

Mallory pushed her glasses up on her nose. "Turn them over and use them next year."

"And next year, I bet you'll be the incumbent," said Jessi.

"I don't know." Mallory looked doubtful. "Besides, even if I do get elected to secretary of the sixth grade, I don't know if that'll count for anything in the seventh grade."

"Next year, run for president," I told Mallory as Claudia, Stacey and Dawn appeared with armfuls of posters. "I can recommend a group of campaigners experienced in supporting presidential hopefuls."

"Good grief, Kristy," teased Stacey. "You're starting to talk like a politician."

"Or a newspaper!" Claudia let her posters slide to the floor. "It's almost time for registration and the big vote. Are you nervous, Mal?"

"Yes."

"Ah – an honest politician," teased Dawn.

"I'm a little nervous about the eighth grade presidential race," I confessed.

"You did the right thing," said Mallory. "You don't have to worry now."

But Mary Anne understood straight away.

"It would be unfortunate if the best person didn't win," she said.

"You mean it would be the *pits* if Grace Blume did," put in Claudia. "And she might."

"She's definitely spent the most money on her campaign," said Stacey. "For Grace, it's a big popularity contest. Too bad."

"Especially if she wins . . . but then again, what if Alan wins?"

"No way, Kristy."

"Pete could win," said Mary Anne.

The bell for registration rang.

"Time to vote for Mallory," said Jessi. "Come on, Mal."

"Good luck, Mallory," said Stacey, and the rest of us chimed in with "good lucks" of our own. Then we headed for our registration classes to vote.

I voted for Pete. I wondered who else did. Mary Anne did for sure.

The day was nerve-racking, I'll admit it, even if I wasn't a candidate any more. But Mallory *had* to win. And I'd decided who had to win as eighth-grade class president, too.

Finally, during last period, the school tannoy system crackled to life.

And for once, it worked — sort of. Or maybe it just sounded clearer because everybody became absolutely quiet in order to listen.

The head teacher began with the sixth grade, starting with treasurer. Secretary was next: I held my breath. . .

"And," (crackle, static) "sixth-grade secretary . . . Mallory Pike."

I let out a whoop. "All right, Mallory!" I didn't even care when everyone turned around to stare.

Then we had to listen to a lot more snap, crackle, static as the winners of the rest of the sixth grade and the seventh grade were read aloud. "Faster, faster," I muttered, but it didn't help.

Finally: "And the new pres-(screeech) the eighth grade is . . . Pete Black!"

What a relief. I didn't let out a whoop, but I was suddenly very glad Pete had run for class president.

School was over after that, and for the last few minutes, while everyone else was talking, I thought about Pete's campaign. I wasn't crazy about his platform. But he'd made some good points (especially the ones that were similar to mine!). And he was serious about the job. Also, he *had* said he'd liked some of the other candidates' ideas. Maybe I would catch up with Pete later and congratulate him and go over my ideas in detail . . . just in case he wanted to use them.

Yes. The best person had definitely won.

I was on time for our meeting that afternoon. But I wasn't the first to arrive. Everyone except Mallory had arrived ahead of me.

"Hey," I said. "What's the deal?"

Everyone stood up and applauded.

"You did well, Kristy," said Mary Anne. "We're proud of you. And . . . welcome back to being merely incredibly busy – instead of out of your mind."

"Thank you," I said. Just then, Mallory stepped through the door.

We stood up and applauded again, while Mallory turned pink.

"Speech, speech!" cried Jessi.

"No way!" said Mallory, grinning.

Then the phone rang. I sat in my chair and called the meeting to order, and Claudia began to hand around tropical-flavoured jellybeans, marshmallows and fruit cookies (they're sweetened with fruit juice so Stacey can sometimes eat them, and Dawn does, too).

It was good to be back to normal. Towards the end of the meeting, I said, "You know what? Remember Pete said he thought the pupils should be the ones to choose the class play?"

"Um-hm," said Claudia around a mouthful of jellybeans.

"So?" asked Stacey.

"Well, listen. Suppose we get to do *Our Town*? And suppose I could audition for the role of Emily, and get it? wouldn't that be *fantastic*?"

A moment of silence greeted me. Then Mary Anne groaned, Mallory and Jessi started to laugh, and everyone else joined in.

I realized what I'd done.

"Well," I said. "If it's not softball season, I might. . ."

"Kristy!" said everybody together.

"Meeting's over," said Stacey, when she stopped laughing. "Come on."

"Where?" asked Mallory.

"To celebrate your victory, Mallory! Surprise! We planned everything. Charlie's going to drive us into town. We're going to pig out." Claudia scrunched up the empty jellybean bag, buried it in her wastepaper basket, and jumped to her feet.

"Wait a minute," I said, "let me see if I can fit this into my schedule. . ."

"Kristy," said Mary Anne. "Come on!"

Laughing, we all trooped out to celebrate Mallory's victory.

MALLORY AND
THE DREAM HORSE

The author gratefully acknowledges
Jahnna Beecham
Malcolm Hillgartner
for their help in
preparing this manuscript

1st CHAPTER

"Yankee Doodle went to town a-riding on a pony, stuck a feather in his hat and called it Mack and Roni!"

"Claire," I giggled, "I think it's *macaroni*. You know, like the noodle."

"Noodle!" my sister squealed as she clutched an old mop from the basement. "That's what I'll call my horse."

Claire patted her mop on the head and said, "Good Noodle." Then, singing at the top of her voice, she galloped around my bedroom.

Well, it's not really *my* bedroom. I share it with Vanessa, another sister of mine. We have to share rooms because there are so many of us Pikes. We have (are you ready for this?) eight kids in our family. Add two adults and you've got a pretty crowded house.

I'm Mallory Pike. I'm eleven and I'm the

oldest Pike. Then come the triplets Byron, Adam and Jordan, who are ten, and Vanessa, who's nine. Nicky's eight, Margo is seven, and Claire is five.

All of us Pike kids have brown hair and blue eyes, but I'm the only one who has curly reddish hair. I am also the only one with a brace (lucky me). Plus, I have to wear glasses.

Being the oldest is not as great as it might sound. Lots of times my parents expect me to help out with babysitting, which I don't mind doing, but not all the time. For a while I felt as if they were really taking me for granted, but we worked it out, and now they always schedule my sitting jobs just like we do in the BSC.

What's the BSC? It stands for the Babysitters Club, which is the greatest group of friends anyone could have. But I'll tell you about that later.

Anyway, it was a Saturday and Jessi Ramsey, my best friend in Stoneybrook, Connecticut (and the world), was at my house for the day. We were doing what we usually do on rainy Saturday afternoons – talking about horses.

Jessi and I *love* horses. In fact you could say we are horse-crazy. We love to read books about horses. Our favourites are those by Marguerite Henry, who wrote *Misty of Chincoteague*. But we'll read any book about a horse. One day I hope to be a great author and write and illustrate books about horses of all kinds – mustangs, quarter horses, Appaloosas, Clydesdales, percherons – you name it. I love them all.

While I would like to be an author, Jessi wants to be a ballerina. And she will be. I'm sure of it. First of all, she's got the perfect dancer's body – slim, long legs, a beautiful neck and graceful fingers. Second of all, she has already danced several leading roles in ballets in nearby Stamford. We (the rest of the BSC and I) always go to her performances, and boy is she good.

Jessica (that's her formal name) has a younger sister, Becca, short for Rebecca, and a baby brother, John Philip Ramsey, Jr., which is a very big name for such a little boy. Everyone calls him Squirt. Jessi's Aunt Cecelia lives with her family, too. So altogether the Ramseys have six people living in their house. We have ten. That's one of the main differences between me and Jessi. Also, Jessi is black and I'm white. It doesn't matter to me, but it did to some people in town when the Ramseys first moved to Stoneybrook. They really had a tough time at first, but that's all in the past. Now things are much better for Jessi and her family.

Anyway, Jessi was lying on my bed with one of her legs extended in the air. It nearly touched her ear. (Ow!) Jessi always does stretching exercises when she's sitting around so that she'll stay supple for ballet. I've got so used to it that I hardly notice it, any more. She was reading *Misty of Chincoteague* again and I was sitting cross-legged on the floor, reading the ending of *Black Beauty* for the two hundredth time, when Claire burst into the room, straddling her mop.

"Whoa! Whoa!" I said, after she'd circled the room several times. When Claire pulled her mop (I mean, horse) to a stop, I asked, "What are you doing riding Noodle in the house?"

"I'm practising for the circus. I'm the bare-back rider." Claire pointed proudly at the mop handle. "See? No saddle."

"I think your horse could do with some more oats," Jessi said, trying to keep a straight face. "He's a bit skinny."

Claire put her hands on her hips, and her mop-horse clattered to the ground. "He is *not*. He's perfect."

"Claire," I said, pointing to the mop lying on the carpet, "you've dropped your horse."

Claire looked at the mop and declared, "Noodle is resting. He's very sleepy." She stifled a yawn as she spoke.

My parents were at home, so I wasn't officially on babysitting duty, but I knew when Claire needed a nap. I picked up Noodle in one hand and guided Claire out of the room. "Meet me in the recreation room," I called to Jessi over my shoulder. "We'll make popcorn and watch *The Black Stallion* again."

"Great!" she replied. *The Black Stallion* is one of our absolute favourite films.

"But I have to practise my riding," Claire protested feebly as I helped her onto her bed.

"Noodle's too tired," I explained, laying the mop on the floor beside my sister's bed. "He just needs a quick nap and then he'll be ready to do higher leaps and gallop even faster around the ring."

"You really think so?" she murmured, snuggling her head into her pillow.

"I know so." I draped a light quilt over Claire and then tiptoed out of the door and down the stairs. It was very quiet upstairs, but downstairs was a different story.

Vanessa, Margo and Nicky were playing so loudly in the dining room that it was hard for Jessi and me to hear our film in the recreation room. Finally we just turned down the volume and talked about our favourite subject: horses.

"Okay," Jessi announced as she stretched her legs out to the side, practically doing the splits. (Double ow!) "If you could choose your dream horse, what would it be?"

"Oh, boy." I sank back into the overstuffed chair by the television and thought for a second. "He'd have to be an Arabian. They're the nicest. A pure white one with a long flowing mane and warm brown eyes."

"A pure white Arabian," Jessi sighed. "That sounds wonderful."

"He'd be extremely clever, so if I fell off his back and broke my ankle in the woods, he'd know to go and get help."

Jessi chuckled. "Just like Lassie."

I tossed a pillow at Jessi. "You know what I mean."

Jessi grinned. "Mine would do sweet things like bring me his bridle and count to ten with his hoof."

"Mine would live in a stable in my back garden and we'd go riding every day. And we'd enter horse shows all over the country and win."

"But you'd have to know how to ride first," Jessi reminded me.

"Well, of course I'd take lessons," I said. "As many as I wanted and as often as I liked."

It's funny. Both Jessi and I dream of having our own horse and riding every day, but neither one of us has ever had a single lesson.

"Remember that old film with Shirley Temple called *The Little Princess*?" Jessi stretched forward and put her elbows on the floor. "She played a rich girl named

Sara Crewe in Victorian England who had her own pony."

I nodded. "And she went riding every day." I leaned back and sighed. "I'd give anything to be Sara Crewe and have my own horse."

"Me, too," Jessi murmured.

I sat up and squeezed my eyes closed. "All right. I'm going to count to ten, and when I open my eyes I'll have my dream horse, riding lessons and contact lenses."

Jessi squeezed her own eyes shut. "When l open my eyes, I'll have my dream horse, riding lessons, and I will dance the role of the Sugar Plum Fairy in *The Nutcracker* next Christmas."

We held our breath and started counting, but before we could reach ten, Nicky burst into the room, wearing a pair of swimming trunks. An old pink bathmat was draped across one shoulder. He'd pinned big black paper spots on to the rug to make it look like leopard fur. He pounded his chest with his fists and let out a deafening yodel. "I'm Tarzan, King of the Apes, and I can wrestle alligators."

"Nicky!" I protested. "Can't you see we're doing something very important here?"

Nicky's shoulders slumped and I felt awful. "But that's okay," I added. "Because I have never seen an alligator, let alone one that wrestles. Where is it?"

Nicky cupped his hands around his mouth and let out another loud yodel. Margo entered the room, a sheet wrapped around her shoulders. She held our hamster Frodo cupped in her hands. Frodo had a little green felt cape tied around his shoulders and didn't look very happy about it.

"Here's the ferocious alligator, Tarzan," Margo said, handing the hamster to Nicky.

Nicky clutched the animal to his chest and said, "Thank you, Margo the Magnificent."

"Margo the Magnificent?" Jessi repeated.

"Yes!" Margo grandly swept her sheet over one shoulder. "I am the world's greatest magician," she announced. "I can turn apples into oranges and lots of other things into ordinary household items. Want to see?"

Jessi and I looked at each other and tried not to giggle. Margo sounded like a TV advert.

"Wait a minute!" Nicky bellowed. "First they're going to watch me wrestle Frodo – I mean, the vicious alligator." He dropped on to his knees and tried to make Frodo sit still on the carpet.

Margo ignored him and pulled an apple out of her sheet, then put it on the coffee table. "This is just an ordinary apple," she said. "I simply wave my magic cape across it—"

I bit my lip to keep from laughing as Margo struggled to hold the sheet in the air while she switched the apple with an orange that was hidden beneath her other arm. The orange slipped out of her fingers on to the rug and rolled towards the hamster, who bolted out of the way beneath the sofa.

"Oh, shoot!" Margo muttered. "I keep messing that part up."

"Now look what you've done!" shouted Nicky. "My gator's escaped."

"Never fear, Reena's here," Vanessa cried from the doorway. She was dressed in a pink leotard and tights. "I walk the tightrope at the top of the tent. I carry a pole that is straight, not bent." Vanessa writes poetry and likes to rhyme when she talks. She rolled a strip of pale blue ribbon out in front of her and pretended to walk along it, carrying a broom as a balance stick.

"Give me that stick," Nicky said, gesturing for his sister to hand him the broom. "I'll nudge Frodo and get him out from under the sofa."

Vanessa executed a perfect turn on the ribbon and headed back to the door. "As soon as I get off the tightrope, I'll give you my pole," she called over her shoulder.

"No, I need it now." He grabbed Vanessa around the waist, and she wobbled wildly from side to side.

"Don't do that, Nicky!" she cried. "Can't you see I'm working without a net? Stop!"

The two of them tumbled on to the carpet in a tangle of knees and elbows. While they wrestled, Margo continued to struggle with her disappearing orange trick.

Jessi doubled up with laughter.

"What's so funny?" I called over the racket.

"Your family," she replied. "It's like a looney bin in here."

Then Claire galloped into the room on her mop-horse Noodle, her eyes still puffy with sleep. "Is it showtime?" she cried. "Why didn't somebody tell me?"

As Claire rode her horse into the chaos, I grinned and shouted back to Jessi, "Make that a three-ring circus. The Pike Family presents The Craziest Show on Earth."

2nd CHAPTER

It was almost five o'clock on Monday when I realized that no one in my family had collected the post. Usually Margo and Nicky fight over who gets to bring it from the postbox, but they were in the back garden inventing new talents to show each other.

The postbox was filled with the usual stuff – a few bills, a couple of catalogues, a yellow envelope from a sweepstakes place that read, "*You* could be a winner!" and a flier for a sale at the local supermarket. I was just about to drop it all on the table by the front door when a green-and-white brochure slipped out and fluttered to the floor.

I bent over to pick it up and couldn't believe my eyes. There was a picture of an elegant thoroughbred and an equestrian dressed in English riding clothes. They

293

were posed beside a ring made of rails and posts painted a crisp white.

"'Horse Riding Lessons, English Style',"
I read out loud. "Classes starting soon at Kendallwood Farm, Connecticut's finest riding school." I looked at the address and gasped. Kendallwood was on the outskirts of Stoneybrook, just an easy bike trip from my house. "This is wonderful!" I exclaimed. "I can ride a horse without owning one. Every week!"

I clutched the brochure to my chest and spun in a circle, not knowing whether to race through the house looking for my mother, or run to the phone to call Jessi. Luckily, before I did any of those things, I glanced at the clock on our mantelpiece. It said ten past five.

"The Babysitters Club!" I gasped. Our meetings start promptly at five-thirty every Monday, Wednesday and Friday afternoon at Claudia Kishi's house. If I hopped on my bike, and left that instant I would have a few minutes before the meeting began to tell Jessi about my wonderful discovery.

I carefully tucked the brochure in my jacket, grabbed my bike, and pedalled as fast as I could to Claud's house.

This is probably a good time to tell you about the Babysitters Club and how it got started. There are seven of us in the club. Jessi and I are the youngest (we're in the

294

sixth grade) so we're called junior officers. The other five members are Kristy Thomas, Claudia Kishi, Mary Anne Spier, Stacey McGill and Dawn Schafer. They are thirteen and in the eighth grade.

It was Kristy's idea to start the club, which is probably why she is also the chairman. Kristy got her great idea over a year ago when her mother couldn't find a sitter for her younger brother, David Michael. Kristy listened to her mother dial number after number with no luck. And that's when the brilliant idea hit.

"Why not have one number where a parent can reach several sitters at one time?" Kristy thought. So she talked to Mary Anne, Claudia and, eventually, Stacey. Together they made up advertising fliers and passed them out to everyone they knew. They decided to hold meetings in Claudia's room, since she has a phone of her own. And soon the calls were pouring in! In fact, things grew so busy that they decided to add a few more people – Dawn, Jessi and me. Now we have even added associate officers, Logan Bruno and Shannon Kilbourne. They don't attend meetings, but they're ready to fill in if the rest of us are busy.

Our meetings are half an hour long. Subs are collected by Stacey on Mondays – the money is for fun things like club parties and sleepovers. It also helps to cover

Claud's phone bill and to replace items in our Kid-Kits.

What are Kid-Kits? Just another one of Kristy's brilliant ideas. (She's got a million of them!) Each of us found a cardboard box that we decorated with paint and fabric and other art supplies that Claudia gave us. Then we filled the boxes with toys, crayons, puppets and games from our own houses. Kristy thought that children would much rather play with somebody else's toys than their own. And she was right! The kids love them.

Another great idea of Kristy's is the club notebook. It's like a diary in which we write up each job that we go on. It's really useful because we find out if a kid has developed a new fear, or is having trouble at school, or is allergic to something and needs to take medicine. Some of the members think writing in the notebook is a pain, but I really like it.

Each member of the BSC is a real individual, which I think makes for a perfect club. Kristy, our chairman, is outgoing and filled with terrific ideas. Her mum was divorced but then she married Watson Brewer, a genuine millionaire, and the Thomases moved to this huge mansion across town from the rest of us. Now, in addition to her three brothers she has a stepbrother, stepsister and an adopted sister. Kristy doesn't care that much about how she looks and can generally be found wearing jeans, trainers, a poloneck shirt and a sweater (it's almost like her uniform). Kristy's big love is sports, which is why she coaches a junior softball team called Kristy's Krushers.

Mary Anne Spier is our club secretary and Kristy's best friend. But the two of them couldn't be more different. While Kristy is outgoing, Mary Anne is very shy. Her mum died when Mary Anne was a baby, so her father brought her up all by himself. (He used to be really strict and not let her wear anything too adult, but that's changed. And boy, is Mary Anne relieved!) Mary Anne is also very emotional. She cries at the drop of a hat. I'm not kidding. I've even seen her cry at a sad TV advert. And she's a romantic. In fact, Mary Anne was the first one of us in the BSC to have a steady boyfriend. (Logan Bruno. He's one of the associate officers I told you about.) Besides being Kristy's best friend, Mary Anne is also Dawn Schafer's best friend. And stepsister. It was really strange how that happened.

You see, Dawn used to live in California, but when her parents got a divorce, her mum decided to move Dawn and her brother Jeff back to the town where she grew up. So that brought Dawn – with her waist-length blonde hair, blue eyes and perfect skin – to Stoneybrook.

Dawn dresses in her own unique style –
we call it California casual. Also, she is a
total health food nut. The sight of a ham-
burger makes her gag. And she loves
mysteries and ghost stories. That's why it
was absolutely perfect when her mum
bought this great old colonial farmhouse
that actually has a secret passageway in it.

Soon Dawn and Mary Anne became
friends at school. Then they discovered
that Mary Anne's dad and Dawn's mum
had been high school sweethearts. Can
you believe it? So, of course, the two of
them decided to get Mr Spier and Mrs
Schafer back together. It worked like a
charm. They fell in love all over again, got
married, and that's how Dawn and Mary
Anne ended up as stepsisters.

Oh, one more thing. I told you Mary
Anne and Logan Bruno were dating. Well,
Dawn is now dating Logan's cousin, Lewis.
Sort of. It's hard to call it dating since he
lives in Louisville, Kentucky. But they write
to each other and, as Dawn says, they
definitely have a strong friendship.

There are two more members of the
BSC: Claudia Kishi, vice-chairman, and
Stacey McGill, treasurer. They are also
best friends. Claudia is Japanese-American
and drop-dead gorgeous. And very arty.
She makes her own earrings and tie-dyes
her own T-shirts. Claudia can put together
strange combinations of clothes – like one

298

of her father's old shirts over tie-dyed tights, with a big belt and a funky waistcoat – and look like she stepped out of a fashion magazine. She's not a great pupil, but she more than makes up for it in talent. Her parents think she just needs to apply herself to her schoolwork, but I think part of her problem is that her older sister, Janine, is a major brain. I mean, we're talking genius. I think Claud thinks that since Janine has taken care of the brains category, she'll concentrate on art. And boy, does she ever. Pottery, drawing, painting, sculpting – you name it, Claud can do it.

She does have one flaw. She's a junk food addict. At every BSC meeting you can count on Claudia to have a bag of Twiglets, Maltesers, or crisps for us to snack on. All of us except Dawn, who turns up her nose at chocolate, and Stacey, who can't eat sweets.

Stacey is diabetic, which means her body is unable to process sugar. She has to give herself these injections (ugh!) every day. Stacey is also the ultimate in cool. She used to live in New York City, so she is very sophisticated. Claud calls her the Queen of Dibbleness, which is our word for ultra cool. Stacey perms her thick blonde hair and wears sparkly nail polish and earrings that Claudia designs. She's very pretty but a little on the thin side. That probably has a lot to do with her strict diet. Can you imagine always having to count calories and monitor your sugar intake and give yourself injections? I couldn't do it. No way. But Stacey seems to manage all right and stay cheerful about it, too.

So those are my friends. The people who have helped me through the crises in my life – like when my dad lost his job. They've also shared my successes – like when I won the award for Best Overall Fiction at Young Author's Day at school. Now I couldn't wait to tell them about horseback riding lessons at Kendallwood.

It was five-twenty by the time I reached Claud's house. I didn't even ring the doorbell but raced upstairs to her room. Kristy was already leaning back in the director's chair, her visor on her head and a pencil over one ear. Claud was rummaging through her desk drawers, looking for a bag of sweets that she'd sneaked into her room when her mum wasn't looking. Jessi had arrived a minute ahead of me and was just taking off her jacket.

"Jessi!" I could barely keep from shouting. "It's happened. My dream has come true!"

Jessi blinked at me, mystified. "You've won a million dollars?"

"No." I chuckled. "Look." I thrust the brochure into her hands, and while she read it, I said excitedly, "Well, not my whole dream. I mean, I don't have my own private horse and stables and riding lessons. But this is the next best thing."

Kristy leaned forward in her chair while Claudia stopped her search for sweets to stare at me. I tried to explain. "See, Jessi and I decided we wanted to be just like Sara Crewe, who is really Shirley Temple in the film called *The Little Princess*."

"This is going right over my head," Kristy said, turning to Claud. "How about you?" Claud shrugged. "She's totally lost me."

I realized I wasn't making any sense. So I took a deep breath and tried once more. "Jessi and I want a horse. We also want to take riding lessons. Well, I got this brochure that says Kendallwood Farm is offering riding lessons. They're just on the edge of town and – " I pointed to the price – "they're not too expensive."

Jessi's brown eyes shone as she raised her head and grinned at me. "I'm going to sign up for lessons, too."

"We could do it together." I squeezed her arm happily. "Wouldn't that be fun?"

A slight frown crossed Jessi's brow. "Of course, I'll have to talk to my parents first."

"Oh, me too," I said. "But they'll say yes. They just have to."

"All in favour?" Kristy lifted her pencil like a gavel.

Jessi and I smiled at each other and shouted, "Aye!"

"Opposed?"

Claudia looked under the bed as a joke and shook her head. Kristy tapped her pencil on the desk. "Then it's settled. You'll both take riding lessons."

At that moment the numbers on Claudia's digital clock switched from 5:28 to 5:29. The door opened and Dawn and Mary Anne rushed into the room, followed by Stacey. They called hellos to everyone and took their seats. Jessi and I dropped on to the floor at the foot of the bed as the clock numbers switched to five-thirty – and the meeting began.

I barely remember it because all I could think about was riding lessons at Kendallwood. The phone rang quite a few times as people called to arrange for sitters. In between calls, Stacey collected our subs, which she put in a manila envelope. Mary Anne diligently recorded the jobs in the record book as they were arranged.

I landed a job sitting for Nina and Eleanor Marshall on Wednesday afternoon; Stacey got a weekend job with the Arnold twins; and then Kristy, Jessi, Claudia and Dawn each booked jobs. But I have to admit I wasn't paying much attention by that time. I was still thinking about the thoroughbred in the brochure. I pictured myself perched on his back, looking elegant in my red riding coat, hard hat and long black boots.

Before I knew it, it was six o'clock and Kristy was waving her hand in front of my face. "Yoo-hoo, pardner!"

"Pardner?" I repeated, blinking my eyes in confusion. "What are you talking about?" "Mal has returned to the planet," Kristy cried triumphantly. Then she put her hands on her hips and said, "I've only been calling your name for the last three minutes. Where've you been?"

"Sorry," I said, blushing. "I think I was daydreaming about riding."

"Well, in case you haven't noticed," Kristy said, pointing to the clock, "the meeting's over. Time to saddle up your horse and head back to the corral."

Kristy grinned at the rest of the club members, who began to laugh. Even though the joke was on me, I think I was the one laughing the hardest.

3rd CHAPTER

Ding-dong!

I pressed the bell at the Marshalls' house on Wednesday afternoon, and the door swung open before the ringing had stopped.

"Mallory! Hooray! You're here." Four-year-old Nina Marshall stood smiling in the doorway. "Come on in, but be careful not to step on Blankie."

"Blankie" was a huge greyish baby blanket that was draped over Nina's arm and was being dragged on the floor beside her. The edges were frayed where the satin border used to be. I realized that the blanket had once been pale blue, but lots of use and probably hundreds of washings had given it the faded grey colour.

"Hi, Mallory," Mrs Marshall called from the kitchen. "I've just put two small pies in the oven for the girls for dinner. They'll be ready around five o'clock. Eleanor is taking a nap but she should be getting up any minute now."

"How are her ears?" I remembered that Eleanor had suffered from ear infections when she was younger. I'd had to give her medicine for them many times.

"They're just fine." Mrs Marshall smiled, pleased that I had remembered to ask. "I think now that she's two, we're past all that."

I watched Nina cross into the study, dragging Blankie behind her. She called over her shoulder, "Come and play Barbies with me, Mallory."

Mrs Marshall smiled at her daughter and then turned back to me. "Nina has just started nursery school," she said in a confidential tone of voice. "The children attend three times a week, and today was her second day."

"Oh? How'd it go?" I remembered watching my brothers and sisters go off to their first days at school, and how scared and excited they had been.

Mrs Marshall pursed her lips. "I can't really tell. Normally, she's very talkative, but she's kept awfully quiet about this."

"Come on, Mallory!" Nina called from the study.

Her mother chuckled. "You two have a good time. I'll be back in a couple of hours."

I waved goodbye to Mrs Marshall and, after checking to make sure Eleanor was still sleeping soundly upstairs, joined Nina in the study. She had laid two Barbie dolls and a pile of clothes on the floor.

I picked up one of the dolls and set it on my lap. "How about if we pretend that Barbie is going to her first day of school, just like you did?"

Nina blinked her blue eyes at me and shrugged. "Okay, if you want."

"Right. School can be fun." I chose a pair of red-and-white-striped tights and a long top made of sweatshirt material for my doll. (Claud would have been proud.) As Nina dressed her Barbie, I asked gently, "Have you had fun at school, Nina?"

Nina shrugged once more. "I don't know."

I tried another question. "What did you and your friends do today?"

Nina was busy putting a long sequinned dress on her doll, so she didn't look up when she said, "I don't have any friends."

I walked my doll across the carpet to her and pretended to make her talk. "Oh, Nina, you'll have lots of friends. It's only your second day of school."

Nina walked her doll towards mine. "It doesn't matter what day it is," she said. "I won't ever have any friends."

Hmm. "Gosh, Nina, don't you like the kids at school?" I made Barbie say.

Nina walked her Barbie doll to a big pink plastic car and put her inside it. "Some of them. But they don't like me."

"Oh, I bet that's not true."

"It is so." This time Nina's lower lip stuck out in a pout and it looked as if she was dangerously close to tears. "They don't like me *or* Blankie."

"Blankie?" I pushed my glasses up on my nose and looked at the drab old blanket that lay across Nina's lap. "You take Blankie to school?"

Nina nodded vigorously. "Blankie goes everywhere with me."

I could just imagine Nina dragging that big old faded blanket to school and what the other kids must have thought about it. I asked in my gentlest voice, "Do the kids tease you?"

"Maybe." Nina's voice was barely audible. She picked up the blanket and held one frayed corner against her cheek and the other part under her arm, as if she were protecting it.

I knew how much Nina liked her Blankie, but I also knew how cruel kids can be. I tried to suggest some solutions to her problem.

"Blankie is such a big blanket. Have you thought about taking a different blanket to school with you? One that's smaller?"

Nina's eyes widened in horror at the

idea of a substitute. "No, I want my *real* Blankie. He goes everywhere with me."

"Maybe you could take Blankie to school but leave him in your locker."

"No, he'd be lonely." She hugged the blanket even closer to her, as if she thought someone might try to steal it from her.

I hated to admit it, but I was stumped. It looked like Nina and her blanket would never be separated, so I gave up trying. Anyway, at that moment I could hear Eleanor in her cot upstairs.

"Nap finished!" she shouted from her room. "Mummy! Nap finished!"

I placed my doll back in her case and stood up. "I'll get Eleanor and then why don't the three of us go outside and play?"

Nina's face brightened in a sunny smile. "That would be fun." She returned her doll and the clothes to their case and began busily putting them in her wicker toy chest.

Eleanor was standing in her cot when I reached her room. Her hair was sticking out in all directions and she had that big-eyed look of surprise that little kids have when they first wake up.

"Hi, Eleanor," I said, smoothing her hair. "It's me – Mallory."

She tried to repeat my name but what came out sounded more like "Mow-ee".

I lifted her out of her cot and, as I changed her nappy, asked, "Would you like to go outside and swing?"

She rubbed the sleep from her eyes with the back of her fist and grinned. "Outside. Swing."

Nina and Blankie met us at the back door and the three of us went outside. The Marshalls had set up a swing with a slide in their back garden. Eleanor made a bee-line for it as soon as I opened the back door. Nina followed right behind her, still clutching the big grey blanket.

Eleanor stood by the swing and held out her arms to me. "Up. Please." I lifted her into the swing and we watched as Nina and Blankie made their way up the steps of the slide. The blanket was so big that Nina could hardly hold on to the railing as she climbed.

"How is Blankie going to go down the slide?" I called as I gave Eleanor a gentle push in the swing.

"We go down together." Nina laid the blanket across the slide, then sat in the middle of it and wrapped herself up as if she were in a sleeping bag. "It makes you go really fast."

She was right. Nina whizzed down the metal slide and rocketed off the bottom, landing (luckily) in a soft mound of grass. Then she untangled herself from the blanket and raced for the swing next to Eleanor's.

"How is Blankie going to get on the swing with you?" I asked.

"Easy." Nina folded the blanket into a long shawl and wrapped it around her shoulders so that she looked like a football player with padding around her neck. Then she backed towards the swing and sat down.

"That's amazing," I said. Nina had obviously had a lot of practice with Blankie, and it was easy to see how tough it was going to be for her to leave her "friend" at home.

The timer went off in the kitchen and I clapped my hands together. "Chow time!"

Eleanor, Nina and Blankie (I was now starting to think of Blankie as a third person) raced for the back door of the house. The kids took up their positions around the kitchen table, with Blankie sitting in his own chair this time, next to Nina. I served them their pies, and they were still eating when Mrs Marshall came home.

As she looked through her wallet, I cleared my throat, all ready to tell her about Nina's possible trouble at school. But then I noticed the clock in the hall. I only had five minutes to get to the BSC meeting! (Did I tell you how strict Kristy is about starting on time? She absolutely hates it when any of us is late.) I decided I'd have to talk to Mrs Marshall about Nina's Blankie problem another time. I ran all the way from Rosedale, where the

Marshalls live, to Claud's house on Bradford Court.

It's a good thing I did get there on time because the phone started ringing non-stop the moment our meeting began. Every single member of the BSC booked a job. In fact, we were so busy we even had to call one of our associates to see if he could take a Wednesday afternoon job. Mary Anne volunteered to make that call.

"I'll phone Logan," she said, already dialling his number. "I don't think he's busy on Wednesday."

"You never know," Claud teased. "He may have a date or something."

Mary Anne stuck out her tongue at Claudia, but before she could say anything, Logan answered the phone. While Mary Anne made arrangements with him to take the Wednesday afternoon job, Jessi whispered to me, "Have you talked to your parents yet about riding lessons?"

I shook my head. "Tonight's the night. I've been working on a strategy."

"Strategy?" Jessi raised one eyebrow.

"Yeah. I can't ask about something as important as riding lessons without having worked out the details first. Dad will ask a lot of questions, and I have to be ready with answers."

Jessi grinned and shook her head. "Mal, you amaze me. I was just planning to ask my parents straight out."

"That might work, too."

Mary Anne had hung up the phone, and now Kristy was making an announcement about buying new items for our Kid-Kits, so I quickly whispered, "No matter what happens tonight, I'll phone you."

"Right!"

4th CHAPTER

Dinner at the Pike house can be pretty chaotic at times, and Wednesday night was no exception. Nicky and Margo started a kicking war under the table, which ended with Margo in tears and Nicky banished to the other end of the kitchen. The triplets kept spooning mashed potatoes into their mouths and showing me what that looked like. I wanted to yell at them, but I had to keep a cool head. Tonight was the night I planned to ask my parents about taking riding lessons.

My mum had just finished wiping up Claire's spilled milk when my sister knocked her glass over again. I leaped to my feet and cried, "I'll clear it up this time, Mum. You stay there."

"Thanks, Mallory." My mother leaned back in her chair with a sigh of relief. "Now isn't that nice?" she asked the table in general. "Life would be a lot easier around here if you all followed your sister's example."

My father, who'd seemed totally oblivious to everything that had been going on during dinner, looked up from his roast beef. "I think Mallory wants something."

Sometimes I'd swear my dad can read minds. I didn't think I had been that obvious.

"Every time Mal gets extra helpful," my father continued, "it means she's about to ask for something," he said to my mother.

I thought back to the time I had asked to get my ears pierced and remembered that I'd dome a major clean-up job that night, too.

"Okay, you caught me," I admitted. "But what I want to ask is really important to me. Probably the most important thing in the world – so I want you to be in a good mood."

Jordan chose that moment to press his fingers against Adam's cheeks. A cloud of mashed potatoes exploded across the table.

"Oh, gross!" Vanessa screamed, pulling tiny bits of potato out of her hair.

"Jordan!" my father said in his sternest voice. "That is *not* acceptable behaviour. One more stunt like that and you'll spend the rest of the evening in your room."

"But Dad," Jordan said in a hurt voice, "Adam's the one who kept stuffing potatoes into his mouth."

314

Mum closed her eyes briefly. "I don't care," she said. "Now stop playing with your food and finish your dinner."

I shot my brothers the most disgusted look I could muster and then turned back to my father. "As I was saying before we were so *rudely* interrupted, these riding lessons mean more to me than anything."

"Riding lessons," my mother repeated as she busily wiped Adam's mashed potatoes off the drinking glasses and serving bowls. "That's the first I've heard of this."

"An advert came in the post on Monday," I explained. "I've spent the last few days trying to arrange my schedule so the lessons won't interfere with anything. Just a minute."

I hurried into the hall to the front cupboard, where I had placed the chart I'd drawn the night before.

"Visual aids," my father said, chuckling, as I returned carrying the white poster board. "Very impressive."

"Thanks." I beamed at my father. I knew I'd scored a big point. "I want you to know that I've thought about this quite carefully."

My chart was really a graph, with the days of the week listed along the side and times of the day listed across the top.

"See, I've put in all of the BSC meetings on Mondays, Wednesdays and Fridays," I explained, "an hour and a half each night for homework, my once-a-month visit to the orthodontist, and – " I put special emphasis on this part – "*my duties at home*. I could easily take the beginner's riding class: It's at ten o'clock on Saturday mornings. I'll just get up an hour earlier to do my chores."

My father wiped his mouth with his napkin and pushed his chair slightly away from the table. "That's fine, but what's this going to cost?"

I knew that sooner or later we'd get round to the bottom line. I gulped and told them the price, quickly adding, "But it's a bargain compared to other stables. And because it's so close, you wouldn't have to drive me. I could ride my bike."

"Hmm." My mother stood up and started clearing the table. I decided to wait until all my brothers and sisters had left the dining room. Then I'd hit my parents with the next step of my bargaining strategy.

Bargaining is a skill that I'm just starting to learn. Once I went to this flea market and saw this really great old jewellery box. The price was $7.50, which I thought was too high, so I offered the man $3.75, which I knew was too low. The owner and I finally agreed on a middle price – $4.75 – which was just right. I also used bargaining when I got my ears pierced. I asked my parents for everything – contact lenses, a new wardrobe, a haircut and pierced ears, knowing they'd never go for it all. When they finally agreed to a haircut and pierced ears, Mum and Dad thought they had saved themselves a ton of money. Which they had. Only they didn't know that all I really wanted was the pierced ears. The haircut was a bonus. I know it sounds sneaky, but it wasn't. Exactly.

I had told my parents the full price for the riding lessons. I waited till we'd loaded the dishwasher and Dad was drinking a cup of coffee before I made my next offer.

"I know that riding lessons cost a lot of money, especially with eight kids in our family." I didn't mention the added hardship of when my dad had been out of work, and we'd had to use up a lot of our savings.

"But if *I* pay for half of the lessons out of my babysitting money, then they really won't even cost as much as Jordan's piano lessons."

My mother and father exchanged glances that showed they were considering the idea. That's when I hit them with my final offer. "It wouldn't have to be for the whole year. Just the beginner's course – eight lessons."

"Well." My father took a sip of his coffee and thought for a moment. "If it's what you really want. . ."

That's when I lost my cool. I sprang out of my chair and wrapped my arms round my father's neck, nearly knocking his coffee cup out of his hands. "It's what I want more than anything in the world. Please! Oh please, oh please!"

My mother laughed at the sight of my father trying to juggle his coffee and hug me at the same time.

Even Dad was chuckling when he said, "Okay, Mallory, you have our permission."

"Since it's only for eight lessons," my mother added. Then she said, "But you really will have to pay for half of it. We can't afford it otherwise. Are you sure you want to do that? That would use up most of the money you've saved from babysitting."

"I don't care!" I danced happily around the room. "I'm going to learn how to ride. At last!"

"Then it's settled," my father declared, sounding a lot like Kristy at the Monday meeting. "You're taking riding lessons."

"Yippee! I have to phone Jessi right away."

I took the stairs three at a time and nearly broke my leg tripping over the phone cord on the landing. I was so excited that my hands shook as I dialled her number.

"Jessi!" I shrieked into the phone, when she answered. "I'm going to have horse riding lessons. They said yes!"

"That's great, Mal."

Jessi's voice sounded oddly flat. I asked worriedly, "Did you talk to your parents?"

"Yes. And they said no."

Then I understood why she didn't sound very happy about my good news.

"Didn't you tell them how much the lessons mean to us – I mean, you?"

Jessi gave a tired sigh. "Yes. But they pointed out that my ballet lessons and babysitting already take up most of my time. They think horseback riding would just be too much."

"That's awful, Jessi."

I felt awful for my friend. But I also felt bad for me. I'd had these wonderful visions of the two of us, best friends, riding our horses around the ring, winning medals at riding competitions."

"Listen," Jessi said after a long silence, "I'd better go. I have a lot of homework to do."

I hung up the phone but barely had time to think about how disappointed Jessi must be, because I was surrounded by four Pike kids, all shouting at once.

"Guess what, Mal, guess what!" Margo squealed. "We're going to put on a talent show."

"But you did that on Saturday, didn't you?" I said, trying to put the phone back on its cradle.

"That was just for you and Jessi," Vanessa said. "And anyway it was more of a circus. This one is going to be a real talent show for the whole neighbourhood."

Margo tugged on the sleeve of my T-shirt. "We'll hold auditions and everything."

"Just like *Star Search,*" Nicky added.

Vanessa showed me a yellow sign-up sheet. "We'll choose the best acts and then put the show together."

"Of course we four get to be in it," Margo explained, "because we thought of it."

"It'll be the biggest thing that ever hit our neighbourhood," Nicky said, giving Claire a high five.

Half of me was still thinking about Jessi and how awful it was that her parents had said no. The other half was trying to imagine how four small children would manage to hold auditions, organize rehearsals and get all those kids to turn up for the performance. But I didn't want to sound discouraging.

"That's a terrific idea," I said brightly. "I hope you lot can do it."

Margo folded her arms firmly across her chest. "We *will* do it."

I hate to admit it, but at the time I honestly thought their talent show would never *ever* be put on.

5th
CHAPTER

"I'm Lauren Kendall," the riding instructor announced in her clipped British accent. "And I'd like to welcome all of you to Kendallwood Farm."

Saturday had finally arrived, and I was about to have my first riding lesson. I couldn't believe it. I, Mallory Pike, was standing in a riding ring, holding the reins of a beautiful chestnut mare called Isabelle. I wanted to pinch myself to make sure this wasn't just a dream. Around me in a semicircle were eleven other new riders, each holding the reins of their horses while we hung on to our instructor's every word.

Lauren Kendall was tall and slender, with straight dark hair that she wore pulled back in a silver hairslide at her neck. You could tell she spent a lot of time in the sun because her face was deeply tanned, with little smile lines around her sparkling green eyes. In her English riding togs – black boots, jodhpurs, white blouse and fitted green jacket – Lauren Kendall looked as if she had just stepped off the cover of *Horse and Rider* magazine. I thought she was the coolest person I'd ever seen. I made a silent vow to be just like her when I grew up.

"I'm calling today's lesson 'Taking the Reins'," Lauren said. "We'll learn how to mount and dismount safely, and how to walk and trot."

All in one lesson? I thought. Goosebumps immediately rippled up my arms. I imagined myself as an accomplished horsewoman – jumping, doing dressage, riding in shows, maybe competing at the Kensington Stakes one day. My horse, Isabelle, seemed to sense my excitement. She flared her nostrils and snorted several times.

"All right, class." Lauren stepped up to the centre of the ring and tapped her riding crop against the side of her tall boots. "Let's form a circle and lead your horses round the ring by the reins."

As I walked my horse into place behind the one in front of me, I had my first good look at the rest of the kids in my class. I had been too excited to pay much attention to them before. There were four boys and seven other girls. The girl leading the bay ahead of me, a blonde who looked about my age or a little older, caught my eye and I smiled shyly.

She didn't smile back but just raised an eyebrow and murmured, "Nice outfit."

I looked down at my clothes and then back at the class. I could feel my face redden as I realized that my outfit was completely out of place. Lauren Kendall had told me on the phone to wear an English riding habit if I had one, but if I didn't, just to make sure to wear boots, a helmet and gloves. And that's what I had done. I had put on my red plaid shirt and jeans (they looked great when I wore them trail riding at Camp Mohawk) and a weathered pair of winter boots. I did have an old riding helmet that my mum had borrowed from one of her friends, but it looked as if it had been run over by a herd of elephants. My gloves were a worn out leather pair that my dad said he didn't need any more.

This wouldn't have been so bad if someone else had been dressed like me, but the others were wearing full English riding habits, just like Lauren's. They had on the same tight jodhpurs, and most of the girls wore blouses with high collars. (I read in a magazine that those shirts are called rat-catchers, which is a pretty weird name but seemed kind of appropriate for the snooty girl in front of me.) They were wearing the same high black boots, and velvet riding helmets, which are called hunt caps. As we completed our circle, I forced myself to fix my attention on Lauren.

You're here to learn to ride, I told myself. Not to enter a fashion contest, so just forget about the others.

"That's fine," Lauren said. "Now move to the left side of your horse and prepare to mount up."

I circled Isabelle, making sure to pat her nose and whisper, "Good girl." Then I slipped my left foot in the narrow stirrup and swung my right leg over Isabelle's back.

I felt as if I were sitting on top of the world. I'd ridden Western style before, but that felt so clunky compared to sitting on this English saddle. Now there was just a small piece of leather between me and my horse.

"Sit tall. Chins high. Backs straight." Lauren barked the commands and we responded. "The reins are held loosely in your hands, threaded between your little finger and the one next to it. Elbows in. Very good, class.

I smiled. I had mastered holding the reins. Horseback riding was going to be easy.

"Take a deep breath. And let's walk our horses round the ring again."

We circled the edge of the wooden enclosure, and I muttered to myself under my breath. "Back straight, reins loose, chin up." Suddenly I noticed Lauren was walking beside me. She chuckled at my mumbling and added, "Breathe, Mallory. That's very important. Wouldn't want you keeling over in the middle of the ring."

Some of the other kids laughed at her joke, but I didn't feel embarrassed because Lauren added, "That goes for all of you. Remember, riding is fun. Try to relax and enjoy it."

This time we all laughed. Once again I had a chance to look around me. And that's when I saw him. My dream horse.

He was an Arabian with a beautiful head and delicate nostrils. He was nearly all white, with a white mane and tail and a light dappling of grey that made his coat look like marble. His rider was a sombre, dark-haired boy with glasses who didn't seem to realize that he was riding the most beautiful horse in the world.

"All right, class," Lauren called, as we circled the ring. "I want you to gently squeeze the sides of your horse with the inside of your boots. We're going to attempt an easy trot. The most important thing to remember about trotting is to keep your heels down and toes up."

"Heels down and toes up," we repeated. "Heels down. Toes up."

"Rise with the motion of the horse, rocking your pelvis forward and back as the horse trots," Lauren said as we rode past her around the ring. "This is called posting. That'll keep your teeth from banging together, Kelsey," she called to the snooty girl.

I gloated secretly, even though my own teeth were doing a pretty good job of clacking against each other in time to Isabelle's jolting movement. After circling the ring twice I felt that I was getting the hang of trotting. I stole a look out of the corner of my eye at the beautiful Arabian horse behind me. His thick mane was flowing in the breeze, and for a moment I pictured myself in brand-new riding clothes, sitting on his back in front of hundreds of spectators.

"Now, this is the tricky part, class," Lauren called. "I'm going to ask you to reverse direction."

Half of the class started turning their horses before she could give the order to the other half of the class. And for a moment it looked as if we were going to have a head-on collision. Lauren waved her crop in the air and bellowed, "Halt!"

We yanked on our reins and managed to pull our horses to a stop. Lauren was laughing. "That was a close one," she cried. "Oh, I wish I had that on tape!"

That made us giggle, and I beamed at my classmates. I knew I was going to love the next eight weeks.

Lauren explained the proper way to stop a horse, told us how to reverse direction without colliding with the other horses, and suddenly the hour was up.

Then came my favourite part of the whole day: the cool down and grooming. First we walked our horses around the stable yard. Then we took off their saddles and after slipping off their blankets, curry-combed and brushed their coats until they shone.

I managed to groom Isabelle beside the Arabian. I was certain he belonged to the boy with the glasses. A horse like that was too beautiful just to be part of a stable. It took me a while to get up the courage, but finally I said, "That's a beautiful horse you have. What's his name?"

"Pax." The boy pushed his glasses up on his nose. "But he's not my horse."

"He's not?" My eyes widened. "You mean he belongs to Kendallwood Farm?"

The boy nodded. "All the horses in our class do."

This was great news. That meant that I might get to ride Pax at my next lesson. I could hardly contain my excitement.

After class, I hopped on my bike and pedalled as fast as I could to my house. I didn't even stop to take off my coat or say hello to my family but ran straight up stairs and headed for the phone. I had to tell Jessi about my fabulous day.

As soon as I heard her soft hello on the other end, I blurted out in a rush, "Jessi, my lesson was wonderful. There are twelve kids in my class and my teacher is Lauren Kendall, and she used to ride with the Olympic riding team, and she is so beautiful. Can you believe it?"

"That's great, Mal."

I launched into a breathless description of the lesson, starting with when we were assigned our horses and ending with when we groomed our horses in the stalls. I went over every single detail but one. I left out feeling like a complete dork in my outfit. I didn't want Jessi to think I'd had a bad time.

"And here's the best part," I went on. "I met my dream horse."

"Oh, really?" Jessi sounded a little distracted, but I thought she must be helping her mum make lunch or something. So I continued my rave report about Pax.

"He's everything we hoped he'd be, Jessi. A white Arabian with a wonderful personality. You should have seen him trotting around the ring with his head high. He looked as if he was dancing. Oh, you would have loved him!"

I waited for Jessi to respond. When I didn't hear anything, I asked, "Jessi? Are you still there?"

"I'm here." Her voice sounded distant and cold. I realized something must have happened at home and maybe I had phoned her at a bad time. I probably would have realized that straight away if I hadn't been so excited about Pax.

"Listen, Jessi, you sound pretty busy," I said.

I thought that would be the perfect opportunity for her to tell me what was wrong. Instead she just said, "Yeah, I really am. I'm sorry, Mal, but I'll talk to you later."

I opened my mouth to say goodbye, but the line clicked off. That was weird. It wasn't like Jessi to be rude. I stared at the receiver, listening to the dialling tone. Finally I hung up.

A disturbing thought came to me. Could I somehow have done something to make my best friend angry with me?

6th CHAPTER

Tuesday

You late? I think I've got a problem. I sat for the Marshalls today and Nina just wasn't herself. You know how happy and helpful she can be. Well, she just sat in her rocking chair in the living room and stared at the floor. Mrs. Marshall was quite worried about her. Mal, was she like that when you sat for her last week? I *thought I'd talk to you guys before I did anything about Nina.*

Jessi's entry in the notebook was pretty weird. If she wanted to know about Nina, why didn't she just phone me? I could have talked to her about Blankie. I decided she must have been too busy with her ballet lessons and sitting jobs to phone me, and that we'd have time for a good talk after the next BSC meeting.

Anyway, Jessi went to the Marshalls' house on Tuesday afternoon. Mrs Marshall met her at the front door and kept her on the front porch for a few minutes so they could talk without Nina or Eleanor overhearing them.

"Jessi," Mrs Marshall said in a hushed voice, "Nina is having some problems at nursery school."

"What's the matter?" Jessi asked.

"I'm not sure." Mrs Marshall pushed a strand of hair off her forehead. "But I received a note from her teacher today saying he thought Nina was uneasy about something, but he wasn't sure what."

"Did the teacher try to talk to Nina about it?"

Mrs Marshall nodded. "Yes, but she wouldn't open up to him."

Jessi tilted her head. "That's strange. Usually Nina likes to talk."

"I know." Mrs Marshall sighed. "But she won't even tell *me* what's wrong. She just mopes around the house."

"Well, I'll see if I can find out anything," Jessi said.

"That would be a great help." Mrs Marshall started to lead Jessi into the house, then added in a whisper, "In the meantime, don't be surprised if she gets a little tearful about things."

Jessi nodded. "I understand."

While Mrs Marshall got her coat from the hall cupboard, Jessi peered around the corner into the living room. Eleanor was on the floor in front of the television, happily watching *Sesame Street*. But Nina wasn't even looking at the TV. She was just sitting in her chair in the corner, clutching her huge, grey blanket.

"Hi, Nina."

Jessi waved, but Nina looked at her without smiling. When Eleanor noticed Jessi, though, she hopped to her feet, and waddled towards her with her arms open wide.

"Hello, Eleanor." Jessi scooped her up and groaned good-naturedly. "Boy, are you turning into a big girl," she told her.

Mrs Marshall poked her head into the living room from the hall. "Bye-bye, kids. You be good for Jessi and I'll be back in a very short time."

"Bye, Mummy." Eleanor put her hand to her mouth and blew kisses at her mother. Jessi noticed that Nina barely mumbled goodbye.

Once the front door had shut, Jessi turned to Nina. "Now it's just the three of us," she declared cheerfully. "What shall we play?"

Nina shrugged. "I don't know."

Jessi carried Eleanor into the hall, where she had left her things, and said, "My Kid-Kit has some pretty fun stuff in it today. Maybe we should take a look at it."

This time Nina looked up, but she still didn't budge from her chair. Jessi carried the box to Nina's side and put it down next to her.

"Here, Nina," Jessi said as she lowered Eleanor to the floor. "Why don't you open it up?"

Nina slid out of her chair on to the rug, pulling her blanket into a huge ball on her lap. She opened the box up listlessly and peered inside. As she rummaged through the box, Jessi noticed that Nina never let go of the blanket at any time. She decided to ask her about Blankie – at the right moment.

That moment came when Eleanor and Nina found a brand-new pack of crayons in the box, and Nina started colouring a paper doll. She relaxed a little. Jessi watched her for a moment, then asked in an offhand way, "Nina, did you take Blankie with you to school today?"

Nina drew back as if she'd been pinched. Finally she mumbled, "Yes."

"Did you two have a good time?"

Nina didn't answer. She just methodically took the crayons out of their box and placed them on the rug beside the doll she was colouring. Every now and then she would adjust her blanket around her knees, as if reassuring herself that it was still there.

Jessi decided that the old grey blanket was Nina's problem. Maybe the kids at school were teasing her about it. But how could her teacher not notice that? Especially since Nina's blanket was so enormous. Unless the other children teased Nina behind the teacher's back.

Jessi knew all too well how that could happen. When she first moved to Stoneybrook, some of the kids at school and even a few adults were mean to her, just because of the colour of her skin. Jessi didn't tell her teachers about it, because she was afraid the kids would think she was a tell-tale. Maybe Nina was having the same kind of trouble.

"You know, Nina, when I first moved here, some of the kids at my school weren't very nice to me." Jessi took one of the paper dolls out of the box and picked up a crayon. "They teased me and made me feel so bad that I cried."

334

Nina stopped colouring but didn't look up "Why?"

"Because they didn't like the way I look."

Nina glanced at Jessi, then reached for another crayon. "I think you look fine."

"Thanks," Jessi said. "But my point is that some of the other kids didn't think so. They were unkind to me just because I was different. But soon they got to know me, and now I have lot of friends."

Jessi studied Nina's face to see if what she was saying had made any sense, but Nina just continued to colour. Jessi looked at the doll she was working on and smiled. Talking about skin colour as a problem probably *didn't* make sense to a little girl who had just coloured her doll's face blue and the hands and legs green.

Jessi gave Nina a quick hug and then went to the kitchen to get some lemonade. As she filled the girls' plastic animal cups, Jessi wondered if maybe she should tell Mrs Marshall about Nina's blanket problem and the teasing.

"No," Jessi muttered to herself. "I'd better wait until I'm sure."

Because what if it wasn't the blanket at all? Then Jessi would have caused a lot of concern for nothing.

I'll talk to the BSC first, Jessi told herself. My friends will know what to do.

The girls drank their lemonades, and after they'd finished, the front doorbell rang. Jessi waited for Nina to say, "I'll get it," like most kids do, but she just continued to colour her doll. Finally Jessi stood up.

"Let's see who it is," she said brightly.

Eleanor, who had been more interested in the outside of the Kid-Kit than in what was in it, hopped to her feet and shouted, "Okay!"

"Come on, Nina." Jessi offered her hand to Nina, who tagged along, dragging her blanket behind her.

What greeted them on the front porch made even Nina laugh. There stood Vanessa, Nicky, Margo and Claire, wearing red rubber clown noses and polka dot bow ties. Nicky had hung a huge white sign around his neck.

"*Stars of Tomorrow* auditions," Jessi read out loud. "Are you lot looking for more clowns?"

Vanessa shook her head. "We're looking for all kinds of acts for our talent show. And today is your lucky day. We're holding door-to-door auditions."

Jessi laughed. "That sounds like fun. Nina, do you want to audition?"

Nina leaned against Jessi's leg and shook her head.

"Oh, come on," Jessi encouraged her. "I bet there are lots of things you can do."

"We need every kind of performer," Vanessa said, checking the clipboard she was carrying. "Singers, dancers, clowns, jugglers, trained dogs, elephants—"

"Hold it a minute," Jessi cut in. "Where are you going to get elephants?"

Claire tugged at Jessi's sleeve. "It's pretend, silly."

Jessi smiled down at Nina. "You could pretend to be an elephant. You could drape yourself in Blankie and stick one arm out for a trunk and you'd look just like an elephant."

Nina considered for a second and then shook her head again. "No, thanks."

"Oh, come on Nina, we're all in the show," Nicky cried. "I'm the strong man wrestling alligators. But I also do acrobatic tricks with Margo. Want to see?"

Jessi checked the sky to see if any rain clouds were lingering overhead and said, "Why don't we sit outside in the back garden and watch them perform their acts?"

Everyone hurried around the side of the house. Vanessa, Nicky, Margo and Claire conferred quickly to decide who should go first. From the excitement in their voices, Jessi could tell that showing off their talents to the neighbourhood was certainly more fun than watching other people audition.

Nina spread her blanket on the grass and let Jessi and Eleanor sit beside her.

Jessi, who loves any kind of a performance (possibly because she spends a lot of time on the stage herself), clapped her hands together and announced, "Curtain going up!"

Nicky did a drumroll with his hands against the side of a dustbin while Vanessa stepped in front of the swings and announced, "And now, *Stars of Tomorrow* presents – Nicholas and Margo doing the Wheelbarrow!"

Nicky walked on his hands while Margo struggled to hold his legs off the grass. They circled the swing set several times as Nina, Eleanor and Jessi applauded. Then Margo tripped over the garden hose and stumbled forward, shoving Nicky's face into the ground.

"Hey!" Nicky bellowed. "You've dented my nose." He sat up and everyone saw that his red clown nose had been smashed flat. Everyone began to laugh. Even Nina.

Then Vanessa took her turn. She walked to the swings and stood at the foot of the stairs leading up to the slide.

"Ladies and gentlemen," she cried. "I will now climb to the top of this ten-storey building," – she clambered up the steps until she was standing on the little platform at the top of the slide – "and perform a death-defying slide to the ground below, using no hands, with my eyes closed."

Nina was very impressed by this

announcement. She turned to Jessi and whispered, "Wow."

They watched as Vanessa snapped her fingers at Nicky and ordered, "Drumroll, please."

Nicky beat his hands against the wooden seat of the swing as Vanessa sat down at the top of the slide. She turned to show Jessi and the Marshall kids that her eyes were shut. Then she folded her arms across her chest and began her descent.

Unfortunately, she was wearing shorts, and her bare skin acted as a brake against the metal slide. She hardly moved at all. Vanessa had to scoot bit by bit towards the bottom of the slide. With each jerk her legs made a loud, squeaking sound.

Jessi clutched Nina's hand and whispered, "So much for the death-defying slide. She couldn't go any slower if she tried."

Nina bobbed her head up and down. "She looks like a caterpillar," she giggled.

Vanessa made it gamely to the bottom of the slide and leaped up to take her bow. As the kids cheered and applauded, Jessi thought to herself, "One thing's for sure – *Stars of Tomorrow is* going to be the funniest talent show on earth!"

Now it was Claire's turn. Vanessa raised one arm and announced, *"Stars of Tomorrow"* proudly presents Miss Claire, the greatest juggler in the world."

Claire raced around the corner of the house. In one hand she held a tennis ball and in the other a Frisbee. Jessi thought Claire must have just found them in the garage. Claire tossed the ball and the Frisbee in the air and tried to catch each object in the opposite hand. Unfortunately the tennis ball bounced off her forehead and rolled into Eleanor's lap, while the Frisbee landed on Claire's own foot.

"Yeow!" Claire cried, clutching her toe with her hands. "Owie-owie-owie!"

Normally Jessi would have got up to make sure Claire hadn't hurt herself, but the sight of her in her clown nose hopping up and down on one leg in a circle was so silly that Jessi couldn't help laughing.

Nina clapped her hands and giggled. "She's really funny," she said.

"I bet if you got up there and put on a clown nose," Jessi said, "you could be funny, too."

Nina's laughter stopped instantly. "I don't want to. I'll just watch."

Jessi decided not to push Nina any further. She decided there was still a long time to go before the talent show. Hopefully Nina's problems at school would be solved by then, and she would change her mind and join in the fun.

7th CHAPTER

My second riding lesson, and I couldn't believe my luck! I got to ride Pax, the beautiful white Arabian. My dream horse. And you know what? He was even more wonderful to ride than to look at.

I arrived at the stables early so that I could talk to Lauren and straight-out ask to ride Pax that day. I also wanted a chance to chat to a few of the other kids in my group before the class started. I thought we'd have lots in common – loving horses, for one thing. But it was strange. None of them seemed to want to talk much.

A short girl with frizzy blonde hair and a brace on her teeth was the second to arrive. I marched right up to where she was saddling her mount and said, "My name's Mallory Pike. What's yours?"

She looked pretty surprised that I had spoken to her. "Allison Anders," was all she answered. Then she turned to Lauren and said, "I thought we were required to wear *proper* riding attire for this class."

I felt the tips of my ears turn bright red and my face grow hot.

Lauren must have seen me blush because she said sharply, "Proper riding gear is boots, gloves and a helmet, Allison. And Mallory is wearing just that." Then her tone softened and she added, "This is a beginner's class. There's no sense in spending a lot of money on gear unless you plan to continue taking lessons."

I wanted to say, "Of course I plan to continue riding. But is it my fault my family can't afford to buy me a fancy outfit?" But I didn't. I just took Pax's reins and led him outside.

"Come on, boy," I murmured, nuzzling my head against his neck. "You're a good horse." I shot a dark look back in Allison's direction. "Not a snob like some people I know."

I walked Pax around the stable yard as more and more of my class arrived. The pupils were all wearing what Allison had called "proper" riding gear. Pax, as if sensing my uneasiness, snorted through his nostrils and gave me a nudge in the side with his nose. I stumbled towards the riding ring. When I looked back at him he gave me another little nudge as if to say,

"You're as good as they are. Get in there and let them know that."

I chuckled and nuzzled my face in his neck again. "You're right, Pax. I'm just being silly. All I have to do is talk to them and they'll realize I'm a nice person. Come on."

As I led Pax into the ring, I summoned up my courage and said to a plump girl in front of me, "I just love horses, don't you?"

"Of course," she replied. "I grew up with them. We have eight in our stables."

"You have your own horses?" I was impressed. Then I thought – if she has her own horses, why is she taking beginning riding lessons?

The girl must have guessed from the look on my face what I was thinking. "My parents thought it would be a good idea for someone besides them to give me lessons," she said quickly. "Anyway, I'm just taking classes to learn to ride English style."

"Me, too," I said. "I mean, I already ride Western."

Okay, I'll admit I made it sound like I was pretty good at riding Western style, when all I had done was some trail riding at camp. But I was anxious to make a friend in this class.

"So what's your name?" I asked, casually slipping my foot into the stirrup.

"Megan." She turned a little too suddenly to mount her horse, and he jerked away with a snort. He was already skittish, but she wasn't making him any more relaxed with her sudden movements. Megan gave an impatient yank on the reins and muttered, "Settle down, you silly horse."

As Megan struggled with her horse, I mounted Pax, who stood perfectly still as I swung on to his saddle. I patted his neck and whispered, "Good horse." Somehow I felt much more confident once I was astride Pax, so I called to Megan, "My name's Mallory. If you like, I'll give you my number and maybe we could get together during the week."

"What?" Megan was still trying to get her horse to stand still. "Oh, right." She yanked on the reins once more. "Whoa, you idiot."

I did not like the way Megan was talking to her horse, but I thought she probably knew more about horse discipline than I did, since she had eight of her own. Eight. Can you imagine it? One for each day of the week, with one extra for holidays.

Pax and I circled the ring and I paused several times to introduce myself to my classmates. One girl named Kyle even smiled at me. "I like that horse," she said. "I wanted to ride him today."

"He's wonderful, isn't he?" I patted Pax on the neck proudly. "Maybe you can ride him next Saturday." Secretly I was hoping *I* could ride him every week.

After we'd chatted about Pax, I told Kyle my name and suggested that maybe we could get together sometime. "We're the only Pike in the Stoneybrook phone book," I said.

Kyle nodded pleasantly and I continued to trot around the ring. I'd made two new friends and I was riding Pax. It was a perfect day!

A few moments later Lauren entered the ring and started class. We reviewed our walking and trotting techniques from the week before. Pax was a dream. He seemed to know what I wanted him to do before I even knew it. As the hour went on, I found the courage to wave to several of the pupils. One boy – the one who had ridden Pax the week before – waved back. I decided he seemed like a nice person, so after class, as we were grooming our horses, I made sure I stood next to him.

"Your name's David, isn't it?" I said as I ran the brush across Pax's broad back. When the boy nodded yes, I continued, "Well, I don't know if I told you last week, but my name's Mallory Pike. I go to Stoneybrook Middle School."

"Oh?"

I took that to mean he was still interested in talking. So for the next five minutes I rattled on non-stop. I told him about my family, my best friend and the Babysitters Club.

"Jessi and I have seen practically every horse film that was ever made," I said, carefully pulling a few tangles out of Pax's mane. "My friends say I'm horse-crazy. Which is why I wanted to take this class." It suddenly occurred to me that I hadn't let him squeeze a word into the conversation. "So why are you taking this class?"

"My parents made me," he said. "Riding is a tradition in my family."

"But don't you like it?"

He shrugged. "It's okay, I suppose."

"Oh, you're kidding, right?" I exclaimed. "I mean, how could you ride a beautiful horse like Pax and not think horses are absolutely wonderful?"

David's face softened as he looked over at Pax. "He is a pretty cool horse." He patted Pax lightly on the neck. The horse craned his head around and nuzzled David's palm.

"That tickles." David laughed and pulled his hand away.

"He's begging for a treat," I explained.

Pax whinnied and then we both laughed.

"How many kids are in your family?" I asked.

"I'm an only child," David replied as he scratched Pax between the ears.

"Hey, maybe you'd like to meet my brothers and sisters. People come over to our house all the time. It's like a big circus. I'll give you my phone number and you could come and visit."

346

I know it sounds like I was being pushy, but David was shy and *needed* a little push. Anyway, I wrote my phone number on a Post It from the stable office and gave it to David. He put it in his pocket and said, "Thanks." If he didn't want it, he could have given it back, right?

As I cycled home that afternoon, I reviewed the new events in my life. I was learning to be a horsewoman. I'd ridden Pax, my dream horse, and I'd taken a stab at making some new friends. Megan seemed okay, Kyle was nice and David even had my phone number. One of them would probably give me a call before the week was up.

"Hi, Mallory," said my mother as I came through the back door. "Lunch will be ready in ten minutes."

"Great, Mum, I'm starved." I sneaked a warm roll from the basket resting on the kitchen worktop. "That gives me just enough time to call Jessi."

My mother swatted my hand. "Why can't you wait till the food gets to the table?" she complained.

I laughed and stuffed the whole roll into my mouth. "It tastes better this way," I mumbled.

Then I took the stairs three at a time and reached for the hall phone. I dialled Jessi without even looking at the numbers.

"Hi," I cried when she answered. "It's me."

"Hi, Mal. I was just thinking about you." Jessi sounded like her old self. "What are you doing today?"

"Jessi!" I gasped. "What kind of question is that? I just had my second riding lesson. Remember?"

"Oh."

"It's only the most important thing in my life right now," I pointed out.

"I'm sorry, Mal. I suppose I forgot."

"Well, aren't you going to ask me how it went?"

There was a long pause. Finally Jessi asked, "How was it?"

"Fantastic. I got there early and Lauren – that's my teacher – let me ride Pax."

"Pax?"

"My dream horse. Don't you remember, Jessi? I told you about him last week."

"Oh, yeah. Right."

Suddenly Jessi didn't sound like herself at all. If I hadn't known her so well, I would have thought she was snubbing me. Even so, I tried to tell her about my new friends.

"There's this boy called David. He's got dark hair and glasses and he's pretty shy – but nice. He rode Pax last week. I think he'll be coming over to visit. You should meet him. And then there's this girl called Megan. Her family own eight horses and they have their own stables, can you believe it?"

348

"Really."

Jessi couldn't have cared less about anything I was saying. I was starting to feel uncomfortable.

"Megan will probably be calling me, too—"

"Listen, Mal," Jessi interrupted, "I've got a lot of chores to do today. I'd better not talk on the phone too long. Okay?"

"Oh, well, okay. If you have to go." This was weird. Jessi had never cut me off before. "I just thought you'd like to hear my good news."

"I'd like to, but I don't really have the time. Sorry."

I couldn't help it. My stomach tightened into a hard knot, and suddenly I felt angry. Jessi was supposed to be my best friend and here she was treating me like a stranger.

"Fine." My voice sounded as dead as Jessi's did. "Then maybe I'll see you at school."

I waited for Jessi to say something about getting together over the weekend. Usually we hang around together as much as possible. But she didn't even suggest it. Which made me even angrier. I put the phone back on its hook. Then without thinking I picked it up again and slammed it down hard.

"That's just fine with me," I muttered through clenched teeth. "I don't need your friendship. I can see all my new friends. Like David. And Megan. And Kyle." I picked up the phone again. "I'll show you. I'll just phone them." But when I put the phone to my ear, I realized I didn't know David or Megan or Kyle's phone numbers or even their last names. I put the phone down and shrugged. "Oh, well. They'll phone me."

A week passed and Jessi and I barely spoke. She went to her ballet lessons, and even though we both had babysitting jobs, that didn't explain why we weren't phoning each other. And what about all those new friends I'd made at Kendallwood Farm? Well, I didn't hear from a single soul.

8th CHAPTER

Thunk. I hit the ground so hard the wind was knocked out of me. Has that ever happened to you? It's the most terrible feeling in the world.

It was my third lesson at Kendallwood Farm and I wasn't riding Pax. I was riding Gremlin, the horse Megan had struggled with the week before. I should have known I was going to have trouble when he bucked every time I put my foot in the stirrup. Lauren finally held him until I was able to get in the saddle, but the whole lesson went downhill from there.

First of all, Kyle and David, whom I had expected to phone me during the week, didn't even say hello to me. You'd have thought we'd never met. Kyle did sort of smile in my direction, but that was it. Then Lauren ran us quickly through our lesson – more walking and trotting and reversing directions. Gremlin kept pushing up against the riding rail. I knew exactly what he was doing. He was trying to scrape me out of the saddle. Normally I would have laughed about it with the rest of the riders in my class, but none of them seemed to be aware that I even existed, let alone that I might be having trouble.

"Okay, everyone, today we're going to learn how to canter," Lauren announced from the centre of the ring as we rode around and around her. "The canter cue is an easy one. Simply keep your outside leg where it is, and move your inside leg back about two inches. Then squeeze your horse with your legs."

I was concentrating so much on where my legs were supposed to go that I forgot to keep a firm grip on the reins. When she said, "Squeeze your horse," I did.

Gremlin bolted forward as if he'd been jabbed with a needle. He bucked twice and I flipped backwards out of the saddle. I landed flat on my back. Luckily I was wearing my riding helmet because my head bounced hard against the ground. As soon as I hit the dirt, every muscle in my body seemed to lock and I couldn't breathe in or out. For a second I was sure I was going to die. I lay on the ground in a daze, vaguely aware of the pounding horses and their riders struggling to avoid stepping on me.

"Come to a halt, class!" Lauren shouted. "Halt!"

She raced to my side, and it was only when she reached me that I was able to breathe. I sucked in a gulp of air and sat up.

"Mallory, are you all right?"

I turned my head slightly and saw that she was staring hard into my eyes. I think she was checking to see if I had suffered any concussion. The jolt to my body had been so strong and so hard that tears rushed to my eyes and streamed down my cheeks. It was really embarrassing. I couldn't stop the tears. I tried to cover my face with my hands so the rest of the class couldn't see, but I knew they already had. Then my hands started shaking.

"Mallory," I heard Lauren say in a gentle voice. "Do you think you can stand?"

I tried to answer but my mouth wasn't working right. So I just nodded.

"Here, I'll help you walk over to the bench." Lauren pulled me carefully to my feet. My legs felt like rubber. I could barely control them, so I had to lean on Lauren's arm for support.

What a jerk I was. Crying and shaking like that. Worse, the rest of the class just stared at me as if I was some strange being from another planet. I saw one girl whisper behind her hands to the girl next to her, who giggled. She stopped quickly when Lauren shot her a hard look.

"Amber?" Lauren barked. "Lead the class in trotting until I get back."

Lauren led me to a wooden bench at the side of the ring and asked me to move my arms and legs to make sure nothing was broken. "Are you sure you're okay, Mallory? You had a pretty bad fall."

I wiped my nose. It had started running (naturally), so besides feeling stupid I also felt ugly. "I think so," I said. "But I'm still a little shaky."

Lauren nodded and stood up. "Just to be on the safe side, I'm going to phone your mother and ask her to come and pick you up." She patted me lightly on the shoulder. "I think you've done enough riding for today."

"Thanks," I mumbled, staring at the ground. Normally I would have protested, but I was too woozy to ride my bike home. I felt like a wimp. In the films, whenever a rider takes a fall, he or she always gets right back on the horse, just to show confidence.

Lauren leaned over and whispered, "Listen, every good rider suffers a fall like this. More than once, I hate to say. So there's no need to feel ashamed." She straightened up and sighed. "Besides, I think it's about time that Gremlin retired. He's been giving everyone trouble."

Her words were meant to reassure me, but they didn't. I still felt embarrassed and hurt and angry. I knew that the rest of the kids in my class were thinking I was a klutz. And I was afraid they were right. I closed my eyes, wishing I could just make a wish, and *poof,* I'd be home.

My mum arrived ten minutes later. She leaped out of the car without turning off the engine and ran towards me across the paddock. "Mallory, are you okay? Can you walk?"

I felt a huge wave of relief. I didn't care if the other kids were watching or not. I got up and limped to my mum and let her hug me. I hugged her back hard. "I think I'm fine. I feel shaky and bruised, but Lauren doesn't think anything's broken."

My mother helped me to the car, running around to open the door on my side. "I think we'd better take you to the hospital, just to be sure."

"Oh, Mum," I protested weakly. "I'm okay, really."

"No arguments." My mother hopped into the driver's seat and started the car. "I've already called Dr Calloway. He and your father will meet us in casualty."

On the way to Stoneybrook General Hospital I told Mum about my accident. I exaggerated a little about how bad-tempered Gremlin was, and how he'd bolted when I gave him the canter cue, but I didn't need to elaborate on the description of having my breath knocked out of me. It was vivid in my memory.

My mother listened with a worried frown on her face. She gasped in all the right places and made sympathetic noises when I described how much the fall had hurt. It felt good to be able to tell her about it.

Dad met us at the front entrance and helped me into the waiting room. I could tell he was worried about me because he was treating me as if I were a basket of eggs. "Do you want me to carry you inside?" he asked.

"Dad!" I looked round quickly to make sure no good-looking boys were in hearing distance. "I'm really okay," I reassured him. "Honest."

"That is a dangerous sport," my mum declared while she filled in the insurance forms at the front desk. "You've had a bad fall. We're not leaving here until I'm sure you're all right."

The nurse ushered us into an empty examining room, where we waited for Dr Calloway to arrive. He'd been out at the golf course, so when he came in he wasn't wearing his usual white coat. Instead he had on these bright yellow trousers, an electric blue polo shirt and a visor.

"Sorry to call you away from your game," Dad said.

Dr Calloway waved one hand. "It's no problem." He slipped on his stethoscope, found a small pen light, and ran me through a series of tests.

First he listened to my heart. Then he shone the light in my eyes while asking me to look in various directions. Finally he tested my reflexes by tapping my knees with a little rubber hammer. After about ten minutes he looked up at my parents and announced, "Well, I think she'll live."

I giggled and he grinned at me. "There, you see? Laughter *is* the best medicine." Dr Calloway tucked his stethoscope away and said, "We don't need an X-ray, but you've had a pretty hard fall, young lady. One you probably won't forget."

Boy, was he right about that!

"I'd suggest," he continued, "that you take it a little easier next time. Choose a different horse."

"I'm not sure there should be a next time," my mother said as we were going home in the car.

"I think we should let Mallory be the judge of that," my dad replied. He looked at me in the rear-view mirror and raised his eyebrows. "How do you feel about it, Mal? Do you want to stop your lessons? We'd understand if you did."

"No way!" I blurted out.

After all I'd gone through to get a chance to take riding lessons, I wasn't about to let one fall stop me. Besides, if I left the class, I'd ever see Pax again. How could I stop seeing my dream horse?

357

"I want to keep riding," I pleaded. "Please, Mum, I'll be careful."

After a lot of fast talking my mother gave in – but only on the condition that I would never ride Gremlin again.

She didn't have to worry about that. Lauren replaced Gremlin with a bay gelding named Samson. He was really gentle but *huge*. *So* huge I was afraid to ride him.

But not just Samson. After the accident, I was afraid to ride any horse. Even Pax, the nicest, most gentle horse in the stable. It took all of my self-control just to get on his back. Whenever Lauren would tell us to mount up, I would feel this awful knot in my stomach and a rushing in my head. My legs would ache for hours after each lesson because I was gripping the horse too hard. I could hardly concentrate on what Lauren said to us. With every bounce in the saddle, my mind would scream, Don't fall off! Whatever you do, don't fall off.

Things just got worse and worse. I started to dread the end of the school week. Every Friday night, I'd toss and turn and then on Saturday mornings I'd do everything to avoid going to the stables. It didn't help that the rest of the kids in my riding class pretty much ignored me.

Worst of all, there was no one I could talk to about being afraid. Not Mum or Dad. The lessons had cost them too much.

So there I was. I had got everything I'd said I wanted – riding lessons and my dream horse. And I was totally miserable.

But what I missed most was my friendship with Jessi. A month before, I could have told her how I felt and she would have understood. Now we seemed to be drifting apart, and I didn't know what to do about it.

9th
CHAPTER

It was a madhouse at the Pikes' on Saturday. Claud and I had no idea that Vanessa, Nicky, Claire, and Margo could be so loony.

Come on, Stacey, they're relayted to Mal, arn't they? They have to be Looney Tons.

I'm sure, Mal, that Claudia meant that in the nicest possible way.

I did.

Anyway, Mal was at her riding lesson and we hardly had to do a thing the whole day except—

Watch the intire nayborhood preform.

And laugh.

And laff and laff.

I would have given anything to be able to stay at home and watch the kids rehearse their talent show, but I had made a commitment to riding lessons.

Claudia met Stacey, who lives right behind me, on her front porch that morning. Together they walked over to our house and rang the doorbell. It was answered by one of the triplets.

"Hi, Byron," said Claudia.

"Hi," my brother replied, pulling the door back for the girls. "Come on in. You're just in time for the dress rehearsal for the big talent show."

Claudia and Stacey had heard about the show but hadn't had an opportunity to see it yet.

"Are all of you kids in it?" Stacey asked as Byron led them outside.

"Not me. No way," Byron replied. "Just Margo, Nicky, Vanessa and Claire. They call it *Stars of Tomorrow*."

"Sounds like a big deal," Claudia said.

Byron made a face. "From the way Vanessa is acting you'd think this thing was going to be on national television."

"She's pretty bossy, huh?" Claudia laughed.

"You said it," Byron replied. He motioned towards the door. "They're all out there getting ready."

Stacey and Claud had been hired to sit for all of my brothers and sisters, so Stacey asked, "What are you and Adam and Jordan up to this morning?"

"We're playing Nintendo in the recreation room."

"Well, let us know if you decide to go anywhere, or if you need anything," Claudia called over her shoulder as she followed Stacey outside.

"Okay."

Stacey and Claudia stepped into the garden and gasped. Every inch of the garden was crowded with children and pets.

"The entire neighbourhood must be here," Claudia said.

Vanessa stood off to one side, shouting through a megaphone that she had made out of poster board. The word "Director" was printed in big letters on the side. "Will the contestants for the *Stars of Tomorrow* talent show please stop talking and lend me your ears?"

"We're supposed to give her our ears?" a little girl in a pink tutu with rabbit ears asked the group in general.

Claudia giggled while Stacey knelt beside the girl and explained, "I think she wants you to sit down and listen to her."

The girl hitched up the front of her leotard. "Then why didn't she say so?"

No one seemed to have heard Vanessa's announcement. The kids continued their excited chatter. Finally Vanessa climbed on a garden chair and bellowed, "Be quiet and sit down!"

There was a shocked silence as the kids stopped talking and looked around to see who was shouting at them.

"That got their attention," Claudia murmured to Stacey.

The triumphant smile on Vanessa's face vanished as the chair she was standing on slowly folded in the middle and collapsed. She fell backwards on to the grass with a yelp. The kids applauded.

"Way to go, Vanessa!" Nicky shouted.

"Was that your talent?" another one asked.

"Very funny," Vanessa muttered from where she lay sprawled on the grass.

"I'd better make sure she's okay," Stacey said.

Vanessa was pulling her crumpled megaphone out from under her when Stacey reached her. A grass stain ran down the side of her white tights, but otherwise only her pride had been injured.

"Did that look too stupid?" Vanessa whispered.

Stacey shook her head. "No, you handled it like a pro. But next time, make sure you stand on something sturdy, like a bench."

"Okay." Vanessa leaped up and brushed the grass off her legs. Then she returned to directing the talent contest. "We're going to run through our show, everybody," she called. "I've arranged it in alphabetical order, so Sean Addison – you will go first."

"Where are the other Pikes?" Stacey whispered to Claud.

Claudia stood up. "Margo and Claire are sitting at the front by Vanessa," she repeated. "And Nicky is over there talking to Buddy Barrett."

Stacey nodded. "We might as well sit back and enjoy the show."

Stacey and Claud sat on the ground in front of the *Stars of Tomorrow* stage. Well, it wasn't really a stage. It was just a clothesline with two blankets draped across it to look like a curtain. Claud giggled and pointed as Sean Addison punched at the blankets, struggling for a way to get through. Finally he found the opening and emerged in front of the audience. He was carrying a shiny metal tuba that was almost as big as he was. Sean looked over at Margo, who stared back at him blankly. Then Vanessa jabbed her with her elbow and hissed, "You're supposed to introduce him, silly!"

"Oh!" Margo stood up and shouted, "Sean Addison will now play a classical song on his tuba."

There was a burst of applause and Sean bowed stiffly, then puffed his cheeks out as he began his song.

Stacey listened for a few seconds, then

said, "Hey, that's not a classical tune. That's 'Old MacDonald'."

Claudia covered her mouth to keep from laughing out loud. "I think she meant a song from their class at school."

Sean played the notes perfectly – all except the last one – so the tune sounded like "Ee-ai-ee-ai-YEOW!" But he didn't seem to notice. He bowed solemnly from the waist and stuck out his tongue at Buddy Barrett, who was next.

Buddy didn't bother to come through the curtains. He was carrying too many props in his arms – a hula hoop, a paper bag and a large red ball. His younger sister Suzi waddled after him, tugging on a leash. At its end was their basset hound, Pow.

"Don't worry, I'll introduce us," Buddy said to Vanessa. Then he stepped forwards and gestured with his thumb to his chest. "I am Buddy Barrett, the world's greatest animal trainer."

"Since when does an animal trainer wear a Cub Scout uniform?" Stacey whispered to Claudia.

"When he can't find anything else to wear," Claudia murmured back. "And now I'd like to present Pow, the cleverest dog on earth," Buddy continued, gesturing grandly to the side. "Bring Pow forward, oh, assistant of mine."

"'Oh, assistant of mine'?" Claudia repeated. She would have burst out laughing if Stacey hadn't jabbed her in the side with her elbow.

Suzi Barrett led the basset hound out to the centre of the stage. He sat on his haunches, his long ears dragging on the ground by his front paws, and stared impassively at the crowd while Buddy declared, "This is Pow, the world's only talking dog."

"This I gotta see," said Claudia, giggling. She leaned forward.

Buddy knelt beside Pow and lifted one of his ears. "All right, Pow, here's your first question. What's on top of the house?"

Buddy and the kids stared hard at the wrinkled basset hound. But Pow did nothing. Buddy repeated the question. This time Pow blinked several times and lazily scratched a flea behind his ear with his back leg. Finally Buddy stood up and shouted, "*SPEAK* to me, Pow."

Pow promptly cocked his head and let out a loud, "Woof."

"That is correct!" Buddy handed the dog a biscuit, which Pow seemed to inhale without chewing. "A roof is on top of the house. See how clever he is, folks?"

The kids giggled and then a boy shouted, "Ask him another question. I bet he gives the same answer."

"That's what you think." Buddy grinned at the boy, then turned to Pow and asked, "Okay, how was your day?"

This time Buddy gently nudged Pow in the rear with the toe of his shoe and Pow grumbled, "R-r-r-ruff."

Buddy raised his arms in triumph. "You heard him say it. Pow had a *rough* day."

There was a burst of applause. Then a girl dressed like a radish yelled, "What's the hula hoop for?"

Buddy frowned at her. "I'm getting to that." He turned to Suzi and said, "Assistant, may I have the hoop?"

Suzi ran forward and knelt on the grass, holding the hoop in front of Pow. Pow, however, had decided to lie down, his big head resting on his paws and his ears spread out across the grass on either side.

"I hope this next trick doesn't take too much energy," Stacey whispered to Claudia. "It looks like Pow's falling asleep."

"Pow, the mighty basset hound, will now jump through the hoop." Buddy placed a dog biscuit on the other side of the hoop and clapped his hands. "Okay, Pow – go for it!"

After several moments of intense urging, accompanied by lots of giggling from the neighbourhood kids, Pow struggled to his feet. He strolled over to the hoop, stuck his head through it, and inhaled the biscuit. Then he sauntered to the shady side of the house and, with a tired groan, lay down again.

"I think Pow is letting us know your act is over," Vanessa informed Buddy.

Buddy put his hands on his hips and marched over to the sidelines to give Pow a stern lecture about leaving the stage too soon. In the meantime Vanessa checked her clipboard to see who was on next.

Stacey surveyed the crowd. "If they're going in alphabetical order, it should be Haley Braddock's turn next."

They watched as Haley marched briskly through the crowd up to the stage. She wore sequinned red shorts, a white sailor blouse, a bow tie also covered with sequins, and a top hat. Stacey saw the baton in Haley's hand and said, "I didn't know she was a twirler."

Haley handed Vanessa a tape recorder, then strode to the centre of the stage and lowered herself into the splits. She waited for the taped music to begin, a wide smile frozen on her face. But nothing happened.

Claudia and Stacey heard her mumble, "Start the music." But Vanessa didn't hear her. She was too busy trying to keep Charlotte Johanssen's schnauzer, Carrot, away from another little girl's cat.

Finally, just as Haley was standing up to see what was the matter, Vanessa gasped, "Oh, the music!" She hit the button and "You're a Grand Old Flag" blared out of the recorder, but Haley was no longer doing the splits.

"Wait!" she yelped. "I'm not ready!"

While the two girls hurried to reset the

tape player, Claudia spotted a familiar figure in the Pikes' drive. "Hey, look, it's Mary Anne." She gestured for her to join them.

Stacey squinted at the house. "She's brought Nina Marshall with her. And Nina's brought her blanket."

"Oops!" Claudia and Stacey murmured simultaneously as they watched the huge blanket get caught on the bumper of a car. Nina pulled it free, but Carrot the schnauzer pounced on the tip dragging behind her. He grabbed it with his teeth and tugged it back and forth with a growl.

"My Blankie!" Nina wailed. "Let go!"

"It's a tug-of-war!" Claudia said. Mary Anne tried to catch Carrot, but he was too quick for her. "Come on," Claud said, leaping to her feet.

Claud flung herself at Carrot and held on tightly while Stacey pulled the frayed blanket out of Carrot's mouth. Apart from a few dangling threads, there was no damage. Mary Anne gave Nina a quick hug and said, "There. Blankie's okay."

The tears in Nina's eyes dried quickly as the music for Haley's baton twirling number began again. "I want to watch the show!" she cried.

"All right." Mary Anne gathered the grey blanket into a big ball and handed it back to Nina. "But be sure and keep your blanket off the ground. There are a few more dogs around here who might think it's a toy."

Nina clutched Blankie to her chest as she made her way to the second row. Mary Anne waited until Nina was sitting safely on the grass, then sat down with Stacey and Claud and exclaimed, "Phew! That was a close one. Carrot could have ripped that blanket to shreds."

Stacey nodded. "I know. It's old enough."

"Just getting that blanket here in one piece has been a major event. First Nina practically dragged it through a mud puddle. Then we decided to put it in the wagon and pull it, but it's so huge that it caught in the wheel and got all tangled up."

Claud tucked a strand of her long dark hair behind one ear. "That blanket is a major problem," she observed. "It makes it difficult to do anything and keeps Nina from playing with other kids."

"I know." Mary Anne pursed her lips. "But I'm not sure what to do about it."

Stacey shrugged. "Maybe she'll grow out of it."

"I hope so," Mary Anne murmured as she watched several children scoot away from Nina to make way for the blanket. "I really hope so."

10th CHAPTER

"Mallory, relax," Lauren said to me during my next lesson. "You're as stiff as an ironing board."

I couldn't help it. The horse I was riding, whose name was Twilight, had been restless the whole hour. The first time I gave him the canter cue, he bucked forward just like Gremlin had, and I nearly fell off again. It was all I could do to stay on the horse and complete the lesson.

"All right, class," Lauren called out, raising her arm above her head. "Come to a halt."

Even stopping Twilight was difficult. In my head I went over the command Lauren had taught us. "Sit solidly in the saddle and give a long, firm tug on the reins." I did just that but Twilight ignored me. The rest of the class had reined in their mounts and watched as Twilight and I made one more circle of the ring. As he trotted past Lauren, she reached out and grabbed his bridle.

"Twilight! Whoa!"

The firm tone of her voice stopped him in his tracks. But I wasn't ready for it and pitched forward over his neck. Luckily, I caught his mane and stopped myself from tumbling on to the ground.

"Interesting riding technique," Kelsey murmured as I struggled to sit up straight.

Lauren led me to my position in the circle of riders and whispered in Twilight's ear, "Now you stand there and pay attention."

For the first time that hour, Twilight did exactly as he was told. I couldn't bear to look around because I was sure the rest of the class were laughing at me, so I kept my eyes glued on Lauren, who turned to face the line of riders.

"Class, we have two more lessons left," she announced. "And then this course will be over."

A few murmurs of regret came from the other eleven kids. But I was relieved, although I wasn't about to admit it in front of Lauren or the class.

Lauren held up her finger. "At the end of each eight-week period, Kendallwood Farm sponsors a horse show and every class participates. You'll all get to show off what you've learned over the past two months."

"Oh, no," I groaned under my breath.

"Our show will be the Sunday after the last class," Lauren continued. "Mark it on your calendars and be sure and tell your family and friends. We'll hand out ribbons to the best riders, so I'd advise you to use the last two lessons to sharpen your skills."

While the rest of the class talked excitedly about who they intended to invite, my mind raced in an entirely different direction. I was trying to come up with an excuse for not being in the horse show. Breaking a leg was out. Too painful. Trying to get the measles probably wouldn't work, either. At any rate, *no way* was I going to invite my family or my friends.

While these thoughts were running through my brain, Amber raised her hand. "Lauren, I'd like to make an announcement, please."

"Go ahead." Lauren gestured for Amber to talk.

Amber nudged her horse forward. "This Wednesday is my birthday," she announced, "and I would like to invite everyone to come to my party. It should be really cool. I've thought of some fun stuff to do, and there will be lots of great food, too. I hope you can all come."

Amber happened to catch my eye and she smiled. Suddenly I felt a hundred per cent better, as if the last hour never happened. Amber had invited *me* to her birthday party. Maybe she liked me after all. I was sure she had smiled specifically at me when she said the words, "I hope you can all come."

Lauren instructed us to dismount, and as we led our horses back to their stalls, I murmured happily to Megan, "Amber's birthday party sounds like lots of fun."

Megan, who had been acting as if I didn't even exist, actually grinned. "Amber's parties are always fun."

"Oh, you've been to them before?"

"Yes. Most of the class has. A lot of us go to the same school."

This was news to me, but it explained a lot of things. The other kids already knew each other, which was why I felt like such an outsider. But now that seemed to be changing. I hummed as I currycombed Twilight. I even gave him one of the sugar lumps I had brought for Pax.

"You're not such a bad horse after all, are you, Twilight?" I said.

Twilight stamped his foot as if in reply, and I laughed out loud. Something I hadn't done much of since my second lesson.

I spent the next four days trying to choose the perfect outfit to wear to Amber's party. At first I thought I'd go wild, like Claudia, with tie-dyed tights and a bright purple oversized T-shirt knotted at the bottom, and maybe a big red belt. But then I decided that since I didn't know the kids well I really should dress more conservatively.

Finally Wednesday arrived. My mum picked me up right after the BSC meeting- and drove me straight to Amber's. I didn't want to be late. Her house, halfway between Stoneybrook and Stamford, was a huge old colonial with white marble pillars lining the porch and a big circular drive leading to the front door. Music was blasting out of the back garden as we pulled to a stop.

I checked my hair in the mirror one last time and then turned to my mum. "How do I look?"

I was wearing a gold-and-brown kilt, a matching gold cotton sweater, and penny loafers. Mum smiled reassuringly. "You look terrific."

Boy, was she wrong. The second I stepped through Amber's front door I realized I had made a big mistake. First of all, most of the girls were wearing wacky bright clothes with spiked hair and loads of junk jewellery. The boys looked just as cool. I felt as if I were dressed for Sunday school.

I spun round and tried to catch my mum's attention before she drove away. Too late. The car was just pulling on to the road. My spirits sank as I watched it disappear around the bend. She had promised to pick me up in two hours – so that meant I was just going to have to grin and bear it.

Oh, well, I told myself as I poured a glass of punch at a big oak table covered with sandwiches and pizza. They already think I'm weird because of the way I dress in class. Why confuse them now?

I took my punch, slid a sandwich on to a paper plate, and headed out to the patio. It was decorated with pink lanterns and bunches of neon pink balloons. Two large-screen televisions had been set up at either end and were tuned to MTV. The patio was crammed with dancing kids.

Amber waved at me from the middle of the dance floor. She was wearing a pink-and-black-striped silk top over a pair of hot pink ski pants. I hurried to join her.

"Hi, Valerie," she shouted over the music. "I'm glad you could come."

"Um." I cleared my throat. "My name's Mallory, actually."

"Oops." Amber covered her mouth and giggled. "I'm so terrible with names. Have you met my friends?"

"Not yet," I admitted. I was hoping she meant to take me round and introduce me to them. But Amber waved her hand towards the pool, where another group of kids were tossing a volleyball back and forth over the water. "Just introduce yourself. They're all really great."

"Oh. Thanks, Amber."

The next two hours were agony. I didn't know what else to do, so I edged through the crowd towards the pool. I made a couple of attempts to talk to people, but every time I'd open my mouth to say hello they'd spot one of their friends and disappear. Finally I went back inside.

I spent most of the time hovering around the food table, not because I was hungry but because it gave me something to do. I must have drunk more than ten glasses of punch and eaten half a dozen sandwiches. I bet I strolled out on to the front porch at least fifteen times to see if my mother had come for me early. But no such luck. She was ten minutes late.

"Listen to that music," my mum said as I hopped into the car. "It sounds like the party is still going strong. And since it's a special night, do you want to stay a little longer?"

"*No!*" I practically shouted in her ear. She gave me a startled look and I said quickly, "My stomach feels a little queasy."

"Oh." A knowing smile crossed her face. "Too much cake?"

"And punch." I didn't want to tell her about the party. I was afraid she might say things like, "Well, did *you* introduce yourself? You can't wait for someone else to do it for you, you know." Or, "You should have asked some boy to dance. That would have been a sure way to make friends."

I decided to talk to Jessi about it. I thought she was the only person I knew who'd understand how I felt. I counted the minutes until we got home.

"Jessi, I have to talk to you," I blurted out the second she answered the phone. "The worst thing has just happened to me."

"What's the matter, Mal? Is your family okay?" Jessi sounded like her old self, concerned and caring.

"My family's fine. It's me. I went to this party, and it was just terrible."

There was a long pause. Finally Jessi said, "The worst thing that happened is that you went to a terrible party?"

"I know it sounds stupid. But Amber invited me to her birthday party."

"Who's Amber?"

"She's from my riding class. I'm sure I mentioned her before."

"A girl from your riding class invited you to her party," Jessi said slowly.

"Yes, and it was awful. There must have been fifty kids there. They had these monster video screens, and lots of dancing, and a swimming pool, and a huge table covered with plates of sandwiches and pizza—"

"Sounds terrible," Jessi said dryly.

"No, the party was just fine. The trouble was, I didn't know anyone and—"

"Did you introduce yourself?" Jessi cut in, saying exactly what I would have expected my mum to say.

"I tried, but no one wanted to talk to me. Instead I ended up drinking gallons of punch and feeling stupid."

"Gee, that's too bad."

Jessi didn't sound sympathetic at all. And I felt really silly phoning to complain about a party she hadn't been invited to. But it wasn't just the party I wanted to talk to her about. It was everything – my rotten riding lessons, my fear of horses, and worst of all, the strained conversations she and I'd been having recently. I just couldn't seem to find the right words.

After a few moments of awful silence, I finally mumbled, "Listen, Jessi, maybe I had too much punch or something. I think I need to lie down."

"Okay."

"I'll see you at school tomorrow."

"Okay."

I went to bed as soon as I hung up the phone, but I barely slept. My dreams were full of strange people in riding boots eating mouthfuls of cake, and big angry horses chasing me around swimming pools filled with punch.

11th CHAPTER

My final lesson had been scheduled for Thursday afternoon. I suppose the party hadn't been so bad after all because the kids in my class seemed a little friendlier to me. Amber's birthday party gave us something to talk about. The kids would say things like, "Wasn't Amber's party a blast?" and I would answer, "It was terrific!" But I still didn't feel part of the group. Maybe because I still hadn't got the right clothes. Or maybe because deep down I knew I wasn't comfortable around horses any more. Would I always be afraid of them?

Anyway, as I said, it was my final lesson. I should have been celebrating, but I just couldn't. Why? Because I still had to go through the horse show the following Sunday. Worst of all, my whole family and all the members of the BSC were planning to come to see it.

I had tried to keep quiet about the show, but Kendallwood Farm sent out little notices to our parents. Then my mum told Stacey's mum, and she told Stacey, and that was it. I was stuck.

Now all I could think about was the prospect of making a total fool of myself in front of everybody.

"Mal, you'll be riding Duke today," Lauren called as I entered the stable that morning. My heart dropped into the pit of my stomach.

"Who's riding Pax?" I asked. Even though I had ridden Pax just three times, he was the only horse I felt comfortable with.

"Amber requested him."

I reached for Duke's bridle and reluctantly started to head towards his stall. During the course of our lessons we had been taught to bridle and saddle our horses by ourselves. By now it was such a familiar routine that I hardly thought about it.

I shoved my left hand into the pocket of my denim jacket and felt the carrot I'd brought as a horse treat. I had put sugar cubes in the other pocket. I'd give the sugar to Duke but the carrot was reserved for Pax. Even if I wasn't going to ride him I could at least say hello and give him a treat.

Pax saw me coming and stuck his big beautiful head over his stall door.

"Hi, Pax," I whispered.

He whinnied softly as I rubbed his velvety nose. The warm, moist air from his nostrils tickled the palm of my hand. After I had petted him for a few seconds he snorted and nudged the pocket of my jacket.

"Oh, you clever boy. You knew I'd brought you a snack." I took a step backwards. "Well, maybe I won't give it to you today," I teased him.

Pax tossed his head impatiently and pawed at the ground.

"Okay, okay, don't be such a baby." I giggled, then pulled out the prized carrot and held it out towards him. He devoured it in two bites. "Hey. Slow down." Pax blinked his big brown eyes at me innocently and with a loud crunch finished the last bit of carrot.

As soon as he'd swallowed, Pax nudged my other pocket, where the sugar cubes were. I shook my head.

"Sorry, fella. I have to give those to Duke. That's to make sure he'll be nice to me today."

Pax seemed to understand and pressed his soft muzzle against my cheek. I wrapped my arms around his neck and gave him a strong hug.

"I wish I were riding you in the show," I mumbled into his mane. "Then maybe I wouldn't be so scared."

382

By now most of the others in the class had arrived, and I had to hurry to get Duke's bridle and saddle on. Putting on the bridle is my least favourite thing. First of all, you have to stick your finger in the side of the horse's mouth to get him to take the bit. Then you have to pull the leather part over his ears – which most horses hate – and finally you fasten it under his chin.

Duke was pretty good about it today. He especially liked the sugar cube I gave him as a reward. Next I put on his saddle blanket and saddle. This part can get tricky because many horses will hold their breath when you cinch the saddle under their belly. That way, when they exhale, the saddle fits loosely, which is more comfortable for them, but a disaster for the rider. After a couple of trots around the ring, the saddle slips sideways and you find yourself lying on the ground.

After I had saddled Duke, I led him to the ring and joined the rest of the kids, who were already astride their horses. This was the part I really dreaded – getting on the horse's back. There was no turning back after that. I took a deep breath, then muttered, "Here goes nothing."

I slipped the toe of my boot into the stirrup and, after several hops, managed to swing my leg over Duke's back. Then I grasped the reins and guided Duke out of the stable into the ring.

Amber was the last to join us. She and Pax trotted into the ring and took their position between Kelsey and Allison. Lauren, who had been standing patiently in the centre of the ring, clapped her hands together and smiled at the class. "Well, folks, this is our final lesson. Next week is the horse show, where we find out if anything I've taught you has sunk in.'

A couple of kids giggled and Lauren winked at them. "I'm really proud of all of you, and I know that next week you'll do splendidly."

I wished I felt as confident as Lauren sounded. She clapped her hands together. "So. Our plan for today is to go through the exercises just as you will be doing them at the show."

She instructed us to walk our horses in a circle around the ring. That was easy enough. Duke fell in line behind Kelsey, who was riding Twilight, without any protest, and I breathed a little easier. So far, so good.

"Heads held high, backs straight, elbows in, toes up, heels down," Lauren reminded us. "Good. All right, class. Reverse direction and trot. Be sure to change your diagonal."

"Diagonals," I said glumly. They were very confusing. You have to sit for a beat when you change directions.

"Smooth post, class," Lauren barked.

"Some of you look like a watermelon bouncing around in your saddle."

I was so busy worrying about my diagonal that I completely forgot about posture or style.

"Reverse direction and canter."

Cantering was the last gait we had learned to do. It was the easiest one, besides walking. You simply sat in the saddle and let your pelvis rock back and forth as if you were riding a rocking horse while the horse did an easy gallop around the ring. The hard part was making sure your horse took the right lead – which meant starting the canter with the correct foot. Luckily, Duke did take the right lead and I started to feel a little more confident.

The final exercise of the day was to keep our horses standing perfectly still. Sounds easy, doesn't it? Well, it was a disaster. I think Duke was all pumped up from getting to run and still wanted to canter. He skipped sideways, knocking into Allison's horse. Then he tried to get out of the line we'd formed by backing up.

"Mallory, be firm," Lauren instructed. "You, too, Kelsey."

I stole a glance at Kelsey and saw that she was having more trouble than me, trying to keep Twilight under control.

"Now remember," Lauren said, "the judges will come down the line to check how well you carry yourself, and after that it will all be over."

Several of the pupils let out moans of disappointment, but not me. As it was, it seemed as if the horse show was going to be endless.

If I can just make it through without falling off, I told myself, I'll be happy.

"Miss Kendall?" David raised his hand. "What horses will we be riding in the show?"

Lauren snapped her fingers. "I almost forgot. Thank you for reminding me, David." She took off her hunt cap and, taking several pieces of paper from her pocket, placed them inside. "We're going to draw lots. I've numbered these slips from one to six. Whoever pulls out number one chooses first." As she shook the hat, Lauren added, "But remember, in next week's horse show, the judges will only judge the rider – not the horse. That way no one will have an advantage."

Lauren walked around the ring, and each of us reached into the hat and drew out a piece of paper. I was afraid to open mine. I squeezed my eyes shut and whispered, "Please, oh, please, let mine be number one."

But before I had even opened my paper, Kelsey squealed, "I get to pick first. I got number one."

My heart sank. Of course Kelsey would

pick Pax. He was the perfect horse. But to my surprise she chose a chestnut named Brandy.

"Who has number two?" Lauren asked, looking around the ring. No one said anything, and I realized I hadn't checked my own number. I unfolded it and gasped in surprise.

"That's me," I said, waving the little piece of paper over my head. "And I choose – " I turned and smiled at the beautiful white horse – "Pax."

I didn't even pay attention to which horses the rest of the class chose. I was too giddy with happiness. For one last time, Pax would be all mine. And right when I really needed him. Just in time for the horse show. Things weren't so bleak after all.

12th
CHAPTER

Thursday

The most terrible, awful thing happened at the Marshalls' today. Who would have thought just washing and drying an old blanket could have such disastrous results? Luckily, it wasn't my idea to wash Nina's blanket. It was Mrs Marshall's. I guess once a month she manages to pry the thing out of Nina's fingers and clean it. But even then, Nina refuses to leave Blankie's side. When I reached the Marshalls' house, she was sitting in front of the dryer, staring *at it like she had X-ray vision and could see inside. Mrs Marshall gave me a few instructions and left. Twenty minutes later, disaster struck.*

Dawn's Disaster happened the following Thursday afternoon. I had cycled out to Kendallwood Farm to give Pax a carrot and to try to relax my nerves about the horse show. It didn't help much. Pax was as sweet as ever, but I was still tense. The least little noise would make me jump. It's a good thing I wasn't the one babysitting for Nina. I probably would have cried louder than she had. Anyway, I think Dawn handled the situation perfectly.

What happened was this. While Nina was in the laundry room staring at the dryer, Mrs Marshall took Dawn aside and gave her some last-minute instructions.

"The kids can each have yoghurt and a cracker in about half an hour," she said. "By that time, Blankie should be washed and clean. Just pull it out, give it a quick shake—"

"And hand it to Nina," Dawn finished for her.

Mrs Marshall smiled. "She'll probably take it from you." She shook her head, making a little chuckling noise. "Nina attached herself to that blanket almost the moment she was born. She's never been without it."

"Has she ever lost it?" Dawn asked.

"One Christmas we left it at a relative's house and didn't discover it until two hours later. We had to turn the car round immediately and drive back to get it. Nina was practically in hysterics."

Dawn whistled softly between her teeth. "Wow."

"Wow is right." Mrs Marshall heaved a sigh of frustration. "That blanket has been a big problem. I'm just glad Eleanor isn't obsessed with a blanket or toy."

Mrs Marshall kissed Eleanor, who was playing with several pots and pans on the kitchen floor, and then called goodbye to Nina. After Mrs Marshall had gone, Dawn joined Eleanor, who had put one of the saucepans on her head.

"That makes a beautiful hat," Dawn told her.

Eleanor toddled over to the cooker, where she peered at her reflection in the glass of the oven door. "Pretty!" she exclaimed.

"Nina, come and look at your sister's new hat," Dawn called.

"I can't," Nina replied. "I'm with Blankie. Tell her to come here."

Dawn led Eleanor into the laundry room. Nina was still sitting on a step stool, while the dryer went round and round.

"Look at Eleanor's hat," Dawn said.

Eleanor waved the pan proudly in the air and then banged it twice against the side of the washing machine. Luckily Dawn pulled it out of Eleanor's hand before she could do any damage to the paint. Eleanor hardly noticed the pan was gone. She continued to bang on the washing machine with her bare hand.

Nina covered her ears to shut out the loud, hollow sound but continued staring at the dryer.

"That's concentration," Dawn murmured.

Eleanor stopped pounding on the washing machine and abruptly declared, "Eat. Let's eat."

Dawn checked her watch. Nearly fifteen minutes had passed since Mrs Marshall had left the house. She thought it would be okay to give the girls their snack a few minutes early. "All right, Eleanor. It's time for yoghurt and crackers."

"Yea!" Eleanor followed Dawn to the kitchen.

Dawn lifted Eleanor into her high chair and, taking a carton of blueberry yoghurt out of the fridge, divided it neatly into two bowls.

Eleanor beat her spoon against the plastic tray.

"Here you go," Dawn said, patting her on the head. "And some crackers."

The buzzer sounded from the laundry room, and Nina bellowed, "Blankie is done! Let him out, Dawn. Please let him out."

The way Nina talked, it sounded as if Blankie had been locked inside a little cage.

"He's all by himself," she continued. "He wants to get out. Hurry, Dawn!"

"Just a minute," Dawn said, putting the yoghurt on Eleanor's tray and the box of crackers next to it. Then she ran to the laundry room, where Nina was jumping up and down.

"Careful," Dawn cautioned as she opened the door of the dryer. "Don't you put your hand inside, Nina. This is very hot."

"I won't. Just take Blankie out."

Dawn bent down and peered inside the dryer. She couldn't find the thin grey blanket at first. It was plastered against the side of the round drum. She reached gingerly for a corner of it, trying not to touch the hot metal. "Got it," she said as she felt her fingers close around the soft material.

"Give him to me," Nina cried. "Please!"

A harsh tearing sound echoed inside the dryer.

"Oh, my gosh!" Dawn gasped. She held up a ragged scrap of grey material. It had separated from the rest of the blanket.

"My Blankieeee!" Nina's howl could be heard two houses away. "You killed him."

She snatched the square of material away from Dawn and plunged her hand inside the hot dryer. Then she howled in pain.

Dawn was shocked by what Nina had done, but it took her only a second to spring into action. She scooped Nina up in her arms and carried her into the kitchen, where she turned on the cold-water tap. "Hold your hand under there," she told Nina. "It will make the burn feel better." Dawn was relieved to see that Nina had burned only a fingertip.

Still, tears were pouring down Nina's cheeks. Dawn didn't know if it was because of her finger or because of Blankie. Nina let her know almost instantly.

"Blankie!" she wailed. "I want my Blankie."

Until then, Eleanor had been eating contentedly in her high chair. Now her own chin began to quiver.

"It's all right, Eleanor," Dawn reassured her. "Your sister burned her finger. But it will be all better in a second."

"It's not my finger," Nina pulled her hand out from under the tap and stumbled back towards the laundry room. "I want my Blankie. Please give him to me."

"Nina, I'll get him for you." Dawn ran ahead of her. "Sit on the stool and I'll hand him to you."

Dawn reached into the dryer once more but when she touched the material, the same thing happened again. Blankie pulled apart like candy floss. "This is a disaster," she said to herself.

Nina saw the next torn piece of blanket and let out a scream louder than the first one.

"I'm so sorry, Nina." Dawn reached out to comfort her, but Nina pounded her shoulder with her fists.

"You did it," she wailed. "You killed Blankie."

Dawn stood up. Her mind was racing. She turned back to the dryer, pulled out another square of material, and cried, "Look! This Blankie is the perfect size to fit in your pocket." She leaned forward and stuffed it into the pocket of Nina's T-shirt. Before Nina could say anything, Dawn grabbed another torn square. "And this little Blankie will fit into your bag."

Nina stopped wailing and wiped the back of her hand across her nose. Tears continued to stream down her cheeks, but she was intrigued by what Dawn was doing.

"This Blankie is just right to tuck up your sleeve," Dawn continued cheerfully.

Nina giggled through her hiccups. Dawn found another piece of the shredded blanket and tucked it into Nina's shoe.

"Oh, look, he wants to go for a walk. And this one wants to hide in your back pocket."

The tears dried on Nina's cheeks as she began to enjoy the new game Dawn had invented. By the time Dawn had finished fishing out the remains of Blankie from the dryer, he was hidden all over Nina. This gave Dawn another great idea.

"Hey!" she exclaimed. "Now you can carry Blankie everywhere you go, and nobody will ever know. He's hidden. In fact, you can keep Blankie all over the place – a piece in your room, a piece in your locker at school, a piece in your pocket – and he'll be your secret."

"He's really hidden?" Nina looked up at Dawn and blinked her eyes.

"Come with me and I'll show you." Dawn led Nina to the kitchen, where she scooped Eleanor out of her high chair. Then the three of them stood in front of the full length mirror in the hall. Dawn pointed to Nina's shirt pocket. "See, we know he's hiding in there but no one else will."

Nina giggled and lifted her foot. "I know Blankie's in my shoe, too, but it's my secret."

"That's right." Dawn knelt beside Nina and hugged her close. "He'll always be with you," she whispered, "and no one will know."

13th
CHAPTER

It was Friday – forty-eight hours until D-Day (Dying-of-Embarrassment Day). School had been a blur all week. I could think about nothing but the horse show. I was late for lessons and missed answers in tests that I should have known. I even forgot about the BSC meeting. Luckily, at five-fifteen my mother stuck her head in my room to remind me. I hopped on my bike and pedalled as fast as I could to Claudia's.

When I arrived, Dawn was telling everyone about the Blankie disaster. I caught most of it – how the blanket had disintegrated in the dryer, and how Dawn had saved the day by stuffing little bits of it into Nina's pockets. Dawn was such a good storyteller that even when Claud's digital clock read 5:30, Kristy didn't interrupt to call the meeting to order. Dawn finished her story and we just stared at her, shaking our heads in amazement.

"Boy, Dawn," Claud said, dropping a handful of crisps into her mouth. "You really were thinking fast."

"I had to," Dawn said. "Nina was about to have a major tantrum. I'm not kidding. She screamed so loudly that when I was leaving later that afternoon, one of the neighbours asked me if there had been an accident at the Marshall house."

"That must have been embarrassing," Jessi said.

"It was. But—" Dawn held up her crossed fingers and grinned. "Hopefully it will be worth it."

"If you ask me," Stacey said, "I think Nina will have a much easier time at school from now on."

"We'll all have a much easier time," Mary Anne agreed. "I hate to admit it, but the last time I sat for Eleanor and Nina and Blankie, it wasn't much fun."

Kristy cleared her throat and adjusted her visor. "Then I would like to take this opportunity to congratulate Dawn on a job well done. And to say that this meeting of the BSC is officially called to order."

As if in response to Kristy's words, the phone rang. Claud picked up the receiver and said, "Hello, Babysitters Club. There's no problem we can't solve."

Stacey snorted with laughter. "She makes us sound like a group of detectives."

"Well, in a way we are," Kristy said as Claud scribbled down the caller's information on a pad. "A detective has to be quick on her feet, ready to handle any new situation that comes along, and able to deal with it in a level-headed way. That's what we do."

Mary Anne cocked her head. "You know, Kristy's right. Dawn solved the Nina-and-Blankie problem. And remember when Mallory worked out what was bothering the Arnold twins?"

I smiled, remembering how I'd discovered that the twins hated being treated like little identical dolls. Once I found that out, they were easy to deal with. I turned to Jessi and said, "What about when Jessi learned sign language so she could talk to Matt Braddock, and then all of the kids in the neighbourhood wanted to know Matt's secret language?"

Jessi answered by signing, "Thanks for remembering that."

"Hey!" Claudia dipped her hand into the crisps again. "Let me know when you've finished congratulating yourselves, so Mary Anne can assign this job."

Everyone laughed and then we got down to business. Friday was busy and the phone rang non-stop. All of the activity almost made me forget about the horse show on

Sunday. Almost. Unfortunately, giant but-terflies were still flip-flopping around my stomach.

Mary Anne took a job with the Prezziosos, Kristy agreed to three after-noons with the Barretts, and I accepted a job with the Rodowskys. Then Mrs Marshall phoned.

Dawn had picked up the phone, and when we heard her say "Oh, hi, Mrs Marshall," we fell silent. The Blankie idea had worked out fine on Thursday, but Dawn hadn't heard whether things were still okay. After Mrs Marshall gave Dawn the details for the next job, Dawn asked, "So how was Nina's day at school?"

"Wonderful!" Mrs Marshall replied so loudly that we could all hear her. "She came home grinning from ear to ear. And she didn't seem to mind at all that she could only take a piece of Blankie to school."

"That's great," Dawn replied. "Tell her I said hello."

Dawn hung up and gave us the good news. Then Claudia changed the subject. "So Mallory, how's the *Stars of Tomorrow* talent show coming on?"

I had been preoccupied with my horse show but I had noticed that the kids seemed pretty organized. "It looks as if they're almost ready," I reported. "The triplets helped build a platform in the back garden to use as a stage, and the neighbourhood kids have been practising day and night."

"I bet your mum can hardly wait till the show is over," Mary Anne said with a giggle.

I chuckled. "She's marking the days off on the calendar. Only eight to go."

"So it's really going to happen?" Jessi asked in amazement.

I nodded. "I have to admit that I was sceptical at first, but the kids have organized the show awfully well."

"What about you, Mal?" Stacey asked. "Are you ready for *your* show?"

Her words sent a ripple of fear through me. My shoulders slumped and I stared at the carpet. "I'm as ready as I'll ever be."

Kristy leaned forward in her director's chair and gave me a funny look. "You don't sound very enthusiastic about it."

I hadn't planned to tell my friends just how badly the lessons had been going. I suppose I was afraid they would think I was being silly, but suddenly all of these feelings welled up inside me. One second I was looking at the carpet on the floor of Claudia's room and the next minute my vision got all blurry. Two tears dropped on to the carpet.

Jessi put her hand on my arm. "Mal, what's the matter?"

It was as if a dam had burst inside me

and everything I was worried about came pouring out. I told my friends everything – about my lessons; how much they'd meant to me and how snobby my classmates had been. Then I told them about the fall.

"Now I'm afraid to get on a horse," I confessed. "Any horse. Even Pax scares me."

"That's all right, Mal," Jessi said softly. "A lot of people are afraid of horses."

"But not me." I bit my lip to stop crying. "I couldn't be. I love them. I mean, it's always been my dream to be a writer and live on a ranch with horses."

"You had a bad fall," Kristy said. "It takes time to get over something like that. Once I was hit in the face by a baseball when I was at bat and it took me nearly a year to stop flinching every time the pitcher threw the ball."

"You think I'll get over it?" I asked, wiping the tears off my cheeks with the back of my hand.

"Of course," Jessi said warmly. "But maybe not straight away."

I held my head in my hands. "This is such a mess. I begged my parents to help me pay for lessons. They did, even though I knew they really couldn't afford to. And then I had that fall and I spent the next five lessons clinging to the horse, petrified that I'd fall off again. It was a total waste. I hardly learned anything."

"I'm sure that's not true," Mary Anne said. "I bet you've learned a lot and you just don't know it."

Claudia finished the last crisp and crumpled up the bag. "Frankly, I'm impressed that you're going to be riding a horse with one of those saddles without a handle."

"Handle?" I giggled. "You mean, the saddle horn?"

"That's right." Claudia shook her head. "I don't know how you stay on."

"It's really just a matter of balance and holding on with your knees," I explained with a shrug.

Stacey squeezed my arm. "See? You do know more than you think."

Soon it was six o'clock and time for the meeting to end. Every single member of the BSC wished me luck on Sunday and reminded me that they'd be there to cheer me on. It certainly is nice having friends to support you.

Jessi suggested we walk our bikes halfway home, so we could keep on talking. I was glad she suggested it, because I'd missed her.

"Mal, I had no idea you were so miserable," Jessi said as we neared the corner where we usually split up to go to our own houses.

"I tried to tell you a few times, but you didn't seem to want to hear about it."

It was Jessi's turn to stare at the ground. "I'm sorry, Mal. I suppose I was so jealous of your riding lessons that I could hardly stand to hear about them. Especially when you phoned and said you'd found your dream horse."

"But he really is a wonderful horse."

"I'm sure he is," Jessi said. "It's just that I thought you were bragging."

I gasped. "I just wanted to share my good news with you."

"You told me you had all these new friends who were rich and owned their own horses," Jessi reminded me. "You told me they invited you to fancy parties with giant video screens and swimming pools."

"Did I really make it sound like that?"

Jessi nodded. "And I felt left out."

"I'm really sorry, Jessi. If you want to know the truth, those new friends barely speak to me. I'm not even sure if they know my name, and we've been together for eight weeks. I don't have the right clothes, I'm the only one who fell off my horse, and I'm the worst rider in the class. The only good thing about the entire two months has been Pax."

Jessi smiled. "He does sound like a wonderful horse."

"Oh, he is!" I cried. "I really want you to meet him."

"I will," Jessi said. "On Sunday at the horse show."

"Oh, that." I leaned on my bike's handlebars. "I really wish I didn't have to go."

"You'll do just fine," Jessi said. "It'll probably only take fifteen minutes, and then all your problems will be solved."

"Not quite," I said. "They're starting another class next week."

Jessi shrugged. "Just don't sign up."

"But how do I explain that to my parents?"

"Tell them the truth. You had a terrible time."

"Oh, Jessi, I could never do that! Mum and Dad couldn't afford to let me take those lessons in the first place, but I begged and pleaded until they gave in. If I tell them I hated the class, they'll feel terrible and I'll look like a jerk."

"Hmmm," Jessi murmured, biting her lip. "That's a tough one. Maybe we should go to my house and talk about it for a while."

"I can't," I said. "I have to get home for dinner."

"Have dinner with us," Jessi offered.

That was the best thing she could have said. We cycled to her house, and it was just like old times again between us. We had a lot of catching up to do. Eight whole weeks' worth. Jessi and I talked non-stop through dinner. In fact, we had so much to say to each other that I ended up spending the night at her house.

We didn't solve the problem of what to say to my parents about future riding lessons, but just then it didn't matter. Jessi was my best friend again and I felt great.

14th
CHAPTER

The day of the horse show arrived and I was a wreck. From the moment I got out of bed things went wrong. I slept late, I couldn't find my socks, and my hair was out of control. It was humid outside, and my hair looked like a frizzball, even when I tried to smooth it into a ponytail.

The only good thing that happened that morning was that Lauren Kendall stopped by our house. She had borrowed a riding habit from a friend, and she thought it might fit me. The jacket and boots were a little big but I was thrilled anyway.

"There's no sense being the only one in your class riding in jeans," she said. "We're here to put on a show. This will make you look like a real horsewoman."

"Yeah," I thought to myself glumly. "Until I get on the horse."

Actually, I was grateful to Lauren. I had

been so busy worrying about being afraid of horses that I hadn't even thought how I would look in my Western riding clothes.

"Thanks, Lauren," I said as I walked her to the door. "I really appreciate it."

She smiled at me and said, "Be confident today, Mallory. You've got potential."

Her words should have made me feel better, but my nerves had taken over. Mum tried to convince me to eat some breakfast, but my stomach was doing cartwheels and I was afraid I wouldn't be able to keep anything down. All I wanted to do was get out to Kendallwood Farm so I could see Pax and try to relax.

Claire and Margo helped me get dressed – if you could call it help. Claire tried on all the riding gear. She especially liked the boots, which came halfway up her thighs. Margo paraded around in my hunt cap and coat and then wrestled with Claire over the riding crop. Finally I managed to wrench the clothing away from my sisters and put it on. I grabbed my mother's hairspray and made a last-ditch effort to de-frizz my hair. It didn't help.

Luckily the phone rang and Adam shouted from the kitchen, "Mal! It's for you!"

"Hi, Mal, it's me," Jessi said when I picked up the phone. "I just wanted to call to wish you luck. In ballet we say break a leg. What do they say in horseback riding?"

"Just the thought of breaking any body parts makes me nervous," I said, laughing. "So 'good luck' would be fine."

"How are you feeling?" Jessi asked.

"Like someone's turned on a blender in my stomach."

"That's how I feel before every ballet performance," Jessi said. "But then I make sure I'm very supple and that all my muscles are warmed up. You should do the same."

"You mean, I should do *pliés*?" I asked.

"Yes." Jessi's voice rang with authority. Warming up is one thing she knows everything about. "Do some side stretches," she instructed, "then raise your hands over your head and touch the ground. Then do some slow knee bends."

"I think I can handle that," I said, making a mental list of what she told me to do.

"Then, just before you ride into the ring, take a deep breath and slowly let it out."

"It's funny you should say that," I said. "My teacher, Lauren, is always yelling at us to breathe."

"Well, she's right," Jessi said. "You can't stay loose if you're holding your breath."

Jessi wished me luck a few more times, then Becca had to get on the phone and do the same thing. Finally we hung up, but not before Jessi told me, "Mal, you're my best friend. I'm really proud of you."

Tears stung my eyes (I was turning into a mush, just like Mary Anne) and I mumbled, "Thanks, Jessi. That means a lot to me."

Mum drove me to Kendallwood Farm at eleven o'clock and then went back to the house to get the rest of the family ready. The field in front of the stables was already jammed with cars and horse trailers when my mum dropped me off. I looked at the steady stream of people filing into the benches that had been set up around the riding ring and I gulped.

"Now, your dad and I will be back with your brothers and sisters by twelve-thirty," my mother said.

I nodded, barely hearing her. Just the sight of so many cars had started my pulse pounding. I stumbled towards the stable without even waving goodbye.

"Mallory!"

I turned to see what my mother wanted.

"You forgot something." She held up the velvet hunt cap Lauren had brought over that morning.

I shook my head, trying to focus. If I was going to be this scatty two hours before the show, I could just imagine what I'd be like on horseback in front of a hundred people. A total disaster.

Mum must have noticed the panicked look on my face because she said quietly, "Relax, Mallory. You have plenty of time to get ready. Remember, we're all rooting for you."

I tried to smile confidently but what came out was kind of a sick grimace. After my mum had driven away, I hurried as fast as I could through the crowd towards the stable. I heaved a sigh of relief as I slipped inside the dark shadows of Pax's stall and felt his warm, comforting nose nuzzle my neck.

"I am so glad to see you," I whispered, scratching his head behind his ears. "Now it's time to make you pretty."

I tried to plait Pax's mane but he wouldn't hold still to let me work on him. He kept pawing the ground and impatiently nudging the pocket of my jacket. Then I realized what he wanted. His carrot.

"Okay, you win, you big baby," I said, giggling. "Today, because it's an important show, I've brought you a special treat." I pulled two carrots and an apple out of my tote bag. He pressed his muzzle towards them greedily, but I pulled them out of his reach. "Now, don't just inhale them," I said sternly. "I want you to chew."

And he did, dripping apple juice down his chin. At least it kept him occupied while I plaited his mane. Lauren had showed us how to plait the long, thick strands of horsehair, then roll them up and tie them with little satin bows. Soon a neat row of ribbons was lining Pax's neck. Then I curry-combed his coat until it glistened.

Pax's tail was harder to untangle than his mane, and also more time-consuming, because you aren't supposed to use a comb or brush, just your fingers. I had to separate the strands of hair one by one. But concentrating on the task took my mind off what lay ahead of me – the dreaded horse show.

Finally I saddled and bridled Pax and then stepped back to look at my handiwork. Pax arched his neck and stood proudly, as if he were posing for a picture.

"You already were the most beautiful horse in the stable," I murmured softly. "Now you're the most beautiful in the world."

The blare of a loudspeaker cut through the silence of the stable then, and I heard a voice announce, "Welcome, ladies and gentlemen, to Kendallwood Farm and another splendid afternoon of fine horsemanship from our young riders."

I felt as if someone had thrown a bucket of cold water on me. I left the stall and peeped out of the big doors of the barn. The benches were full, and I could see my mum and dad in the very last row, with my brothers and sisters lined up in front of them.

Instantly I wanted to run – far, far away,

from saddles and bridles and anything having to do with horses or riding.

The speaker crackled again and the announcer said, "Class Number One – that's the pony class – you're on call. Take your mounts to the paddock and warm them up, please. We're now calling the halter class. Will the handlers lead their horses into the ring at once."

Suddenly I couldn't remember when my class – which was Beginning Equitation – was supposed to perform. My throat tightened with panic, and I looked around desperately for someone to ask for help. Behind me Kelsey was leading a chestnut gelding named Brandy out of his stall towards the stable door.

"Kelsey, I don't know when we ride," I gasped. "What am I going to do?"

"Read the schedule, silly," she said, rolling her eyes. "It's tacked to the wall right behind you."

"Oh." I grinned sheepishly. "Thanks."

Kelsey shrugged and left the stable.

I turned and looked at the list of events. So many classes were listed that at first I had trouble finding my own. There were Junior and Senior Jump classes, Hunter Under Saddle (in which the riders showed off their horse's manners), Hunter Over Fences (in which the riders rode their mounts over jumps), and all different levels of show jumping. Finally I saw my own

class – Class Three, Beginning Equitation –
right after the pony class.

I hurried back to Pax's stall and then
led him out of the stable into the bright
sunlight. The paddock was full of horses
and riders. The halter horses had finished
their event and were being led back to the
stables.

Now the pony class was entering the
ring. The riders, who were about eight
years old, were wearing caps, jackets and
high black riding boots like the rest of us.
They looked so serious and cute, just like
Shirley Temple in *The Little Princess*. That
made me think of Jessi, and I scanned the
stands for her smiling face. I spotted her at
the rail of the show ring. She was surrounded by the entire BSC, and once more
my stomach did a flip-flop.

"Beginning Equitation," the loudspeaker
blared above my head. "Class Number
Three is on call in the paddock."

"That's me," I yelped. I grabbed Pax's
reins and led him into the fenced enclosure.

"Mallory," Lauren said as I joined the
rest of my class. "You're here. Good."

"I – I'm sorry—" I stammered, but
Lauren cut me off.

"Don't worry, you're right on time."
Lauren handed each of us a piece of
cloth with a number printed on it, and a
pair of safety pins. "Attach these to your

jackets – top and bottom, please. That's so the judge will be able to tell who's who." Her eyes were bright with excitement. "Now listen, mount your horses and walk them around the paddock. When the announcer calls the class into the ring, enter one at a time and stick to the right. The judge and her assistant – that's the steward – will be standing in the middle of the ring. Once you're all inside, they'll close the gate and put you through your paces. *Do exactly* what the judge says."

Every one of us must have had the same stricken look on our faces because Lauren burst out laughing.

"Don't look so glum! Remember, the judge won't ask you to do anything we haven't done together a hundred times in class. So relax – and *breathe*!"

Twelve nervous riders exhaled at once, and we all started giggling. I walked Pax around the paddock, running over in my mind all the pressure commands for the different gaits. Before I knew it, the loud-speaker was blaring, "We're now calling Class Three, Beginning Equitation, into the ring. Class Four, Intermediates, are on call."

I followed my class out of the paddock. As we neared the entrance of the show ring, I gave Pax a gentle nudge with my heels. He stepped smartly through the opening, and I found myself staring at a sea of faces.

414

I heard a wave of applause start at one end of the benches and turn into a rushing sound that roared in my ears. Crisp images of the event stick in my mind like little snapshots. My family up in the benches, grinning and waving like goons. Jessi and the rest of the BSC by the rail down in front, cheering as I passed by. The judge and her assistant standing in the centre of the ring, their arms crossed, stern looks on their faces.

After we'd all entered the ring and the gate had been closed behind us, the judge said something to the steward, who gestured towards the announcer's booth.

"Walk your horses, please," the announcer said over the loudspeaker.

We did as we were told. We made a complete circle of the ring and then the steward gestured to the booth again.

"Trot your horses, please."

The judge scribbled furiously on her clipboard while we posted around the ring. I tried my best not to look as clumsy and off balance as I felt. "Heels down, toes up!" I repeated over and over. When we reversed direction, a little voice inside me shouted, "Don't forget your diagonal!"

The announcer then called, "Walk your horses, please."

Pax settled into his comfortable walking pace and I let out a long breath of air. So far, so good.

"Canter your horses, please."

I pressed my knee into Pax's side and he obediently changed gaits. Then the announcer said, "Reverse your horses, please."

Pax turned smartly, but I noticed Kelsey had trouble getting Brandy to take the right lead. I didn't have time to gloat because the announcer was already asking us to come down from the canter to a trot. We returned to a walk and then the announcer told us to line up straight across the arena.

I nudged Pax in beside Allison and prayed that he'd stand still like he was supposed to. Megan was near the front of the line, slumping slightly in her saddle. I noticed the judge make a disapproving face and mark something on her clipboard. I sat up as straight as I could, making sure Pax was square towards the judge, just as Lauren had taught us.

We sat there for what seemed like an eternity. Then the judge handed a note to the steward, and nodded and walked quickly down the line of riders.

"You, you, you, you, you," he said, pointing to Allison and four other riders, including David and Amber. Then he turned to me and added, "And you. Pull out and walk your horses around the ring, please."

I was shocked. Barely thinking, I blindly

followed the other horses into the line. The judge made us do everything again, only this time I was the one who goofed up when we reversed directions on the trot. I forgot my diagonal and it took me a second to correct my mistake.

We returned to the line-up and waited anxiously while the judge made a few more notes, then handed her clipboard to the steward, who ran it over to the announcer's booth.

The announcement of the winners came over the loudspeaker: "First place in Beginning Equitation goes to Allison Anders riding Peaches."

The steward pinned a blue ribbon to the bridle of Allison's horse, while the audience applauded. Then the rest of the winners were announced. Amber placed second, a girl named Signe placed third, and David won a pink ribbon for fourth place. Fifth place was announced and then I heard my name blaring out over the speakers:

"Sixth place goes to Mallory Pike riding Pax."

The steward pinned a white ribbon on Pax's bridle and then it was all over. I couldn't believe it. My butterflies were gone and my worries were over. Pax and I trotted back to the barn like a couple of champions.

"Sixth out of twelve," Jessi said later as

she and my brothers and sisters watched me comb down Pax. "That's not bad."

"Not bad?" I groaned. "It's pretty terrible."

"Well, it means half the people in the class were better than you," Vanessa said. "But you were better than the other half."

I laughed. "When you put it that way, it doesn't sound so awful." I spotted my parents making their way towards me from the viewing stands. I whispered to Jessi, "But it's a good excuse for not taking any more riding lessons. Now that they've seen how I ride, they'll know that any more classes would be a waste of money."

Boy, was I wrong about that. My father was beaming when he came into the stable. He scooped me up in his arms and shouted, "Mal, you looked spectacular out there."

"Sixth place." My mother gave me a big hug. "That's pretty good for your first show."

"*First* show?" I repeated.

"Of many," my father added.

Mum squeezed my arm. "Your father and I talked it over and we've agreed to cover the full cost of your next eight lessons."

"You'd really do that?" I asked.

"Absolutely." My father draped his arm proudly around my shoulder. "You're a real equestrienne now."

I looked over at Jessi with a sinking feeling. There was no getting around it; I was going to have to tell them the truth. Jessi realized I needed to be alone with my parents, so she bent down and whispered to my brothers and sisters, "How many of you would like to look at the other horses with me?"

Of course they all wanted to. I flashed Jessi a look of thanks and then, taking a deep breath, faced my parents. "Mum. Dad. I have a confession to make."

"What is it, darling?" My mother was still smiling.

I decided to get right to the point. "I really didn't enjoy my lessons very much."

"What?" Dad looked completely surprised.

"After I fell off that horse, I got really scared," I explained. "I had to force myself to go to every lesson. It just wasn't any fun."

"Well, Mal, that's understandable," my mother replied. "But don't you think a few more lessons will help you get over your fears?"

"Maybe later," I said. "But I – I'm just not ready right now."

Mum and Dad exchanged quick glances.

"Mallory, your mother and I don't want to force you to do anything," my father said slowly. "We just thought that since you loved horses so much—"

"Oh, I still do. I'm just not that crazy about *riding* them."

"Are you sure about this?" my mother asked, studying my face.

"I'm positive. The idea of getting on a big horse again really frightens me. Maybe in a couple of years I'll change my mind."

My mother clasped my hand. "I know that must have been difficult to say, Mallory, and we're really pleased you could be so straightforward with us."

"That's right," my father agreed. "And listen, Mallory, if you do change your mind, we'll be ready to help you out. Because frankly, I think you'll make a fine rider one day."

My father spoke so loudly that several of the riders from my class turned to stare and I could feel my cheeks turning bright pink (partly from embarrassment but mostly because I was happy that my parents were so proud of me).

Before I left the farm that afternoon, I asked Jessi to come and say goodbye to Pax with me. He was in his stall, happily munching on a bucket of oats. I slipped in beside him and he pressed his muzzle against me. I tried to say goodbye but I couldn't make my mouth form the words. Finally I buried my head in his neck and hugged him for a long time. When I looked up, Jessi was wiping her eyes.

420

"He really is the most beautiful horse in the world," she said in a soft voice. "You're so lucky to have known him, even if it was for a short time."

"I know," I replied. "I know."

15th
CHAPTER

"It's showtime!" yelled Nicky.

I couldn't help giggling. It was Saturday morning and the *Stars of Tomorrow* talent show was about to begin. Every room in our house was filled with kids putting on make-up or struggling into a costume.

The triplets had volunteered to be the ticket collectors in the back garden. Byron kept running through the house making announcements like, "We're really packing 'em in!" or, "I think it's going to be standing room only!"

He was right, too. Our back garden was filled with neighbours, their children, and a couple of dogs and cats. The entire BSC had come to show their support. Several of us were babysitting, so we had brought our charges along. Kristy brought her stepbrother, Andrew, and stepsister, Karen, her brother David Michael and little Emily

422

Michelle. They took up the entire front row.

Jessi and I sat behind them with Becca and Squirt and Charlotte Johanssen. Dr Johanssen had phoned me that morning to see if I would mind looking after Charlotte during the talent show. Of course, I said I didn't mind. Charlotte and Becca were just about the only kids in our neighbourhood who weren't going to be in the *Stars of Tomorrow* talent show. But they had been adamant about not doing it. After their miserable experiences in the Little Miss Stoneybrook contest, both of them had sworn they would never appear on the stage again. But they made very enthusiastic audience members.

"Bring on the stars!" Becca shouted, clapping her hands.

Several older kids in the audience heard her cry and started clapping and chanting, "We want a show! We want a show!"

A dismayed look crossed Nicky's face, and he ducked behind the curtains to confer with Vanessa. The curtains were still just blankets, only now big silver stars made of aluminium foil were pinned to them.

The triplets decided to do some crowd control. They ran to the front of the stage and yelled, "Quiet! *Quiet! SHUT UP!*"

"I knew their loud mouths were good for something," I said, giggling, to Jessi.

Vanessa stepped through the curtains, dressed in white tights and my dad's dinner jacket and bow tie. "Welcome to the first annual *Stars of Tomorrow* talent show," she declared, "brought to you by the one and only Pike family."

A cheer sounded from the triplets, who had taken up positions around the audience to make sure there were no hecklers. Then Vanessa gestured grandly to her right.

Nothing happened.

Finally she cupped her hands around her mouth and hissed, "Margo. You're on."

Margo stuck her head around the side of the curtains and blinked. "Now?"

Vanessa rolled her eyes and put her hands on her hips. "Yes. Now."

This sent a wave of laughter through the audience. At first Margo looked shocked and then she started giggling, too. In fact, she was laughing so hard she couldn't read the piece of paper she held in her hand.

Finally Vanessa marched over to her side and said, "Give me that." Vanessa studied the paper and announced, "Our first act will be Sean Addison on the tuba."

Nicky stuck his head through the curtains and called, "Sean can't find his tuba. He's back here crying."

"Well, help him find it," Vanessa shot back, "and tell Buddy he's on."

"I think I saw Sean's tuba in the

kitchen," I whispered to Jessi. "I'll go and get it."

Jessi nodded. "Okay. And I'll go and help Sean."

We left Becca, Squirt and Charlotte sitting on the grass. They were applauding wildly as a grey cat bolted across the stage, pursued by Pow the basset hound. Buddy and Suzi Barrett were both gripping his leash but weren't having any luck getting him to stop.

"Hey!" Nicky shouted to them. "You're not supposed to come on till after you're introduced."

Buddy ignored Nicky and just kept tugging on the leash. "Stop it, Pow," he bellowed. "I mean it."

Luckily the cat made a quick exit through a hedge and Pow's leash caught on a tree by the stage.

Buddy didn't seemed to be flustered at all. With a big grin on his face he turned to the crowd and announced, "I'm Buddy Barrett and this is my dog Pow, the fastest dog in the West. He also talks. Want to hear him?"

"Yes!" the audience shouted.

I made my way through the costumed kids who were clustered on our back porch and stepped inside the empty house. Sean's tuba was just where he'd left it that morning – on the table and, after a quick look around to make sure no other instruments or costumes had been left behind, I hurried back outside.

Buddy and Pow were just completing their jump-through-the-hula-hoop trick. To make sure Pow would make his leap through the hoop, Buddy had brought a large T-bone steak with him. I secretly wondered if Buddy's mother knew what her son was using as bait.

Pow bounded through the hoop without any urging and promptly settled down to devour his steak. No amount of urging could get him to budge from his spot. Finally the triplets rushed to Buddy's aid and the three of them dragged Pow, his steak clasped firmly between his teeth, off the stage.

The audience cheered and, while Vanessa waited for them to calm down so that she could announce the next act, I scanned the crowd. I was truly amazed at the turnout. People were still entering the garden. I spotted Dawn as she paid her admittance. She was carrying Eleanor Marshall on her hip and holding Nina's hand. Dawn waved to me and I grinned back. After passing the tuba to Claire, who quickly took it backstage, I hurried over to say hello.

"Mow-ree!" Eleanor squealed.

"How's the show going?" Dawn asked, flipping her sunglasses to the top of her head.

"It got off to a slightly rocky start," I said with a grin. "But now it looks as if it's going to be a success."

I felt a tug on my sleeve and saw Nina grinning up at me. "Mallory," she said. "Guess what."

I knelt down beside her. "I give up. What?"

"I brought Blankie to the show today."

"Blankie?" I looked up at Dawn, who nodded.

"He's in the front pocket of her shirt," Dawn whispered.

Nina beamed proudly and patted the pocket. "But nobody knows except you and Dawn and Eleanor. It's our secret."

I pretended to pull a zip across my mouth. "Don't worry," I promised. "I won't tell a soul."

"*Ooooh!*" the crowd suddenly murmured. I turned to see what the commotion was about and was startled to see Nicky's head towering four feet above the clothesline.

"He's on stilts," Dawn cried. "I didn't know he could do that."

"Neither did I," I said in amazement. My brother, sporting a red, white, and blue top hat and a white goatee beard, grinned at the audience as my sister announced, "And now, let's hear it for Nicholas Pike as Uncle Sam."

"Yankee Doodle Dandy" blasted out of

the tape recorder as Nicky strutted back and forth in front of the curtains on his stilts. He was wearing a long pair of trousers that completely covered the wooden stilts, so he truly seemed to be an eight-foot-tall person.

"Hasn't Nicky been practising at home?" Dawn asked me.

I shrugged. "He might have been, but I was kind of preoccupied with my riding lessons and the horse show and everything."

My lessons really had taken up a big chunk of my time. I'd neglected my friendship with the members of the Babysitters Club, especially Jessi, and with my own brothers and sisters. But that was over now and I was relieved. Jessi was my best friend again and horses were just a small part of my life. A bit like Nina and her Blankie. She no longer needed to carry the big cumbersome blanket around with her. A small piece of it was just fine. And loving horses from a distance was fine enough for me.

Finally all of the *Stars of Tomorrow* performers took their curtain calls. As Vanessa, Margo, Claire and Nicky stepped forward to take their bows, everyone cheered.

But nobody cheered louder than me.

Need a babysitter? Then call the Babysitters Club. Kristy Thomas and her friends are all experienced sitters. They can tackle any job from rampaging toddlers to a pandemonium of pets. To find out all about them, read on!

Reader beware – here's THREE TIMES the scare!

*Look out for these bumper GOOSEBUMPS editions. With three spine-tingling
stories by R.L. Stine in each book, get ready for three times the thrill …
three times the scare … three times the GOOSEBUMPS!*

Creatures

The Series With Bite!

Everyone loves animals. The birds in the trees. The dogs
running in the park. That cute little kitten.

But don't get too close. Not until you're sure.
Are they ordinary animals – or are they creatures?

1. Once I Caught a Fish Alive
Paul's special new fish is causing problems.
He wants to get rid of it, but the fish has other ideas...

2. If You Go Down to the Woods
Alex is having serious problems with the school play costumes.
Did that fur coat just move?

3. See How They Run
Jon's next-door neighbour is very weird. In fact,
Jon isn't sure that Frankie is completely human...

4. Who's Been Sitting in My Chair?
Rhoda's cat Opal seems to be terrified ... of a chair!
But then this chair belongs to a very strange cat...

Look out for these new creatures...

5. Atishoo! Atishoo! All Fall Down!
Chocky the mynah bird is a great school pet.
But now he's turning nasty. And you'd better do what he says...

6. Give a Dog a Bone
A statue of a faithful dog sounds really cute. But this
dog is faithful unto death. And beyond...

Creatures – you have been warned!